THE FLING

Visit us at www.boldstrokesbooks.com

By the Author

Better Off Red: Vampire Sorority Sisters Book 1

The Fling

THE FLING

by

Rebekah Weatherspoon

2012

THE FLING
© 2012 BY REBEKAH WEATHERSPOON. ALL RIGHTS RESERVED.

ISBN 10: 1-60282-656-0
ISBN 13: 978-1-60282-656-4

THIS TRADE PAPERBACK ORIGINAL IS PUBLISHED BY
BOLD STROKES BOOKS, INC.
P.O. BOX 249
VALLEY FALLS, NY 12185

FIRST EDITION: APRIL 2012

CREDITS
EDITOR: CINDY CRESAP
PRODUCTION DESIGN: SUSAN RAMUNDO
COVER DESIGN BY SHERI (GRAPHICARTIST2020@HOTMAIL.COM)

Acknowledgments

I must thank the following people:

My editor, Cindy. You are a saint.

Olya, the only Russian exchange student my family wanted to keep.

Inna Sysevich. I'm sorry I've forgotten eighty percent of the Russian you tried to teach me, but I'll be back soon for more instruction. And thank you for all the hugs.

And as always, Radclyffe.

Dedication

To Vanessa and Maria.
I know you're not doing it, but you totally should.

And to T, the executive producer of my heart.

PROLOGUE

THE FANTASY FULFILLED

O ksana's nipples were pierced.

Annie had already seen the tattoos that covered her trainer's left arm, and from the occasional slip of fabric, she knew there was more ink across Oksana's stomach and side. But for all of the body art that was revealed as Annie undid the ivory buttons hidden among the white ruffles running down the center of Oksana's short sleeve blouse, the tiny gunmetal barbells going through the hard, pink nipples came as a complete surprise.

A pleasant surprise.

Annie let Oksana open the front closure of her bra. Annie's breasts were way too big for front closure bras. Her cleavage destroyed the clasp if she was bold enough to cough. Oksana's breasts were smaller. Small and perky, and even without the piercings, Annie would have been fascinated by the light pink tips, the same cocoa-pink as Oksana's full lips.

Annie swallowed. She should probably stop staring.

"They don't scare you, do they?" Oksana's soft, husky voice filled the thick air of the hotel room.

"No. Not at all." Annie leaned a little closer and studied the barbells some more. She stopped her hand before her fingers brushed the left nipple. She looked up into Oksana's dark green eyes that were darker and hooded in the golden light from the lamp near the TV. "May I?"

Oksana swallowed and nodded bashfully, her teeth clutching the inside of her bottom lip. The gesture was pretty adorable. Annie smiled and took a deep breath. This was no time for *her* to be shy. This was all her idea. Oksana may have been the actual lesbian, and yes, she'd volunteered, but this was Annie's plan. Annie's fantasy.

They'd met at the bar, greeted each other with the same smiles and the same warm hugs they shared in the gym. They'd chuckled foolishly the entire way up in the elevator, joked nervously about how big the bed was and the awkward placement of the huge desk protruding from the far wall.

Finally, the laughter faded and they faced each other. Annie realized as Oksana looked down at her, still biting that lip, that she would have to make the first move. In all her fantasies and most of her wet dreams, she'd always been the aggressor. She'd always wanted to fuck another woman, to be the fucker, not the fuckee, and with the way Oksana watched her, seemingly reluctant to instigate the first bit of contact, Annie knew if she played her cards right, her *whole* fantasy would come true.

Annie swallowed once more and forced herself to relax. Tonight she wasn't Annie Collins, bride-to-be and line producer on three hugely popular reality TV shows, and Oksana wasn't one of the best personal trainers Los Angeles County had to offer. They weren't almost friends. Tonight, for one night, they were lovers.

Annie licked her bottom lip and leaned forward. She'd skip the fingers and lead with her mouth. Her eyes closed as her tongue curved around the small piece of steel. She moaned when Oksana let out a light gasp. Annie never thought something so basic could be such a turn-on. She was simply licking someone's nipples, but Annie's body reacted instantly and her mind began to wander toward the opportunities these piercings presented. She'd been aroused the moment she saw Oksana waiting for her downstairs, but as the slick skin between her lips began to pucker even further, Annie could feel her own pussy soaking, the swollen muscles between her legs growing thick and hot.

Annie pulled back as Oksana shuddered, and she drew the flat surface of her tongue up Oksana's breast to the height of her ribs.

Oksana took a small, faltering step back, whimpering once more as she grabbed on to Annie's shoulders.

"Are they sensitive?" Annie asked before licking up again then swirling her tongue over the very tip. She switched to the other piercing, hoping the answer was yes. She could easily suck on Oksana this way all night.

"Yes," Oksana pinched out, then drew in a deep breath. Annie followed as Oksana leaned against the bedpost. Oksana began to tremble. Annie took that as a good sign, pulling more of Oksana's breast into her mouth, varying the swirling strokes of her tongue as she wrapped her arm around Oksana's waist. "Annie. Wait."

Annie blinked up, panting as her own lustful need spiked. "Yeah?"

"They're *really* sensitive," Oksana said. "Can we...can we go slower?"

"Sure," Annie replied with a shaky laugh. She knew Oksana was close to coming. She thought that was a good thing, but maybe Oksana wasn't such a cheap date as Annie was. Annie liked coming right away, then coming again. She shook herself slightly. She should have asked what Oksana wanted before she went full force for her chest. Annie took a step back, but Oksana reached for her before she could retreat altogether.

She decided to focus on Oksana's eyes instead of her exposed breasts or where their fingers were touching.

"You're doing fine, but you wanted all night, remember?" Oksana's tone was filled with patience.

"That's the plan."

"Then let's take all night. We don't have to rush," Oksana replied. She stroked the back of Annie's hand, reassuring her that Annie had made the right decision. Oksana was the one.

Oksana got rid of her shirt and her bra then reached for the button on her flared-bottom trousers. Annie followed her cues and pulled her own top over her head and reached for the zipper at the back of her tight skirt. She watched Oksana as Oksana watched her, until they were nearly naked, underwear and shirts, and stilettos and flats in two piles beside the bed.

Annie was nervous about how Oksana would view her body. Oksana had told Annie plenty of times how proud she was of her for reaching the fitness goals they'd set together, but that was praise from trainer to client, not a comment from lover to lover. They had only planned on one night, but Annie wondered what kind of woman was Oksana's type. Was Annie too short? Were her breasts too large?

With their encounter in mind, Annie had examined herself in the mirror earlier that night. Her thighs were slimmer than when they first met. Most of the fullness from her chin was gone, along with some of the weight on her stomach and arms. Her breasts had stayed the same size, though. They drew attention no matter what she wore, and they'd always produced a sense of awe in the few who had seen them bare. She felt so exposed as she tossed her bra to the floor. Nothing would happen between them beyond this night. Still, the temporary terms of their sexual relationship didn't stop Annie from wondering what Oksana thought about her. And not just her body. Maybe Oksana really liked tougher women, with a lot more muscle and some knowledge of power tools. Maybe this was charity for Oksana in more ways than one.

But as Annie looked back up from the clothes at her feet, she saw she wasn't alone in her bashfulness. A light flush touched Oksana's skin as Annie's eyes wandered over her body again. She was so perfect. No hair between her legs, and the sheen of her wetness was obvious from a few feet away. Her full thighs were topped with wide hips. And those piercings. Annie had been waiting months for this chance, mulling the fantasy over for years. Oksana was right; they should take their time. Annie stepped toward Oksana at the same moment Oksana moved in her direction. She matched Oksana's nervous laughter and giggled even louder as they both took a step back. With a shrug, Annie relented and met Oksana beside the bed.

"Is kissing okay?" Annie asked.

Oksana snorted a laugh and returned Annie's sudden smile. "Yes, kissing is allowed. I'm your trainer. Not a hooker."

"Okay. Good." Annie stood on the balls of her feet, an odd sense of glee rushing through her mind as Oksana bent to meet her halfway.

Oksana's lips were soft. When they brushed against Annie's, her whole body turned into a ball of sensation. Her eyes slipped shut and she rose on her toes even higher, bracing herself with her hands on Oksana's hips, leaning closer to Oksana's warm body. She felt the tip of Oksana's tongue and she let her in, let in the warm, wet softness of her mouth.

Oksana's kiss was perfect. Delicate, but confident. Sweet. Annie tried to match her careful skill, kissing Oksana back with just as much patience, with deliberate but gentle motions of her tongue. Oksana moaned.

The sound was enough to encourage Annie further. Stepping back just a little, she never broke contact with Oksana's perfectly full lips as she maneuvered her onto the bed. Annie lowered herself over Oksana's body, straddling her lap as Oksana shifted back on the bedspread.

Annie wrestled with a desperate urge to hump Oksana like a little dog in heat. There had to be more finesse involved. She had no real clue what she was doing, but finally, Annie could put a lifetime of her secret desires and creative daydreaming to good work. And she could ask. Gently, she pushed Oksana back down on the bed. She followed, kissing her way down Oksana's neck, making her own desperate noises as Oksana's fingers caressed her sides. She was enjoying this. Every second of it.

"Tell me what to do," Annie said breathlessly.

"No," Oksana said, letting out a gasping noise. "Just keep doing what you're doing. I like what you're doing."

Annie slipped her hand between their bodies, eager to feel Oksana, and quickly spread Oksana's wet lips. Her clit was hard under Annie's fingers, tiny and hard. Again, she wanted to ask what she should do next. This was all so new, but to save herself from sounding like more of a fool, Annie thought of the ways she liked to be touched, the ways she liked to touch herself. She stroked over Oksana's clit, stroked up and down each side slowly before dipping her fingers lower. Oksana's body lifted off the bed to meet her hand. Annie slipped inside. She shuddered, blowing a heavy breath across Oksana's nipple. She was so wet. There was no resistance, but as soon as her fingers filled Oksana's body, the soaked muscles gripped at Annie's hand. Another shudder traveled down to Annie's pussy. She wanted to come.

"You're a liar," Oksana panted.

"What?" Annie peered up, watching the strain on Oksana's face as her fingers continued to stroke her from the inside.

Oksana laced her hand through Annie's loosely pony-tailed hair. Annie leaned into her grasp and looked up as Oksana brushed her bangs to the side with her other hand. "You've been with a woman before. Hundreds of them," Oksana said.

"I have not." Annie couldn't resist smiling. She added another finger and dug a little deeper.

"Liar." Oksana hissed, her eyes rolling shut. "Oh God…"

Annie kissed her way back to Oksana's mouth and she fucked her with a little more insistence. Annie was close to coming herself, but she wanted Oksana to finish first. Yes, Oksana was doing her a favor in a way, but Annie wanted to make it worth her while.

Another finger added, Annie shifted her palm and stroked Oksana with her thumb.

"Anne…" Oksana whined desperately against her mouth. No one had called her Anne in years, but Annie liked the way it sounded. Annie liked the sound of Oksana's voice. She liked the breathy quality that took over the already sexy tone as she moved closer and closer to orgasm. She wanted to hear it again.

"Are you gonna come?"

"Yes. Fuck. Yes. Please."

"Does this feel good?" Annie rotated her finger slightly, sliding her middle finger in and out while she massaged upward with her pointer.

Oksana grabbed her wrist, stilling Annie's hand. A half second later she came, calling out Annie's name. "Anne," she whimpered over and over. "Anne. Fuck."

A grin broke out across Annie's face. Oksana was so gorgeous and ten times more so when she orgasmed. Annie gave her a moment to come back to herself, tracing soft lines up and down Oksana's thigh, and then she kissed her.

Annie let Oksana roll them so Oksana was on top. Annie gazed up at her, loving the sweet, hot breath Oksana heaved against her chin and throat. Annie was shocked with what she'd just done, the magic she'd worked with her hands and her lips. The night was young. Maybe later—

Annie swallowed then finished her thought aloud, "I want to go down on you."

Oksana smiled this time. "Can I go first?"

Annie shrugged and rolled her eyes. "If you must."

Oksana sat up and ran her fingers along Annie's pussy. Annie's reaction was instant and a little pathetic. She rolled slightly on her back, arching into Oksana's touches. This was a moment she'd been thinking about for a while too—what it would be like to have another woman's mouth on her body. Oksana didn't disappoint. Her soft lips closed over Annie lips and clit. Oksana hummed against her skin, a deep sound of satisfaction sending tingles everywhere.

I guess I pass the taste test, Annie thought before her brain was wiped clean with a fresh wave of pleasure.

Annie hadn't said a word; Oksana read her perfectly. Where Annie had treated her to hard and slow, Oksana devoured her. Rough and quick. Annie's fingers gripped the back of Oksana's shaved head; her heel dug into Oksana's side. She moaned pathetically, chanting swears and Oksana's name as Oksana drilled two fingers inside Annie's cunt and lightly scraped her teeth over Annie's clit. Her thighs trembled.

"Oh yeah. *You're* definitely a lesbian," Annie groaned.

Oksana choked on her laugh, but didn't stop the thrusting of her finger and the rough strokes of her tongue. Annie squirmed as Oksana sucked her clit, flicking the tip over and over until Annie arched hard off the bed, driving her hips against Oksana's face.

"Fuck, Sana," Annie cried as Oksana fucked her even harder. In her haze, she shortened Oksana's name. It sounded strange coming off her lips, but something in her gut, something that craved more— more sex, more intimacy, more than just one night—thought the nickname fit the scene and Annie's desire. "Sana, please. Oh my God! Please don't stop." Oksana followed instructions.

"Yeah," Annie panted. "Yeah!" She came hard. A wet, hot rush she could feel surrounding Oksana's fingers and coating her chin. Oksana pulled her fingers out but kept on kissing and licking until Annie lay helpless on the bed, softly rubbing the back of her head. She'd never been with anyone who had a shaved head before, guy or girl. Annie liked the way it felt.

After a moment, or fifty, when Annie regained her sight, she watched as Oksana pulled herself upright and casually wiped her mouth. Annie followed Oksana up the bed and wrapped herself around Oksana's body as she settled against the mountain of hotel pillows. They were quiet for a while, just holding each other and breathing, heavily at first then softer and slower. The air in the cramped room was still heavy.

"Everything you ever wished for?" Oksana asked after some time. Annie glanced up and met Oksana's eyes before settling her gaze on Oksana's tight stomach. She started tracing the pattern of the birch bark tattoo on Oksana's right side. They hadn't discussed cuddling, but she didn't want to move. She was warm, and Oksana's touch along her shoulder was just as soothing as it was unexpected.

"Yes," Annie answered truthfully. "And just so you know, because of its awful placement, I think we're obligated to fuck on that desk."

Oksana's body shook as she laughed again. "We can do that."

Annie sat up and bit her lip. "Let's do it now."

A text alert pulled Annie out of a deep sleep. She rolled over in the unfamiliar bed and the night, the whole night, came rushing back to her. She smiled and stretched, rubbing her thighs together and contemplating getting herself off just once before she headed to work. She had plenty of mental material to work with now.

Her cell went off again. Annie reached for her phone then smiled at the words that lit up the screen.

No fantasy should have an awkward morning after. I'll see you soon. And yes, I had a great time.

CHAPTER ONE

THE REALITY...SLIGHTLY ALTERED
BY SEVERAL GLASSES OF WHITE WINE

Drunk didn't feel right, but it suited Annie's mood. She took another gulp of her chilled Moscato, swirling the fruity wine around in her cheeks as she pulled up Jeff's itinerary on her BlackBerry. Dublin, Amsterdam, Berlin, and then a few days "drying out" in Paris before heading back to the states. Four more weeks before her fiancé was back in town.

If only she could stay drunk the entire time.

As it stood, Annie was nine months into what her mother insisted be a yearlong engagement to photographer Jeff Treeder. That engagement had been the start of this whole messy situation, and ultimately, the cause of this evening's intoxication.

They'd met years ago, when Annie was fresh out of USC. She was a production assistant on some B movie, and Jeff had offered to do the stills for free to build his portfolio. The first day, they'd chatted while balancing their lunch plates on their knees. Two days later, Jeff walked Annie to her car and kissed her. A week after that, they spent the night fucking on her new futon.

The weeks and months between their first time together and the sunny July afternoon when Jeff proposed to her on the beach passed so quickly, so easily. They never fought, gave each other space and freedom. He was her best friend and the best lover she'd ever had. Not that she'd been with a ton of people before him, but Jeff was definitely the one for her. She proudly wore the ring he'd slipped onto her finger.

Thanks to her mother's thirst for extravagance and her maid of honor's freakish talent for organization, their wedding ceremony would be King James traditional and the reception Martha Stewart perfect with a Laguna Beach twist. It had been Annie's idea for the two of them to do one thing that her mother had no control over. There would be no bachelor or bachelorette parties. Those functions were lame and outdated. At least that was Annie's justification for what she really wanted, and her future hubby was completely on board with her proposed alternatives.

Instead of getting wasted in Vegas, Jeff opted for thirty days traveling around Europe with some buddies on the promise that Annie wouldn't ask any questions once he was back. Her bridesmaids—Megan, Shane, and Feather—thought she was nuts, letting Jeff go off to do God knows what while she sat at home. But Annie hadn't let herself get screwed out of the fun. She'd taken full advantage of her freebie.

One night where she would allow herself to indulge in her longtime fantasy. No veils covered in little plastic dicks. No oiled guys in G-strings. Just one perfect night, just for Annie.

In the beginning, she didn't know where to start. Craigslist couldn't be trusted, and she wasn't sure if she actually wanted to hit the bars. She had a few gay acquaintances, but none she was attracted to. None but her trainer, the very woman assigned to trim Annie down for said wedding.

Annie wasn't surprised by how beautiful her personal trainer was. It was Los Angeles, after all. Head shots were attached to résumés at McDonald's. She and Annie were nearly the same age, right on the cusp of thirty, but where Annie had traded on her traditionally Anglo good looks, Oksana's exotic appearance grabbed your attention, whether you wanted it to or not.

Minutes after meeting her, Annie had to ask where Oksana was from and who had donated the DNA to her light brown skin and her vibrant eyes that reminded Annie of fresh clover. Oksana kept her hair buzzed close to her head, but after seeing it grown out a bit, Annie had to know how someone with her gorgeous skin tone ended up with brown hair that seemed to radiate with wisps of blond in the sunlight. The answer had been a Russian mother and a West African father, but knowing the science didn't diminish the effect she had on Annie. It took three sessions for Annie to get over what was going on from the shoulders up and a few more to get over the intimidation created by Oksana's body.

Her breasts were perfectly shaped, and Annie now knew, deliciously pierced. Her waist seemed impossibly small and her hips and her butt round in a way that could make other women and Barbie dolls worldwide jealous. Oksana was one of those people who shouldn't exist. It wasn't fair to all the plain girls out there to have to compete with her for attention, but she didn't resent Oksana's beauty. In a weird way, Annie was drawn to it, long before they'd come to this agreement. Weeks before she knew Oksana was gay.

Oksana had whipped her into shape in no time. Annie didn't have much to lose, but now thanks to their bi-weekly sessions, her stomach was super flat and her arms flab free for the bouquet tossing. And in that time they'd become sort of close. Annie didn't know a lot about her, but she liked their sessions together, even if they were grueling. She liked the occasional quick phone call they shared. The silly texts here and there.

Annie didn't have a real confidant. There were certain things you couldn't just come out and say to your boyfriend. She could tell Megan anything, within reason, but not this. Megan wasn't homophobic exactly, but she wouldn't understand what Annie wanted and why. She wouldn't understand it was possible to be genuinely bisexual. Like a good hairdresser, though, Annie felt like she could share this little secret with her personal trainer. She trusted Oksana, and boy, was she glad she did. She was nervous the day she blabbed her plan to Oksana. Annie wanted to spend one night, one perfect, sex-filled night with another woman.

It wasn't cheating. She and Jeff had agreed that whatever they did on their night of freedom, or month in his case, was a complete and utter pass. Oksana was shocked at first, but she warmed to the idea quickly, even applauded Annie for wanting to do something different from the typical night of drunkenness with her girlfriends.

That night after their session, Annie walked to her car, her stomach flopping anxiously as she heard Oksana call her name from across the parking lot. She was glad she'd told someone, but she was no closer to finding a playmate, no closer to actually executing her plan. She'd turned to see Oksana jogging in her direction.

"Annie," she breathed as she reached Annie's Prius. "I'll do it."

"Do what?" Annie had asked, shocked because she knew the answer.

"I'll be…the one. If you want."

"You'll sleep with me?" They had laughed. It sounded crazy out loud. Who the hell planned these sorts of things? Annie did, that's who. She had no interest in picking out flowers and nailing down a DJ for the reception, but she still liked her own plans to be tight and flawless. Her mother had taught her that much.

"Yeah." Oksana shrugged. The confidence she usually had in the gym was gone, replaced by this raw eagerness. To Annie it was so sexy. "Could be fun."

"I think so," Annie had replied, trying not to choke on her tongue. Oksana was perfect. Beautiful. Nice. Gay. She wasn't a murderer. She'd seen Annie sweating her ass off and hadn't been completely repulsed. She was willing. And most importantly, she didn't hate Annie for having this idea in the first place. Annie knew how it sounded. That she was just looking for some easy gay girl to try out her bi-curiosity on, but that wasn't it. She wanted someone who wanted her, just for that night and someone she would want too. Mutual, consensual fun.

"Okay." Annie beamed up at her. "Let's do it."

So they decided, after giggling some more at Annie's last choice of words. Oksana requested the night to fit with her morning training schedule. Annie booked the room. And a week later, twenty-four hours after Jeff flew out of LAX, Annie found herself four stories above downtown L.A. in a junior suite of The Hilton

Checkers Hotel, the perfect place for their sexual rendezvous. A safe distance from Oksana's stomping ground of West Hollywood. Miles away from Annie's home in Venice.

The night had been flawless, hot, and intoxicating. In the end, all Annie wanted was more time to explore Oksana's body, more time to drown in her kisses. That should have been the first sign. This whole affair was meant to last one night. One night only, but almost a full day later, Annie couldn't get Oksana out of her mind. The text messages they'd exchanged throughout the day weren't making things any easier. She had plenty to distract her, but all those distractions revolved around a certain wedding. A wedding for some reason she was suddenly dreading.

Annie swallowed hard as the thought and the emotion and the flood of anxiety that rushed over her skin like an eerily cool breeze all met in the pit of her stomach. The mix sent the kung pao chicken surfing in her gut.

Another glass of wine sounded like a super idea, and then as she poured well to the top of the glass, Annie thought it would be best to play another round of the blame game. With a flick of her thumb, she pulled up their text conversation. For this portion of the tournament, the judges found that Oksana was at fault. Oksana had sent the first text of the day, and even if it had been somewhat of a "see you later-good-bye-ish" text, if Oksana hadn't sent that stupid thing in the first place, Annie would have never replied with: *Not awkward at all. You should have stayed.*

Then Oksana never would have replied with: *O rly?*

Annie never would have giggled like a fool as she walked to the hotel shower and she'd never have texted back as she waited for the water to warm up. *Rly. The shower is pretty big.*

Maybe next time was the returned text that made Annie freeze, one step away from the sink. There was not going to be a next time, but at that moment, Annie knew a next time was exactly what she wanted. And now a good way to being shitfaced, sitting on her couch surrounded by take-out and bridal magazines, Annie mumbled the same thought that had passed through her head earlier that day.

Why did she text Oksana back?

That moment, that text, was the text that should have ended this part of their relationship. Annie should have brought them both back to reality, back to their respective roles as client and trainer, a professional relationship that was due to end in exactly two and a half months. Maybe a full three if Annie kept burying her sorrow and confusion in whole bottles of wine and Chinese food. Not to mention the Ben and Jerry's she'd been hoarding for her next cheat day.

She scrolled through the list of electronic bits of forbidden lust. Lust was the right word. Not love. Only pathetic virgins and desperate teen boys fell in love with the person—or in this case, the unearthly angel of beauty and cardiovascular fitness—who'd popped their cherry. Annie was not in love, but she was certainly pathetic. So pathetic she was actually considering texting Oksana again. Why stop now, right?

Back and forth all day, through payroll, through Annie's lunch break, the *Single Dads* scheduling meeting, and immediately after a brief call with her mom. Annie assumed between Oksana's other training sessions, they couldn't seem to stop with the texting. Oksana's nightly dinner with her grandmother and her little sister was the only reason they weren't swapping messages now.

Oksana had only mentioned her small family of three a few times before. Like a good trainer, she kept most of their conversations focused on Annie, but that hadn't stopped Annie from wondering every now and then what the grandmother and the kid sister were like.

The image flooded Annie's mind—the sweet, understanding old woman who loved Oksana for exactly who she was, tattoos and all. And the adorable little sister, fourteen years old or so, perked up in her chair, passing dinner rolls to Oksana as she gleefully recounted her day at school. It wasn't middle America perfect, but it was Oksana perfect, and Annie realized that she was fucking crazy for dreaming up Oksana's personal life and even crazier for maybe, a little bit, wanting to be a part of it.

Annie squinted at the lilac polish on her ring finger and the diamond below then shook her head trying to blur the thoughts away.

Jeff. Jeff was the focus. His rugged good looks. His adorable hipster flare. His gorgeous brown eyes and sweet smile. Jeff had tattoos too. Sexy tattoos that Annie loved. She knew what each one stood for. The Joker on his shoulder showed his dedication to his favorite DC villain. The orchid on his chest was in honor of his late aunt, and the enormous dragon on his back was a commissioned piece from his favorite local artist. Some of the other smaller pieces on his arms and legs were a little silly to Annie, like the Road Runner on his calf (his best friend sported Wile E. Coyote on the other leg.) Okay, the Road Runner was really stupid and kind of unattractive, but it suited the whole Jeff package. A package Annie would love unconditionally until death do them part.

Oksana's tattoos were similar in a way. All tattoos were. Annie didn't have any, but she thought maybe one day she would get one, if she could find some symbol to commit to for life. One like Oksana's that mixed with her femininity. Oksana was definitely femme.

Annie paused for a moment. Femme was the right word. Or was it lipstick lesbian? It didn't matter for this particular conversation, but except for her shaved head, Oksana had a very feminine, almost dainty air about her. That femininity made her hard-edged tattoos that much more intriguing.

The large Cyrillic letters (Annie had looked that up as soon as she got to work) that ran up Oksana's left side, the cutout of the heart on her hard bicep that followed a dashed trail over her armpit then over the curve of her breast and stopped at its exact match, right above her heart. The heart didn't have the typical bulbous curves or the anatomical structure of some of the heart tattoos Annie had seen before. It was all hard lines. Two boxes at the top converging at a pointed base.

See, Annie wasn't that drunk. "Converging" was still part of her vocabulary. She still had her words. There were sunflowers too, in gray and black, and that really cool birch bark that blended into her skin on her right side. More words, more pictures, two silhouettes of grizzly bears on either wrist, and the inner workings of a clock, but the heart had intrigued her the most. She never got a chance to ask about it. Her mouth had always been full of some part of

Oksana, blocked by her own screams of pleasure. Oh, it had been one perfect night for sure, but not enough to wipe out the lifetime she had planned with Jeff.

Annie rolled her head off the back of the couch and eyed the clock on the DVR box.

A lifetime is a long *time.*

"Ugh!" Annie groaned, pounding the sofa with her fist. "Anne. Please get your shit together. You are marrying Jeff. You are marrying Jeff. You *love* Jeff."

In twelve weeks, she would be walking down the aisle toward an amazing guy. They hadn't exactly discussed it yet, but eventually they would have their own cute kids. No doubt much cuter than any Oksana-related little sister. Jeff wasn't much for sentiment or sit-down dinners, but he would make an excellent father. An excellent father and an excellent husband. Twelve weeks and Annie would have her happily ever after.

And in the meantime…

Annie glared at her phone. In the meantime, Annie would become an alcoholic. Or find a new trainer. Yeah, the new trainer thing was a great idea. A guy trainer. An ugly guy trainer with an ugly face and a killer body. A gay guy trainer with a really ugly face that Annie would never, ever considering sleeping with whether she had an agreed upon ho pass from Jeff or not. That would solve all her problems. New trainer, never see Oksana again, never have to look at her beautiful supple mouth again. Work off all this take-out and the seven thousand calories of wine, keep it off, then marry Jeff.

"You're a genius, Anne," she slurred cheerfully, holding her glass up in the air.

A moment later, her cell phone vibrated in her other hand. Annie closed her eyes and prayed this spiraling nightmare would just end already.

"Please be Megan. Please be Megan." She opened one eye, then the other, and calmly set her wine glass down on the table. Then she looked down at her phone.

It wasn't Megan.

I have to call it an early night. Sweet dreams. Annie could almost hear Oksana breathing the words.

"Sweet dreams, my ass," Annie grumbled, sneering at her phone.

That's when it dawned on her. This was a test. A test from the matrimony gods. She worked in television, and movies before that, and not once had she given in to random advances from crew guys and grabby producers, not even the cute ones, because she had Jeff. No other guy compared to him in her eyes. But Oksana presented something new and fresh. Unexpected. Oksana was different, her body a different kind of temptation. Oksana had boobs and killer legs. If Annie could sleep with someone like Oksana, if she could let Oksana kiss her, let her soft hands explore every inch of her body, she could surely turn the other cheek, figuratively of course, and walk right into a peaceful, long marriage.

If she could never think about Oksana's body again…Oksana's breasts, soft and perky, the right size to fit in Annie's palms with those mouthwatering piercings, were nowhere near enough to make her want to leave Jeff. No way. No fucking way. It was sex. That was it. Annie was bisexual, yes, but she had made her choice, and one night was not enough to make her all the way gay, and it surely was not enough to make her have a single second thought about being with Jeff.

The oral sex they shared on the bed. The brutally kinky finger fucking she'd delivered to Oksana on that shockingly sturdy desk was no match for what Jeff could do with his cock. Jesus Christ, the way Oksana tasted. How wet she got when Annie—

Shit. She'd done it now.

Annie slid down into the cushions, cupping herself pathetically through her jeans. She wanted back in that hotel room. She wanted Oksana back between her thighs.

She was drunk and horny and this had to stop. For now, she'd fuck herself into oblivion—another big word she was proud to remember—exorcise the demon out of her pants, then for the next few weeks she'd abstain from any sexual thoughts, focus on work, and what parts of her wedding Megan and her mother would let her touch. And then she'd let Jeff fuck her back to sanity the minute he walked through the door. Three and a half weeks from now.

Annie sat up and chucked her phone across the couch. It skidded across the cushions, bounced off the armrest and skipped to the pink shag carpet under her coffee table. It could stay there. She'd charge it in the morning. No way that evil mobile device of temptation was following her into the bedroom. She corked the wine on the third try and grabbed her glass. She only tripped twice on her way to the kitchen, managed only to spill a few drops down her chin as she finished what she had already poured out. So what if the glass broke in the sink.

She made it to her room without any major incidents. The socks came off and then the jeans and her shirt and bra. Annie collapsed on her bed and worked her fingers into her underwear. She was wet. Absolutely no surprise there. She brought Jeff into her mind, his messy brown hair between her legs as she fingered her clit with one hand and fucked her pussy with the other. It only took fifteen seconds before those thick, dark locks were replaced by a soft bald head, those dark brown eyes suddenly green. All traces of a five o'clock shadow banished to the back of her mind for smooth cheeks and full, pink lips that flashed open to a teasing smile.

Annie came twice before she passed out with her hand between her legs.

❖

"What's wrong with you?"

Oksana put the car in park and swiveled in her seat to face her sister. Kat stared back, her eyes narrowing. Oksana ignored the tongue ring Kat clicked against her teeth impatiently. She also ignored the Sweet Valley way Kat flicked her head back to get her bright green bangs out of her eyes. They slid right back into place, screening the black shadow smeared over the top and bottom of her eyelids.

"What are you talking about?" Oksana asked.

"Something is going on with you. I can tell and so can Baba."

"What? She cannot. I'm fine."

"See? If it was nothing you would have said so. But you know Baba can see something's up with you and so can I. You spent the night out the other night and you haven't done that in like forever, and then last night you wouldn't let your phone out of your sight. You always leave it in the little house when you come up for dinner. So I want to know what is going on with you? Or should I ask, who is she?"

Dammit. Oksana had planned on coming clean to Paulo. Her boss needed to know when she crossed a line with a client. Not that her job was in jeopardy. Oksana's gym, Elite Fitness, had the same rules as any whorehouse. Be thorough, be professional, sleep with as many clients as you want, but never, ever fall in love. Oksana never liked the idea of getting sexually intimate with her clients, but when it came to a certain petite blonde, Oksana wished the option of love wasn't completely off the table.

But that was between her, her boss, and a certain petite blonde, not a conversation she needed to be having at seven thirty in the morning outside her old high school with her little sister. The fact that Kat had brought up her odd behavior was problem enough. Baba Inna would kill Oksana if she knew exactly where she had been the other night. Her actions were irresponsible, and simply put, she wasn't setting a good example for Kat by staying out all night or sleeping with her straight, *engaged* client.

Kat's eyes softened for a moment, a look Oksana only saw when the kid actually let down this tough as nails persona she'd taken on the second she hit puberty. It was the look Kat gave her when she needed Oksana to be honest with her as a sister, not a parent. The look they shared any time their mother bothered to call, the look they exchanged whenever Baba started moving a little slower.

It was a weird role: parent and sibling.

She and Baba were doing an all right job raising Kat. No fights in school. Good grades. Only a few arguments on Facebook here and there over various girls, but all in all, the kid had turned out pretty good, and for a moody teenager, she seemed fairly happy. But when she gave Oksana that look in relation to Oksana's love life,

Oksana felt like a single mom whose only child really wanted her pathetic parent to find love already, for the good of the family.

She'd seen variations on the expression before. The night she moved out to live with Vivian and the morning she'd lugged a duffel bag of her stuff back.

Oksana hated that look. It made her feel trapped and unworthy, like she was failing at this parenthood thing and doing even worse as a big sister. She couldn't *lie* to that look.

"What's going on?" Kat pleaded.

"Okay…" Man, she'd really fucked up. Why did Kat have to be so perceptive? "I was out with someone, but I don't think it's going to work out. We were talking a little bit yesterday, but it's over." Oksana ignored Kat's gaze as it darted to her cell phone nestled in her lap.

"What happened? Why didn't it work?" The look was becoming too much even though Oksana should have expected it. She'd been single for so long, and even though they didn't say it directly, her sister and her grandmother knew she was lonely. They did want her to find someone, but Annie was not that someone.

"She's just not right for me," Oksana replied. Kat regarded her for a moment, the concerned look on her face a bit disturbing. She really wasn't a kid anymore. Oksana had to be more careful before her mistakes turned Kat into the wrong kind of adult. "I promise I'll tell you when I meet someone I want to bring home."

"Okay." Kat unbuckled her seat belt and grabbed her bag. "I don't believe you, but okay. I'm taking the bus with Erica."

Oksana didn't like that turn in the conversation much better. Erica, aka girlfriend number two in as many months, was one of eight kids. Oksana wasn't into the idea of Kat adding to Erica's mother's already heavy after school burden, but with her evening session and Baba staying later at the store, Oksana didn't want the girls hanging out at the big house by themselves. She also didn't like the idea that Erica's mom was so busy with the other children that she didn't have time to catch Kat teaching her daughter the ways of physical love. Oksana had already caught them twice. She held in a shudder as she dished out her orders.

"Home by seven or meet Baba at the store."

"I know. I know." Kat rolled her eyes as she jumped out of the car. "Love you."

"Have a good day."

Oksana counted to ten then rolled down the passenger window. "*Ekaterina, wait,*" she yelled in Russian. Kat paused and looked over her shoulder with wide-eyed horror. Oksana switched back to English for the benefit of everyone in a two-block radius. "I love you too," she shouted.

Kat flipped her the bird and booked it for the side door.

Oksana's smile held until she pulled away from the high school. This shit with Annie, whatever it was, had to stop.

As soon as she read the text Annie had sent her a few minutes before.

One night. It was supposed to last one fucking night, and now it was stretching into two days. When Annie came to her with her silly idea, Oksana wanted to be annoyed. Who the fuck did she think she was anyway? At first glance, she was a snobby, rich brat from the OC who had her parents' wallet wrapped around her little finger, but she found that Annie was the exact opposite. She was funny and smart as hell and hot. Really hot and short. An angel of Oksana's secret shame. She was a sucker for short women.

The day she'd taken Annie on as a client, she knew she'd have a hard time keeping her thoughts professional. Annie was too attractive. Her beach babe next door package was complete with natural bleach blond hair and sky blue eyes. Her lips looked soft and inviting enough to suck on. Her smile was infectious. Annie didn't need a trainer. Her body was amazing, plump and soft in all the right places with a huge rack and a round ass that shouldn't belong to a girl that little. Almost immediately, Oksana could tell Annie was intelligent with a hint of a sick sense of humor, qualities that Oksana loved in a woman. She had to ignore the ache in her nipples and between her legs, a cruel tug and swell that always fired up during their sessions together, set off by Annie's smile, her laugh, and maybe her ass. Annie was off-limits. She was a client. She was straight, straight enough, and she was engaged.

Even if Annie was just some ignorant straight woman who thought she could borrow a lesbian for a night, Oksana couldn't see past the silver lining. Staring her in the face was her chance to fuck Annie Collins. The best thing to walk through the doors of Elite Fitness in the time Oksana had been working there. Or ever.

It took some time, but she was finally over Vivian. Or more accurately, the way her ex-girlfriend had left things between them. Oksana's heart had been broken. Her sense of trust torn and spat on, and when the wreckage had been cleared away, Oksana and everyone around her knew she needed some time before she put herself back out in the dating game. The standard few days to cry over a relationship lost turned into a few months of self-pity, which turned into a year of self-reflection and another three years of refocusing her energies. In all, four sexless years. She'd been a little gun-shy when it came to being with someone new, but not long before she met Annie, Oksana was ready to try again.

It was time for her to get back out there and find something good, something healthy for herself that didn't involve shuttling teenagers to the beach or conversing with an elderly chain-smoker who'd had fond memories of the Cold War. She loved her grandmother and her baby sister, but for what she was feeling, they weren't enough.

She wanted love again, real love this time, and great sex with her own girlfriend, not someone else's fiancée. When Annie came to her with her prenuptial confessions, Oksana could not ignore the tiny voice in the back of her head screaming at her to go for it. This was the moment she had been waiting for, not just to indulge in the fantasies of Annie she'd been harboring since the moment they were introduced; it was also an opportunity to move on, to shake herself out of this sexual slump.

At the time, this "play date" with Annie seemed anything but risky. It seemed like fun with absolutely no risk of commitment. The perfect mix to help Oksana dust off that part of her life. But sleeping with Annie was not the thing to do. She should go out and date someone single, someone who was gay. Problem was, she wanted Annie Collins so badly her mind erased every logical reason for staying far, far away from her.

Oksana rolled her eyes at herself as she stopped with the flow of traffic right on the edge of West Hollywood. Things were a mess now. A huge mess. Her innocent little one-night stand was now something else. It was a distraction, and suddenly it was a point of interest for Kat. God, and Ronnie. Her best friend would have a field day mocking Oksana's ass if she knew she'd actually fucked a straight woman. An engaged straight woman. She had less than a future with Annie. If things went well, Annie would get married and they would never see each other again. If things went poorly… Oksana didn't want to consider those humiliating possibilities.

This was a *huge* fucking mess.

The parking lot of Elite Fitness was almost full at eight a.m. Oksana pulled her Tahoe to the rear and deftly backed it in the free spot between Paulo's Ferrari and the ivy covered wall of the smoothie place next door. After she cut the SUV off, she dared a look at her cell phone.

Hope you slept well. I got wine tanked and fell asleep with my fingers in my crotch. Can you say classy?

"Fuck," Oksana grumbled through gritted teeth.

Another text that shouldn't have been sent, but was because as good as Oksana was at pleasing a lady in bed, she was absolutely terrible at subtle brush-offs. She texted Annie and Annie texted her back, back and forth like Kat and her friends, and now, on day two, Oksana needed it to stop. It was great, immature, reckless fun and a disaster waiting to happen.

Annie was her client, nothing more.

"This ends now. Now. Right fucking now," she announced to no one.

Before she could talk herself out of it, she opened their message log. She looked through their texts, thought of the way Annie had kissed her, the way they'd fucked.

Those should have been my fingers. Oksana typed then hit send. And then her stomach plummeted into her ass. She wasn't ready to cut things off.

Oksana had feelings for Annie; she had from the first joke they'd shared, but soon she would have to blow her favorite client off because in twelve weeks that client would be married to the man who completed her world. A man who was smart enough to hold out for more than one fuck.

Don't do that, she scolded herself. It was much more than a simple fuck. She and Annie had come pretty damn close to actually making love. She'd had some passionate sex with Viv before the bitch disappeared, but it hadn't been nearly as passionate or fun as the sex she'd shared with Annie in those short hours.

Oksana's phone vibrated again in her hand.

Now I'm wet. Thanks.

A knot tied itself in Oksana's chest as her thighs pressed into the leather seat. She let the sensation fester for a moment before she shook off the arousal and grabbed her bag from the backseat. She had to come clean to Paulo, and if this shit didn't resolve itself, it was time to find Annie Collins, her beautiful, brainy producer, a new trainer. After they shared a few more texts.

Chapter Two

The Awkward Workout After

For no good reason, Annie was hiding in her car. Using a half-assed conversation with Megan as an excuse, but it was an excuse either way. She was hiding from Oksana. Stalling maybe. Not hiding. Actually, it was more like she was just taking her time walking into Elite Fitness. She was late. She knew it, but she wasn't ready to face Oksana yet. She didn't know what to say. She didn't know how to act. How do you behave when you see someone you've just had sex with? Someone you'd spent the last thirty hours exchanging dirty texts with. And these texts were dirty. Like "I want to fuck your pussy again" dirty. How do you act natural around someone after they spell something like that out so clearly, then send it to your phone? How do you go back to calm and casual when the texts you've sent were just as explicit? Annie didn't know, so she was hiding until she came up with a plan.

It had been ages since she'd had a sexual encounter with someone new. Annie had wanted to jump Oksana's bones for months, but now she knew how Oksana kissed. She knew how smooth her thighs were and how her toes curled when she came. She wanted to experience all of Oksana again. Right after they worked out. As soon as Annie got up the nerve to leave her car.

"Annie? Annie!" Megan screamed into the phone.

"What?" Annie replied.

"What are you doing?" Hiding. Plotting. Drenching my own underwear with thoughts of Oksana's nipple piercings.

"Nothing. What did you say?"

"We have to do something before your wedding," Megan said. She was speaking for Shane and Feather. Megan took her maid of honor duties seriously. Annie's mother was obsessed with the grand adventure, the venue, and the number of guests, but Megan helped keep everything tasteful. The invitations, the dress, the small gifts for various participants and family members, Megan had seen to all of that. There would be no mistakes on her watch, but she knew Annie was the bride and she wanted to make Annie happy. She was shocked that Jeff had taken off to Europe, still she was perfectly fine with skipping any semblance of a bachelorette party. Shane and Feather felt like they had been robbed. Megan hadn't let them do anything beyond trying on their dresses. Their whining wouldn't change Annie's mind. She had what she wanted.

"Really, it's okay." Then Annie heard Shane's voice in the background.

"Shane thinks we should go to Lucky Strike and get wasted while we bowl," Megan said. Annie watched as an older woman, Mrs. Barstein or Farstein or something walked into Elite Fitness. She was actually running late.

"Annie?"

"What?" She finally turned off her car. She had to go inside.

"Where are you?" Megan asked, annoyed.

"I'm about to work out."

"She's working out," Megan repeated for Shane. "Hold o—"

"What's the name of your gym?" Shane asked in a rush. Annie's fingers froze, clutching her keys.

"Why?"

"I'm looking for a new trainer," Shane said. "Quick got asked to do stunts for some lame movie and that's all he talks about now. He's driving me nuts." Annie had met Shane's trainer, Quick, once. He was a great trainer and a total jerk. Shane was smart to look for someone else. Anyone else but someone who worked with Oksana. She knew their time together was limited, but Annie wanted that time to be theirs. The last thing she needed was Shane coming up with the bright idea of joint sessions or something just as intrusive. The thought of even running into Shane while she was with Oksana made Annie break out into a nervous sweat she imagined still smelled like wine and Chinese food. She needed more time.

"Oh. Uh, I remember my trainer saying they are booked till the end of the summer," Annie lied.

"Shit. Okay. Here's Megan."

"No, actually I have to—"

"Hey." Megan was back on the phone before Annie could make her escape. "So we're going bowling. Just to get Shane to shut up."

"Sure. Let me just see what my schedule is like."

Megan scoffed and Annie immediately knew why. "We both know it's not worse than mine." Megan worked a shade under a thousand hours a week in the legal department at one of the major studios. The fact that her boss had let her leave work early that night was a small miracle. No doubt she'd mapped some sort of work-related errand into her escape.

"Right. Well, we'll figure it out."

"Okay. Kisses!" Megan said in her best valley girl voice. Annie laughed.

"Bye."

Annie ended the call and slipped her phone into her bag. She felt so bad. Like a little kid getting away with something less than a crime, but enough to be punished for. She was lying to her friends and Jeff, sort of, even though he'd technically agreed to what had happened between her and Oksana. She felt like a criminal for wanting more.

Annie climbed out of her car and was reminded how unseasonably humid it had been when she left her office. The heat from the day lingered as the sun began to set. She pushed aside any further preparations and walked, shoulders back, right into Elite Fitness. Immediately, her eyes landed on Oksana as she busied herself re-racking a few low-pound weights across the room. She didn't see Annie, giving her a few more seconds to hide her anxiety as she walked toward her fate.

The gym was busy, but like usual, the noise level was kept to a minimum, just some light bass pumping through the speakers overhead. Through the glass windows on her right she saw that spinning class was well under way. She smiled at the owner, Paulo, as he chatted with Mrs. Barstein or Farstein, who seemed in no hurry to actually begin her workout now that she was indoors. Two guys who always worked out together were side by side on treadmills facing the street. They looked strangely similar. They were both ripped, dark hair cut the same way, naturally tanned, good-looking in this uniform way. Annie couldn't tell if they were a couple who had transitioned to that looking and dressing alike phase, really good friends who'd met their match, or brothers. Maybe she'd ask Oksana when she ran out of things to say.

She tripped over the edge of the mats as she stared at their twin glutes and when she righted herself and the spike of adrenaline cleared, she was feet away from a grinning Oksana. It was a friendly smile, familiar, but she wasn't flirting.

"I see I didn't convert you completely," Oksana said. Annie shrugged off the comment, having pushed the gym rats out of her mind. Her thoughts and her whole body focused on Oksana and Oksana seemed to notice. *This* part felt like a scene from a movie. Annie entered this odd cone of silence. She couldn't hear anything, but she could feel the beat from the music above them. The air was too cool to carry anything beyond the rubber scent of the weights and the mats, but she was searching for the smell of Oksana. Her memory found it immediately and it filled Annie's nostrils and rolled over the surface of her tongue. She licked her lip. Oksana's skin suddenly grew darker but brighter at the same time.

Annie imagined if she had hair, Oksana would do something adorable with it like anxiously tuck it behind her ear. But instead she gently tugged at her studded earring and glanced at the floor. "Hi," she said, just as sweetly.

"Hi," Annie replied. She moved closer, too close, but Oksana didn't move away. "I feel like I should say something inappropriate."

"Like what?" Oksana asked. She swallowed as if preparing to be horrified.

"Like how beautiful you look today."

Oksana looked away, blushing even more, but Annie could see her smiling as she ducked her head. "Can we please just work out?"

"I'm sorry. Sure. Let's work out." Oksana kicked a foam roller to the middle of the floor and motioned for Annie to sit down on the mat. Annie plopped down on the floor and slid the roller under her calves.

"So."

"What am I supposed to say to you?" Oksana asked.

"I don't know, but this is lovely weather we're having."

"It is. Any plans for the weekend?"

"Yes." Annie smiled. "I'll be doing my best to remain appropriate." Something changed between them then, like the ice had been broken and they slid easily into their workout.

Beyond her usual instructions, Oksana was unusually quiet as Annie stretched. She flinched every time they touched. When she gripped Annie's hands to stretch her back, Annie noticed her palms were cold and a little clammy. Annie sensed she was more nervous than uncomfortable, but all the things that came to mind to say to help soothe Oksana would get her tossed out of the gym and Oksana fired, so she kept her solutions to herself. They barely made eye contact as they walked over to the treadmills. Annie almost asked about the jogging twins, but she thought better of it. Maybe she was coming on too strong.

She settled into a brisk walk, then poked Oksana in the shoulder. "You okay?"

The confidence seemed to settle back into Oksana's shoulders. "Yeah. I'm glad we've already got your money. You don't need me anymore."

"What do you mean?"

"Look at yourself." Annie glanced down at herself then up at her reflection in the window. "You're in perfectly good shape. I'm sure your dress fits like a glove."

Annie didn't want to think about her dress. "Are you trying to get rid of me?"

"No. We don't like to give refunds."

"Oh, well, as long as you have my money."

Oksana chuckled lightly, tapping the monitor on the treadmill. "I'll be right back. Don't touch that incline."

"I promise I won't."

She looked forward again and watched Oksana's reflection as she headed to the other side of the gym and disappeared into their main office. When Oksana came back she seemed like her old self, the person Annie had grown to know before their one night together. The shift in her demeanor Annie took as a sign to really back off. She was acting like she had no control over herself, flirting with Oksana in the gym, but as their workout continued Annie couldn't ignore the way Oksana was looking at her when she thought Annie wasn't looking back. She felt so aware of her body and even more aware of the way Oksana was watching her. As she counted through sets and waited for Annie to catch her breath or take a drink of water. Annie couldn't ignore it. Once they were finished, Annie took a chance, thinking Oksana's response to a request she'd never made before would give her the answer she needed.

She wiped her face one last time then shoved her jacket into her bag. "Walk me to my car?"

"Okay." Oksana followed her silently to the door. No one seemed to notice them slipping out, not that they would have cared, but it was that type of secret they shared. A silly part of Annie thought everyone knew or was at least trying to figure them out.

When they reached the parking lot Annie fought the urge to take Oksana's hand. They weren't on a date. They were outside Oksana's place of employment. Talk about inappropriate. As they turned to each other in the shadows near Annie's car, she felt the climate change. The air of innocent, albeit, sexual flirting was gone, but so was any sense of professionalism. Somehow, at least for this moment, something between then had turned serious. Annie could feel it. She could see the look of consideration on Oksana's face. She could tell Oksana was just as anxious to see what would happen next.

"So, I'll see you this weekend?" Annie asked.

"First thing in the morn," Oksana said, looking down at her sneakers. Annie looked from Oksana's face to her hands that were braced on her waist so her elbows were out. They were silent for a few moments, then Oksana looked up.

It wasn't anything Oksana did or the adorably quizzical expression that touched her face as she looked back at Annie. There wasn't any practical reason for Annie to step any closer than she was, and she should have done the exact opposite of putting her hands on top of Oksana's. The only thing going through her mind was that she should kiss Oksana. So she did.

Oksana had been wrestling with what to do about Annie all day. She held off on telling Paulo the truth. He asked her a hundred times if she was okay, pointing out that from the moment she walked in that morning that she'd been acting strangely for the past couple days. But she had no clue how to tell him the truth because she wasn't ready to come clean yet. Coming clean meant facing the fact that she'd made a mistake. This wasn't how reconstructing your love life was supposed to go. There were rules for this sort of thing. Like both people should probably be single. Still, she couldn't ignore the texts she found at the end of every hour. She had to respond to them. She couldn't remember the last time she'd actually been wet all day long. She wasn't ready for that part to end either.

She'd decided to see how things played out once they were around each other again. No one could argue that texting and speaking face-to-face were not on the same level when it came to applying heavy meaning to communication. She wanted to see if Annie was using their distance as a way to keep her fantasy going a little longer or if, once they were together, Annie would keep up whatever this game was between them. Oksana hated admitting it to herself, but she was enjoying this game. At least until Annie actually showed up at Elite Fitness.

Oksana shouldn't have been that shocked by her aggressive behavior. Annie had been blunt all along, but for some reason Oksana wasn't prepared for it. She'd convinced herself that Annie would start spouting some nonsense about her wedding, but she didn't. She even went as far as to change the subject every time Oksana brought it up. This scared Oksana a lot. She did not want to start having feelings for Annie. Real feelings beyond the "I desperately need to have sex with your fingers and your mouth" type feelings that Oksana had been fighting every moment since they met. She needed Annie to have some reason. She needed Annie to push her away before she fell into something that ended with her looking like a fool.

Instead, she followed Annie out to the parking lot, something she'd never done with a client before. Instead of telling Annie they needed to end this thing between them, they were kissing. It was kisses like this that she had been warring with since she'd woken up that morning. Annie's lips that made her forget where she was and who she was supposed to be, or how responsible. Kissing Annie was like waking up again, like feeling joy for the first time. Joy and fireworks in your crotch.

She thrust Annie against the wall, pushing them both further into the darkness, and as Annie moaned, Oksana slid her thigh between her legs. It went on for some time, not an overwrought, sloppy meeting of tongues and lips, but this perfect caressing of mouths. Holy shit, Annie could kiss, and if they had been somewhere else, Oksana never would have stopped.

"You tell that sweet Bettino I say hello," Mrs. Barstone yelled from across the parking lot. Oksana jumped back, separating herself from Annie, and was instantly relieved that Annie seemed to understand what was happening. They were breathing heavy, smoothing their clothes, Annie fixing her hair. Mrs. Barstone climbed in her Volvo without a glance in their direction.

"I should probably get going," Annie said as she exhaled.

"Yeah, okay. I'll see you later." Before things got really awkward, Oksana hugged her and left her to dig for her keys, but instead of walking calmly back into the gym, Oksana ran. She didn't want to be left outside alone.

❖

Hours later, Oksana was still lost in the fog of that kiss. She wondered how it happened, how she could be so careless to kiss Annie back, right out in the open like that. Mostly, though, she was unnerved by the kiss itself.

The kiss was loaded. The whole situation had been filled with danger, but the kiss changed the name of the game. This was no longer innocent fun. They had both achieved their initial purpose. Annie knew what it was like to be with a woman and Oksana had banished an embarrassingly long sexual drought. But that kiss— Oksana could feel it the moment Annie pressed against her—it was a kiss that was asking for more.

Oksana did the one thing she knew she shouldn't; she thought about the possibility of more. But what could they have? Nothing. Annie was capitalizing on her free pass. She was taking advantage of that freedom, and Oksana was playing right into that selfishness. Not that it was wrong for Annie to explore herself before she settled down for good, but it was wrong for Oksana to be a part of it.

Annie's whole existence was dangerous, and the more aggressive she became the more Oksana saw Vivian in her. Vivian had pursued her the same way.

Things with Annie wouldn't end the same way they had with Vivian, mostly because Oksana and Annie weren't really together, but Oksana saw herself getting hurt if she wasn't careful.

"Sana."

"Hmm?" Oksana blinked, looking away from their mastiff, Vasily, who had been the focus of her blank stare.

"Baba's talking to you." Her grandmother, Inna, was a great caretaker and guardian, but she was slightly terrifying. She was exactly five feet tall and she was almost as wide. Like Kat, she liked coloring her hair. Tonight her pumpkin-shaped head was adorned with fruit punch red waves, cropped short. She rarely stopped smoking, and she only spoke English if she absolutely had to. And she didn't like being ignored.

"Oh." She switched to Russian as she addressed her grandmother. She glanced at Oksana over the laundry basket between them. *"I'm sorry. What did you say?"*

"You have a girlfriend now."

"What?"

"Give me that shirt. You'll never fold it."

Oksana handed the shirt over and grabbed for a towel out of the basket. *"Who says I have a girlfriend and how come I don't know about it?"*

"Ekaterina tells me there's a girl, and I believe her because all night you've been out in space."

Oksana turned to her sister, who was half hanging off the recliner and shot the brat her own look. A look that said Kat had violated the sister code.

Kat shrugged and spoke in Russian, the little suck up. *"What do you want me to say? You've been out in space all night. You daydream. You ignore your baba when she is speaking to you."*

Oksana narrowed her eyes and switched to English. "I'm going to kill you." She turned to Baba Inna. *"I'm not seeing anyone."*

"You are thinking of someone."

Oksana didn't answer or lie. She knew her grandmother could interpret her every expression.

"Give me your phone."

"It's...I left it in the little house." Oksana shifted, covering her phone with her leg.

"It's right there," Kat said before she could stop herself. She was just crapping all over the sister code tonight. Oksana was going to find some reason to ground her very soon.

"Seriously?"

"Sorry."

Oksana pulled out her phone and handed it over. She'd never regretted teaching her grandmother how to use anything more in her life. As if he felt her pain, Vasily left his spot by the TV and wiggled his giant body between her feet and the couch.

Momentarily comforted by the only mammal in the room who hadn't turned on her, Oksana watched, absolutely sick to her stomach as Baba went through her text messages. Baba didn't say a word or make a face, but Oksana knew exactly what see was seeing. Finally, Baba handed the phone back. She picked up a pair of Kat's jeans

"*You help no one by lying.*" She'd said those words before.

Choked up but tearless, Oksana helped her grandmother take care of the rest of the laundry, ignoring Kat's apologetic looks from across the room.

Once they were finished, she kissed them both good night and headed back to the little house.

Her cottage behind Baba's enormous Craftsman had been rented out to random relatives of the local Russian community until Oksana turned eighteen and claimed it as her own baby sister-free zone. Baba didn't rent it out while she was living at Vivian's.

Kat followed.

"Sana, wait!" Kat called after her. Oksana stopped and waited. "What's up?"

"I'm sorry. Really. Are you mad at me?"

"No, but…" Fuck, this is what she hated. If she and Kat were closer in age and if Oksana wasn't damn near her mom she could say something like "keep my secrets and I'll keep yours," but she couldn't do that.

She pulled Kat into a tight hug. "No, but let that be a lesson to you. Our grandmother *can* read."

"I promise I won't rat you out again."

"Good. Go to bed."

Oksana waited until Kat was back inside before she turned and unlocked the door to her place.

The little house was quiet and empty. Oksana changed for bed, checked her e-mail, and before she finally made up her mind to go to sleep, Oksana sent Annie one last text. One last long text.

Hey, are you there? She typed. Annie responded not even ten seconds later.

Yeah. Just lying in bed. My hands are above the covers. I swear. I don't think we should do this. It's been more than one night.

Twenty painful minutes went by before Annie replied. Oksana knew she had done the right thing. She didn't like lying to her family and she didn't like lying to herself even more.

You're right. I'll talk to you later.

Good night.

After that, Annie didn't text back.

Part of Oksana regretted not handling this in person, but she knew she wouldn't be able to say exactly what needed to be said. Now the guilt didn't matter. Their fun was over.

CHAPTER THREE

THE NEED FOR CLARITY

There were no tears, but Annie's throat and her eyes burned so badly she was surprised she wasn't crying all over herself.

She read the text again and again, reread Oksana's "fuck off" and her own stupid response, and all she wanted to do was cry. The entire situation was backward. A single text message should not hurt this bad. Oksana shouldn't mean so much, but as Annie stared at the very final message from her and her own acceptance of what Oksana was really saying, she realized that Oksana meant something to her. She considered why crying seemed like the only sensible reaction and she wanted to cry even more. Her body gave out and two fat tears rolled down her cheeks. Two more immediately followed. She wiped her face and blew out a deep breath.

Why was this happening? She was supposed to be the happiest girl this side of the valley. She had a great job, friends, and an amazing fiancé she was about to make hers forever. And the fantasy—it was fulfilled. She got exactly what she wanted. She got her one night and it was perfect. Oksana was perfect. And it ended exactly as it should have, maybe just not when. Annie realized it was the kiss. The texts were one thing. Flirting never hurt anyone, but the kiss must have suggested to Oksana that Annie wanted to continue some sort of relationship between them, outside of their workouts. Annie had asked for one night and Oksana had delivered.

She played along, but Oksana wasn't attached. She wasn't making cases for why one more time together wouldn't hurt. Annie's whole plan had gone exactly as planned with extras thrown in. So why the hell was she crying?

Two years ago, Jeff forgot her birthday completely. He usually forgot until the day of, never asking what Annie wanted or what she'd like to do, but still he managed to pull something together that always made her smile. For her twenty-seventh birthday, he'd forgotten altogether. Megan and Feather saved the day, taking her out for dinner and a movie.

When she got back to her place, Jeff was sound asleep in her bed. He never said a word about it, and Annie never cried about that particular birthday.

Oksana, in an epic feat of responsibility, politely closed the door to any more flirting and innuendo, any more public make-out sessions, and Annie was pushed to a desperate breathing episode in the parking lot of her office, complete with those thick orphanage tears. Luckily, her early crew had already arrived. She had another hour of insanity before her executive producer strolled through the parking lot and witnessed her wiping her face like her cat had just died. She didn't need that.

She had crossed a line with Oksana at some point, and Oksana had tried to put it right.

Why was this making me so upset, she wondered as she pathetically scrubbed her face.

Annie knew why, but she couldn't conceptualize what her heart was telling her. She really did have some sort of feelings for Oksana, but in the sobering sun of this Hollywood morning, Annie couldn't nail down exactly what those feelings were or where they had come from. But she had to. Annie hated uncertainty. The black-and-white nature of her relationship with Jeff was one of the main reasons she loved him so much. He loved her with no theatrics and she loved him with no demands.

Maybe Annie needed a friend who wasn't involved with the wedding, wasn't part of the hometown group of friends, someone who had no stake in Jeff. Or maybe it was something more. She knew plenty of people who weren't involved in the wedding and plenty more people who absolutely couldn't care less if she was attracted to women and still engaged to a guy. But Oksana had been the one she'd come clean to and the one she'd slept with. Annie had never been honest with anyone the way she had been honest with Oksana. That had to count for something.

Or maybe Annie really was gay. God, what did that even mean? She wasn't gay. Jeff or not, she loved guys. Penis was a good thing, but Oksana...

Their time together had been unusually comforting. There were a few moments where Annie was nervous, but all her nerves revolved around making Oksana happy, getting Oksana off, not maximizing every minute of her freebie for the sake of walking faithfully back to Jeff. And the kiss they'd shared? She'd never kissed Jeff like that. There'd never been that sort of heat. Did she really have romantic feelings for Oksana, or did the experience of being with another woman awaken something in Annie that she'd honestly been ignoring?

What did that mean for her and Jeff?

He'd been her one and only adult relationship, and maybe sixty years ago when suffering in silence or suicide—okay, now she was getting bleak—were more suitable options than divorce, she would have pushed all these emotions down with a stiff upper lip, but...

Annie refused to give the next thought more steam. She couldn't.

She shook her head and closed her eyes. She should have dated more men, and for fuck sure, more women. She'd had seven years to reason with that tiny voice in the back of her mind that told her she was craving more than what any guy had yet to give her, but Jeff was sweet and easy. And she'd agreed to spend the rest of her life with him.

Oh God. Fat tears rushed faster down her face. She'd become that idiot girl, the one who waits till the last possible moment to try to get to know herself. Talk about selfish.

Annie needed to sort through these feelings. She ached for Oksana's touch, shivered still every time she thought of the caresses they shared or the way Oksana's fingers felt inside her pussy, but would she react to another woman the same way?

There was only one way to find out.

Jeff had taken his month, and now she would use the remaining time she had to herself. She'd have to test all theories. Hurting Jeff was the last thing she wanted to do, but she wanted to strap on her garter and walk into a false marriage even less.

No. She loved Jeff and she was going to marry him, but she had to know exactly what she felt and why so she could be honest in her marriage, not some confused mess. She had to be sure—

"Holy shit!" Annie gasped. A knock on her window scared the rest of the thought from her mind. It was Esther, her production coordinator. She frowned at Annie with blatant concern and motioned for her to roll her window down. Annie pressed the button and used that whole second to wipe her face again even though it was pointless. Esther had already seen the tears.

"Hey." Annie swallowed.

"Are you okay?" Esther squatted so she was looking up at Annie.

"Yeah. Sorry. Just…"

"Is it Jeff?" Esther's gasp was pretty impressive.

Annie's laugh forced out a few more tears. "No, it's not Jeff." It was much, much worse.

"You want to talk about it?" Esther was good listener and a pretty good friend, but what was Annie supposed to tell her? Confessing feelings about your trainer when you were supposed to be very focused on your future with someone else fell right into the "Problems with Jeff" box of issues.

"Actually. Not really. Sorry. It's not a talking about it will make it better kind of situation."

"Well, here." Esther handed Annie a tissue. "Pace told me they got some awesome footage last night." Another reason Annie didn't want to open up to Esther. She was dating one of the camera guys. She loved her crew, but they really didn't need to know about her screwed up love life. Correction, her screwed up sex life. This had nothing to do with love.

Annie wiped her eyes again, trying to get herself together.

Esther rubbed her shoulder and smiled hopefully. "Meta fell off the go-go booth at The Maypole and the guys got the whole thing on tape. You wanna see?"

Annie laughed for real this time, but still felt a twinge of pain. She usually checked on the night crews, but she'd been so unreasonably upset about Oksana's final text she'd forgotten. She had to go in eventually, and having Esther as a physical buffer might be a good idea.

"Okay." Annie sniffled and opened her door.

❖

Annie followed Esther toward the commotion in the back of the office. Her camera guys were always rowdy in the morning. It didn't matter if they didn't get their full turnaround or not. Between the Red Bull and cigarettes, and surely a few grams of coke here and there, they were always amped and ready to go.

Just as she found them most mornings, Justin and Johnny Dangerous, as they liked to call him, were prepping A and B cam respectively. Brad, their sound guy, was casually checking his battery packs, but unlike normal mornings where Pace was busy running around like a nut making sure his guys had everything loaded into their vans, he was cuing something up on the monitor.

Ryan, the other camera operator, turned as they entered the room. "Annie, you have to see this shit."

"E told me." Just then Esther handed her a cold bottle of water and another tissue.

Pace turned around at the mention of his Esther's nickname. He caught on to Annie's blotchy face right away. "Hey," Pace said as he looked at her carefully.

"I'm fine," she mouthed back, before she took a rather refreshing sip of water. Pace nodded and turned back to the monitor. He got it and he let it go.

"Okay. Brad, this'll teach you to ditch me for the fucking Discovery Channel," he said.

"It was more money," Brad laughed, winking at Annie. She scowled at him. She just allocated the money; she didn't fund the shows herself.

"Whatever. Suck my bag. You're never leaving me again," Pace replied. "Okay. Watch this. Six years doing this reality shit, and this is the best fucking face-plant I've ever seen."

Annie watched as the unedited clip started up. *Just Dance* had the second highest ratings of their shows, coming in right behind *Single Dads*. The show followed Meta Rogers, a J. Lo wannabe who had made a decent name for herself after choreographing a major tour. She was nuts. A complete bitch, a camera whore, and the bisexual Annie never wanted to be. She was ratings gold.

On screen, Annie watched her dancing erratically on a raised block just off the dance floor. A go-go boy in nothing but a pound of Vaseline and some briefs danced behind her, but Meta wasn't sharing the spotlight. As the camera panned up, Meta's feet passed out of the frame, but before Pace said another word, Annie could tell that Meta was running out of space on that four-by-four box. Suddenly, Meta slipped. The crowd was already parted to make room for Pace with his camera. There was no attempt to catch her, and BAM! Meta thwacked her face right into the floor.

Annie's hands flew to her mouth. "Oh my God! Is she okay? Why didn't you guys call me?" she asked as the rest of the crew laughed hysterically.

"She's fine." Pace chuckled. Annie watched as a few guys helped Meta to her feet then breathed a sigh of relief as Meta brushed off her jeans and revealed that all her teeth were in her mouth.

"Wait. Pace, you turned in your tapes last night, right?" Annie frowned. As hilarious as this footage was, it should have been on its way to the post-production office a good eight hours ago.

"Busted," Justin snickered.

"Pace!" Annie nearly popped a blood vessel.

"I did. I did. I just made a copy of this." He smiled like the network wouldn't fire his ass then sue the shit out of him if this footage was leaked prematurely.

"Delete it. Now."

"What's going on?" Jewel, the office assistant, came flip-flopping into the room. Annie couldn't stand the twenty-year-old brat, but she was great on the phones, and as long as she was blowing Sergio, their executive producer, she wasn't going anywhere.

"We're watching Meta eat shit." Johnny laughed with an unlit cigarette hanging from his lips. Which reminded Annie. She reached into her bag and tossed him a fresh pack of menthols. Amends for the shitty day rate they were getting.

"Ma'am." He nodded with a smile and slipped the pack into his utility bag.

"This time. In slow motion," Pace announced, and like that, they watched as Meta went down at a thousand frames per second. It was brutal. "I will delete it. I know legal'll shit a fucking brick if they find out."

"Oh, wow." Annie shook her head while they watched Meta's face meet the floor again. That had to hurt. The viewing audience would love it. "Where was this?"

"The Maypole, that gay bar over on Crescent," Jewel answered.

Right, The Maypole, the trendiest gay bar in town. Esther had gotten location clearance the week before, but Annie had been so wrapped up with Miss Fantasy Fulfilled that she'd been letting simple details like where her crew was going slip. All the more reason to wrap her mind around these feelings, toss them in the ocean, and never think of Oksana again.

"The Maypole…" she muttered to herself as Pace played the clip at double speed. It was funny every time.

Annie had never been there before, but…she had an idea.

She turned to Jewel.

"Do you know if they have a ladies' night?"

Jewel gave her that duh look that made Annie feel old. "Yeah. Thursdays I think. So today. Have you been crying?"

"Shush, Jewel. Are you going to have a bachelorette party?" Esther smiled in the most unnerving way.

"No, I was just wondering."

"Bummer."

But she was going to head out for more ladies only entertainment. She did need to know for sure. Was it Oksana she craved or women in general? If her relationship with Jeff had even the slightest chance of being in danger, she needed to figure that out and fast. Throwing herself into a sea of women seemed like the best place to start. Or the worst place ever for Annie to be when she was emotional and vulnerable. Either way, she needed to put herself out there while she had the chance. And if that didn't work, if Oksana was truly the thing, the ugly man trainer idea was still on the table.

❖

"Who do I have to fellate to get another day?" Stewart asked. Oksana watched her client mop the sweat off his face. He was more than ready to pump up his sessions, but she'd been waiting for Stewart to make that decision for himself. That was their deal; he'd bust his ass if Oksana wasn't a complete bitch during their hour together. They'd expanded his comfort zones together. He worked like crazy, shed a ton of weight, safely, and slowly, Stewart became the first client Oksana considered a friend.

Oksana smiled and whacked him gently on the leg. "I think you might enjoy your sucking time with Paulo a little bit more than with me."

"Mmhm, you know that's right. I'm still too big boned for him, but just give me one chance." Oksana's laugh barely covered her grimace as Stewart licked his lips. Stewart was awesome, but the thought of him on his knees—gross.

She kept her bone jokes to herself and helped Stewart up off the mats.

"I'm headed back there now. What's your best day?" Oksana asked. She rocked on her heels a little, thoughts of Stewart porn overshadowed by how proud she was of him. Sure, vanity was at play, but Stewart was genuinely trying to change his life and his health for the better.

And not trying to fuck you—again. Or making you crazy with his bottomless blue eyes. Or kissing you right out in the open. And you definitely wouldn't be worrying about if he is going to text you again tonight while you lie awake in bed thinking about those bottomless blue eyes.

Great. Oksana rolled her eyes at herself. *Made it a whole twenty minutes not thinking about Annie. Oh, God, please ask for Saturday morning. Please. I'll bounce Annie in a heartbeat if it'll help me shake these fucking meat sweats she's giving me.*

"Let's do—what's that face, chickie?"

"What face?" Oksana snapped her spine straight and frowned down at Stewart.

"You have a time in mind?"

"No. No. What's good for you?"

"Let's do Saturday…" *Oh God, yes!* "Let's do Saturday afternoon. Noon work?"

Three months ago, the answer would have been no, but she'd taken on Saturday mornings for Annie. Damn it. "Yeah. Noon is perfect."

Stewart smiled wide, showing off a massively chipped tooth. He had a few million dollars to fix it, but he never had. He had his reasons, which Oksana totally understood and respected. That didn't stop Oksana from staring at it constantly, which she knew was rude, but the imperfection comforted her for some reason.

"No, noon is good." It would put her home by the time Kat finally decided to roll out of bed, and they could still have the rest of the day together. Saturday morning would have been better. Stupid Annie.

"Good. I'll see you then. And stop scowling," Stewart said, tapping the corner of his eye. "You'll line."

❖

Paulo was behind his desk, pretending to work. He didn't keep the books, and outside of the seasonal classes, the four trainers on staff arranged their own schedules with their clients. Odds were he was cruising the Internet or playing poker. Oksana lingered in the doorway until he looked up from his monitor.

"Come in. I hate when you do that," he said, letting his Italian accent slip a little. It was always strongest during business hours.

"Sorry." Oksana collapsed on his couch and stretched her legs out in front of her. It always took a little while to get out of stand and encourage mode. She watched the subtle light changes from the monitor dance across Paulo's bronze face for a few moments, and then she stopped being a punk.

"I slept with Annie Collins."

Paulo froze, but he didn't turn. "Will she be a problem?"

For me, yes. For the gym... "No." Oksana thought of that final text. It hurt like hell, but Annie had gotten the point, and as far as Oksana knew, they were on for Saturday. Annie's wedding was still on.

"Good." Paulo relaxed and spun his chair in Oksana's direction, his running shorts bunching a bit over his muscular thighs.

Paul Taylor was a dark-haired, corn-fed, farm boy from Missouri. After a career in acting didn't pan out and he realized fucking other men was much better when it wasn't in exchange for bit parts, he took on a new persona: Paulo, Italian fitness master.

Oksana, one other trainer, and Paul's partner, Bettino, an authentic Italian, were the only ones who knew the truth.

When he spoke again, Paulo was gone. "Was she any good?" he asked with a glint in his eye. Oksana liked it when he let his Midwest out. He seemed more honest in their conversations then and she felt less like the only foreigner in the room.

"It was fucking amazing."

"How'd that happen anyhow? Her wedding's what, two months out?"

"A little more. She..." Oksana hesitated before she told the whole truth. "She kissed me last night in the parking lot."

"Okay *that* kind of shit can't happen."

"I know. I know!" Oksana groaned, rubbing her face. "I told her last night. No more of, I don't know, whatever it was. It's over."

"Good. I hate straight people." Paul rolled his eyes and leaned back in his chair. "Well, at least you got some. It's been a while."

"Thanks."

"Don't mention it," Paul replied, flashing a handsome grin. "How about a new victim?"

"Stewart asked for Saturday, noon," she told him before he committed her elsewhere.

Paul grabbed a pen and scribbled that down. "Won't be a problem. I got a call from Overhouse this morning. They are casting *Angels of the Prairie Run*."

Oksana had heard a while ago that the film adaptation of the *New York Times* bestselling novel had started pre-production. She'd actually read the book. The historical drama was a quick break from the biographies she'd been gobbling up in her free time. The book was pretty good. Hopefully, the movie would be good too.

"When they're ready, they want us to train their leads. It may be nothing major, but…"

"I know. They have to be a believable nineteenth century skinny, not runway skinny."

Paul tapped his nose. "Right on the head, sweetie. What do you say?"

All the clients of Elite Fitness were high-end, but the other trainers had issues getting starstruck. Oksana would take a fork to the eye before she got in bed with an actor. Plus, she felt like she owed Paul after the Collins affair.

"I'm in." A new client was always a fresh start, exactly what she needed.

"It might be early mornings," Paul said. "Very early, but I'll give you your afternoons for the contract. I'll have Martin handle the Pilates class."

"Deal."

"It might be a while or it might be soon, but they're willing to pay for you."

"Oh? So you *didn't* want me?"

"I always want you, but you were requested by name." Not unheard of, but…

"Who's the reference?"

Paul pretended to search for the info in his day planner. Oksana humored his silliness.

"A Miss Ronnie Ramirez."

Oksana's laugh echoed through the office. "That bitch!"

❖

Sixty-five minutes on the treadmill, a hundred or so crunches and push-ups, and eight not-so-innocent peeks at her cell phone later, Oksana wandered into the big house in search of food.

"Come here," Baba Inna grumbled in her native tongue. The old woman knew how to throw her voice. Oksana had no clue how, some elder Russian proverb about being invisible in the woods and heard across the fields, but her voice still echoed down the main hall, just daring Oksana to take her time. She was still irritated with Oksana's cell phone antics.

She cursed herself for letting the front door slam and Oksana walked into the kitchen to find Kat cleaning her plate into Vasily's dish. He came for a sniff then cleaned the rest off with his tongue.

"You walk him tonight," Baba told Kat as she lit another cigarette.

"Baba, no," Kat whined, slouching dramatically against the corner.

"I'll do it," Oksana offered. The dog was the size of a small truck and protective of Kat. She was perfectly safe walking him at night, but Oksana wanted to get away from Baba's mood as soon as possible.

"No, it's her turn. She wanted a puppy. The puppy became a dog and now she walks the dog," Baba said.

Kat switched to English, which she only did to piss off their grandmother.

"I hate this." She dropped her plate in the sink and stormed out of the room. "He takes the biggest shits." She had a point.

Oksana watched the dog enjoy his dinner of scraps, pretending she didn't feel her grandmother's glare drilling a hole in the side of her head. Baba Inna ashed her cigarette in the sink and walked to the stove. Oksana finally sat at the table.

Baba Inna brought her a plate piled high with steak, potatoes, and onions. She often joked that Oksana's grandfather had passed on his appetite, his Viking blood, and his height to both his grandchildren, but the truth was, being a trainer was as active a career as most people thought. In her down time, Oksana had to keep herself in shape. If she didn't eat like a trucker, she'd be fabulously underweight and undesirable as a trainer. She had to be slim but healthy, which meant eating mountains of Baba's starches and proteins and fats. Traditional Russian cuisine was not for the weak, and certainly wasn't a diet she'd recommend to a client, but Oksana loved it. As she stuffed her mouth, Baba grabbed her phone off the table.

Fear was quickly replaced with relief as she remembered the final texts her grandmother would read. She replaced the phone next to Oksana's elbow then just stood there.

"Who is she?" Baba Inna asked after an uncomfortably long silence.

Oksana swallowed, then filled her fork again. *"A client."*

"You love her."

"No." Oksana took another bite and considered how to phrase more of the truth. Baba was already irritated. Her tempers were subtle, but the fact that they were having this conversation at all proved that Baba had noticed Oksana's recent behavior and she wasn't impressed. The truth didn't necessarily need details though.

"She's engaged. I made a mistake."

"There is no mistake. You love her. Your eyes are terrible liars."

Oksana's throat wanted to close. The last time they'd talked like this, it was about Vivian. Baba told Oksana not to move in with her. They hadn't known each other long enough. Oksana insisted it was the right step in their relationship, but in the end it turned out Oksana didn't know Vivian at all.

This time Oksana knew her side of the argument was for the best.

"I like her," she said. *"But I don't love her. It was a mistake and it's over."*

Baba let her clean her plate in silence, but when Oksana's cell vibrated on the table, Baba snatched it away again. The third night in a row she'd brought her phone up for dinner. She really wasn't being slick, and worse yet, of all the people who could have texted her, she prayed it was Annie coming around for another chance. At what, she didn't know, and she knew she shouldn't think about.

Once she rinsed her dishes, Baba handed back her phone. *"Awful, awful liar. Call Ronnie."* Baba patted her gently on the butt and sent her on her way.

❖

"You love me, yes?" Ronnie cackled over the phone.

Oksana tossed the keys to the little house into the bowl by the TV and turned on the light. She dropped her bag on the floor and started to undress. Her nipples needed some air and some gentle, loving attention. She ignored the idea of Annie doling out that attention and the rush of heat and moisture between her legs.

"No. Miss Ronnie Ramirez, you dick. What did you do?"

"I got you another A-list client. That's what I did. That's seven this year. You should buy me something," Ronnie said.

"Three, and you have plenty of money, dick." Oksana smiled as she kicked off her shoes.

She and Ronnie had a wonderful love/hate relationship. Outsiders thought they genuinely didn't like each other, but that was just how they connected. Ronnie didn't give you a hard time if she didn't love you, and Oksana was grateful for every moment of the friendship she'd shared with Ronnie and her girlfriend Noelle. They both stuck with Oksana through all the bullshit with Vivian, and even though Ronnie was completely to blame for Kat's green hair and piercings, she had been there to help Oksana pick up all of her pieces.

After she was over this initial round of sulking, she could definitely use some quality time with them both. After she was done sulking and masturbating. Stupid Annie.

"Plus, we don't know if the lucky winner will be A-list. Could be a nobody on the rise," Oksana said before she pulled off her shirt. She missed a little of what Ronnie said under the muffle of sweat-dampened cotton.

"—o. I'm thinking totally crazy, method A-lister. You're in for some fun, and since you really do owe me, we're going out tonight."

"Um, no."

"Uh, yes. Noelle locked herself in her studio. I'm lonely and useless. You need to keep me company," she said dryly. Ronnie was a successful hair stylist and bitch to boot who desperately loved Noelle. She knew that Noelle needed her space to focus on her paintings, though it didn't stop Ronnie from pouting when she wasn't around.

Oksana groaned. She wanted to sleep. Actually, she wanted to mope and stare at her phone. She wanted Annie to crack. That was the truth. She wanted Annie to call or text or something, and she wanted to be available for the possible moment of weakness.

Exactly why you should go! Finally, a part of her brain was making sense. She rubbed her nipple through her sports bra then grabbed a towel.

"Give me twenty minutes."

Thursdays at The Maypole were perfect. The weekend crowd wasn't gumming up the line to the restroom and they didn't have to wade through the sea of women who came in to take advantage of the half-priced drinks offered every ladies' night. Ronnie hated ladies' night. They weaved through the line, skipped flashing their IDs because Oksana had trained the owner on and off for a while now, and slipped into the bar. She tried not to think about Annie as Ronnie ordered her drink.

She soaked in the music. The Gaga/Britney mash-up was blasting so loudly it vibrated her eardrums and her bones, but she didn't feel like dancing. There were a few women in the crowd of gay men, but Oksana knew them all and she wasn't interested. True quality time with Ronnie it would be.

"So what's going on with you?" Ronnie raised her voice. *Fuck.* There was no point in fighting this. Everyone could tell she was off. She'd mentioned Annie to Ronnie and Noelle before, said that she thought Annie was hot, and immediately told them she was taken when Noelle's eyes lit up at the prospect of matchmaking. At the time, they all agreed: get Annie fit and trim for her wedding dance, then send her packing. But no. Oksana couldn't keep her mouth shut or her hands to herself, and once again, she was screwed. Hopefully, one day Oksana would know a train wreck when she saw one.

She turned around and put her forehead on the bar. After a few deep breaths, she stood and faced her. Ronnie put her drink down. She knew this was serious.

"I fucked the reality show producer. The straight, engaged reality show producer," Oksana said over the Gaga.

"Fuck you. You're lying."

Oksana shook her head and took a sip of Ronnie's drink. She winced and set the glass back down. It was more Red Bull than vodka.

"I fucked her and then I started texting her. It got out of hand."

"And?"

"*And* it got out of hand. So I put a stop to it."

"Let's go sit." Ronnie liked to get comfortable before she laid into you. Oksana followed her toward the edge of the dance floor. "I Facebook stalked her, but there's no real picture," Ronnie said over her shoulder. Which was true. Oksana had looked her up too, but instead of the lick-able blond bombshell, there was a picture of Aileen Quinn from the 1982 film version of *Annie*. It was cute, really.

"Yeah, she—" A familiar laugh coming from the dance floor stopped Oksana right in her Converse. "Oh shit." Pure terror snaked up the back of Oksana's neck.

"What?" Ronnie asked.

Annie was what. Oksana peered through the throng of moving bodies and spotted the person she *needed* to avoid. Yup, it was Annie all right, smashed between two go-go boys.

Oksana should have left. She should have dragged Ronnie, or ditched her if she resisted, and headed right back home, but something wasn't right about what she was seeing.

Annie admittedly never hung out in West Hollywood. "Work, then my body craves the beach," she'd joked a few times. Plus, aside from the two glistening employees grinding up against her, Oksana got a feeling that Annie was alone. There were no friends looking on, no other girls dancing close by. But it was more. Something wasn't right about the way Annie was moving.

"Is that her?"

"Yeah," Oksana gasped.

"She is hot, and *dios mío*, she's wasted."

Ronnie was right. It was barely ten thirty, and Annie was blasted off her ass. And she'd been drunk the other night too.

Oksana stormed across the dance floor. One of the go-go boys caught her eye and grabbed the other guy by the shoulder. They both looked in Oksana's direction before scurrying off to their pedestals, knowing full well a woman moving with purpose when they saw one. Annie kept dancing. She looked so beautiful as she swayed to the music. Her hair swept up in a ponytail, her tank top showing off her smooth shoulders and neck. Wisps of her bangs stuck to her forehead with sweat.

Gorgeous.

Oksana steeled her nerves as she reached for Annie's hand, ignoring the heat that shot up her arm the moment they touched. Annie spun around, and the second she realized whose fingers were gently gripping hers, her face lit up like the Hollywood sign.

"You came!" she shouted gleefully. "I mixed up the nights, and then one Mojito turned into four and then—I just love Gaga!"

Oksana leaned down so she wouldn't have to yell. "Annie, are you alone?"

"Yeah, but it doesn't matter." She threw her arms around Oksana, who thanked her good balance for keeping them upright. She shivered as Annie nuzzled her face between her breasts. "I wanted you to come and you came."

Despite her dread, Oksana's arms went around Annie and she pulled her closer.

Beside them, Ronnie was laughing her ass off.

CHAPTER FOUR

THE FURTHER COMPLICATION OF THINGS

Annie woke with a harsh gasp, her heart thumping hard at the base of her throat. She'd had one of the dreams where you trip, and the momentum of the fall and the desperate reaction to save yourself jerk you awake. Annie sniffled sharply as she lifted her head off the pillow. She rubbed her face, and just as quickly, she flinched.

She wasn't in bed alone.

For a short moment, she closed her eyes before she turned. She'd gotten drunk, but not that drunk. She remembered where she'd gone, how she'd gotten there, and how she'd gotten home, exactly who she'd been elated to see, and that very person was the same person who had driven her tipsy ass and her hybrid all the way back to Venice. It definitely wasn't a matter of who, but a matter of what next?

Annie's instincts, light years ahead of her brain, made her whip her shoulders around to face Oksana.

She was sitting up in bed, above the covers, her head tilted back against the wall. Her breathing was steady and her eyes were closed, but she wasn't sleeping. A muscle in her jaw twitched like she was trying to hold still. Annie looked her over for a moment in the light coming from her closet. Oksana was still in her white low-top Chucks, and her short pleated skirt and a white tank top. The bra she had on was navy blue, the same color as the skirt. Annie's eyes ran the length of Oksana's long body once again, from her feet crossed at the ankles hanging just off the bed, up to the gunmetal studs in her ears. Finally, her gaze settled on Oksana's left breast.

Her nipple was hard and the rounded edges of the piecing were prodding against the fabric.

"Are you still drunk?"

Annie looked up at the dry sound of Oksana's voice. Her eyes were still closed.

"No." Annie cleared her throat and tried to explain further. She'd made a thorough ass out of herself, and the last thing she wanted to do was piss Oksana off even more. There had been a few too many drinks, but a full dose of crazy and adrenaline had lead to her ridiculous showing at The Maypole. And now there was no hangover, just a lot of embarrassment and a little bit of dehydration.

Slowly, Annie crawled out of bed and stood. Looking down, she closed her eyes and breathed out even more nonsense. Oksana had helped her get changed for bed. One of Jeff's Nikon T-shirts covered her down to her knees. More of the night before came flashing back, the awkward ride home where Annie *would not* shut up, Oksana's concern about her open yard fence and her broken garage door. Her concern about Annie in general. She looked up at Oksana again whose eyes were still closed. No part of this could be good.

"Please don't leave. I—"

"Okay," Oksana replied calmly. Annie hesitated a moment before walking out to the kitchen. What the hell was wrong with her? She'd pounced on Oksana like a cracked up leech at the club, given her the freaking lazy motorboat in front of her friend, and ultimately scared Oksana so badly that putting Annie in a cab clearly wasn't an option. Annie chugged down a glass of water as she leaned against the counter. The clock on the stove glowed four thirty a.m. in neon green. No plan. She didn't have one, but somehow she had to convince Oksana to let her apologize. It was too early in the morning to think of anything beyond that.

Annie stepped back into her bedroom to find Oksana in the exact same position. Eyes still closed, head still tilted back. Annie had to know.

"Why did you stay?"

Oksana opened her eyes. "I watched a friend puke in his sleep. He's fine, but it scared the shit out of me. You seem to be drinking a lot lately. Not that I'm around you enough to make a comparison, but you know…"

"I'm a pain in your ass, but you didn't want me to die."

Oksana pursed her lips and nodded. "So what happened?"

"I…uh…I needed some clarity."

"About?" Oksana scowled.

"I wanted to know how gay I am." *Yes, Annie. You just said that.*

"I was wondering why you weren't wearing your ring. Ladies' night is Friday night."

Annie glanced down at her bare finger. It felt wrong leaving the diamond at home, but she couldn't test her theory if she was sending out signals that she was taken. Just going over that logical move in her head made Annie feel like the lowest piece of shit and she felt even worse when she looked up and caught Oksana's eyes as they flashed with hurt.

That was enough for Annie, the lingering look on Oksana's face. It was jealousy and it turned Annie on like no other look could. All it took was one step into that club and she knew the confusion she was feeling wasn't about women in general. It was about Oksana. The one person who had taken care of her and was now visibly pissed that Annie had gone out lady hunting. This round went to Oksana.

Crossing the room at lightning speed, Annie all but dove headfirst into Oksana's lap. Seconds before their lips mashed together, Annie didn't miss the small fact that Oksana had reached for her too, her arms wide open to catch Annie the moment she saw that she was on the sexual charge.

Their kiss was heated and rough. All tongues and lips and teeth. Annie scrambled across Oksana's lap, straddling her stomach as Oksana moved them further onto the bed. Annie sat back just long enough to tear off her shirt and Oksana's tank top before she attacked her mouth with renewed desperation.

Oksana kissed her back with just as much passion, moaning as Annie sucked on her swiftly swelling lips. The same sounds pushed up from her throat as Oksana pawed at her ribs, gripping the suddenly hypersensitive skin of Annie's back, maybe hard enough to bruise, but she didn't care. She couldn't fight her need anymore. Oksana wanted her too, no matter how she tried to end their relationship the night before, despite her anger with the way this night had played out, Annie could feel it in the way they touched, the way Oksana's tongue moved inside her lips. Oksana wanted to be with her, if only for tonight. Oksana could have made her way back home once she dropped Annie off.

Maybe her friend could have followed them, but Oksana had stuck around and Annie wanted to know why. She wanted to take this force between them to its limits, and in the morning if things were really over between them, both personally and professionally, she could take that defeat face-to-face, not over text message. If it was coming, she wanted real closure.

But that end would have to be dealt with later, when Annie could focus and think. Roughly groping one of Oksana's breasts in one hand and gently stroking the nipple and piercing of the other, Annie couldn't think of anything beyond this moment. Nothing beyond Oksana's breath mingling with hers and the wetness pooling in her underwear mattered.

Suddenly Annie jumped off the bed. Oksana looked like she was trying to regain some sense of composure, to calm her panting, but she lost that battle as soon as Annie yanked off her sneakers. Her hands went right to her nipples while Annie grabbed her hips and tugged her further down the bed. She might have been short, but their weight sessions had paid off. The swift yet gentle move of aggression registered as shock in Oksana's heated stare and the look sent another surge of pleasure down to Annie's pussy. She watched as Oksana tweaked her nipples again, arching off the pillows. Annie didn't say a word as she flipped Oksana's skirt up over her stomach and pulled down her panties. Oksana watched her in the dim light. It had been a long night for them both. Slight bags were starting to form under Oksana's eyes, but they still raged with fire, her lips still wet from their kiss. Annie would definitely attack them again, after she latched onto Oksana's clit.

Annie tried her hardest to be gentle, but she had to taste Oksana. She sucked on her pussy, drawing her tongue over every inch of skin she could reach. It was a fine demonstration of clumsiness, Annie knew. She was all over the place, but she couldn't get enough of Oksana's taste or her smell. Her own pussy clenched and released, aching for its own turn at attention, but that ache just spurred Annie further. Her ass bounced in the air, her thighs squeezed together. Her fingers pressed inside Oksana's hot sweetness, and as she pumped in deeper and faster, Annie glanced up only to be trapped by Oksana's dark gaze. They stared at each other and it was clear that at least *this* encounter was no mistake.

She had no fucking clue what she was going to do. She'd never wanted to touch Jeff this way, never reacted this way to their closeness, never coated her own underwear at the sounds he made when she searched his body. They'd never taken that kind of time. Annie knew she would come eventually, but it was Oksana's pleasure she craved, her body she yearned to be wrapped around, thrust inside of. She sucked harder, using her tongue to stroke over Oksana's hardened clit and her fingers to bring her closer and closer to climax. Annie knew she had her when Oksana's hand dropped from her nipple to the back of Annie's head. Oksana gripped her hair in her fist and ground her crotch down on Annie's face.

Out of nowhere, *Annie* came.

Annie's eyes slammed shut as Oksana continued to ride her mouth. She trembled, gripping Oksana's hip to keep herself steady. Almost immediately, Oksana cried out under the weight of her orgasm, her pussy spasming around Annie's fingers. Annie savored the feeling of filling another body, of being inside Oksana, a feeling she'd been craving for so long. After a few moments, Annie scrambled up her body. Oksana took her in her arms again and let their legs intertwine as their lips met. Oksana licked her mouth clean, the bold move making Annie shudder and moan again.

It took some work on both their parts, but the kissing didn't stop as Annie managed to shimmy out of her underwear and help Oksana out of her skirt and bra. Oksana pulled Annie down on top of her and brushed Annie's hair out of her eyes. Annie gently stroked the short hair on the crown of Oksana's head. Oksana sighed as Annie swallowed nervously, her desire bubbling up from her stomach as her body pressed Oksana's into the sheets. She was ready for more, but she wanted Oksana to say it was okay.

"Fuck me again," Oksana breathed.

"I just want to touch you," Annie replied, her breathing just as heavy. This was more than fucking for Annie. With a slight nod, Oksana seemed to understand. She met Annie in the middle and they kissed again. This time the kiss was tender and drawn out, with gentle caresses up and down Annie's back, teasing passes over the cheeks of her ass soon had her body grinding slowly against Oksana's thigh.

She whimpered, massaging her swollen lips over Oksana's heated skin, feeling Oksana's own juices ease across her body.

Annie rode her slowly at first, their lips and tongues always in contact, their teeth always exchanging gentle nibbles and bites. Soon the pressure became too much. That first orgasm had only been a hint of what touching Oksana's soft skin could make her feel. Now that there was real contact, Annie's pussy throbbed almost painfully at the hint of more.

She broke from their perfect kiss and rested her forehead on Oksana's shoulder as she pressed herself harder and harder to her body, bringing them both closer. This time Annie came explosively, her eyes momentarily blinded by the pleasure, her throat driven hoarse as she called out Oksana's name again and again. Oksana gently gripped her chin as she shuddered against her chest and brought their lips back together. More slow kisses, deep and penetrating in a way Annie knew she would distantly regret.

Annie was spent, but she wasn't done with Oksana yet. She pressed her fingers back between their bodies. Her lips went to Oksana's right nipple. She sucked and licked the hard pink tip with just the right amount of force.

She filled Oksana, three fingers this time, quickly plying another orgasm from Oksana while she continued to lap at her sensitive breasts.

Once the room righted itself and they could breathe again, Annie rolled them under the covers and spooned Oksana, her own breasts securely pressed against her back. She felt Oksana tense for a moment, but Annie loosened her grip and gently rubbed her stomach with reassuring strokes. Soon Oksana's muscles seemed to relax in Annie's arms, and not long after, Annie could hear her light snores. Annie lay awake for a little while longer, enjoying the feeling of a full bed and a soft, warm body. Oksana's body.

She still had no plan, but now she had answers. She was definitely a little bit gay and she wanted more time with Oksana.

❖

Annie's eyes fluttered open, and this time her gaze landed on the sleek body on the edge of the bed; the soft, trimmed hair; and the perfectly toned back. Oksana pulled her tank top over her head then paused.

Annie was afraid to move. This was the awkward morning after she'd been wanting to avoid, but now things were more complicated. There were feelings that could no longer be ignored, but there was still a wedding on the books and still a fiancé to return.

"I have to get going," Oksana said quietly. She turned slowly and looked over her shoulder at Annie. Her expression was hard to read. Annie saw the hesitation and the anxiety, but there was a glimpse of hope in those eyes.

Annie glanced at the clock. "It's six a.m." She still had three hours until she had to be at work.

Oksana turned back around and reached for her sneakers. "I have a session at seven thirty."

"Oh. Well…" Annie scrambled for something to say. "Wait, how are you getting home?" Annie had acted like a real jackass. The chance encounter had been an answer to her prayers, and the sex exactly what she had been after, but ultimately, she'd trapped Oksana and stranded her in Venice. *Bravo, Annie. Bravo.*

"My friend Scooter is outside."

"Oh!" Annie jumped up and searched around for something to wear. She could feel Oksana's eyes on her. She waited patiently while Annie dug up some shorts and a shirt.

"Ready?" Annie asked once she was decent. "I mean, right. Let's go."

With her clutch purse in hand, Oksana followed Annie to the living room, and when she released the lock to the front door, they faced off in the pre-dawn gray of the Venice morning.

"Thanks for bringing me home." Annie didn't want to offer an apology. The last thing she wanted Oksana to think was that she didn't enjoy the time they'd spent together. What she really wanted was for Oksana to stay. She wanted to make her breakfast, or buy her breakfast at least. She wanted to be with her until the last possible second.

"It's fine," Oksana said, looking down at her Chucks. "Just be more careful next time."

"There won't be a next time." Annie laughed nervously, then cursed herself. "I didn't mean—" She took a deep breath. *Okay, dumbass. Use your words.* She could feel it; Oksana was closing up. "I'll see you again?"

Oksana frowned. "Yeah. Tomorrow morning."

"Right..." Annie was drawing a blank. What the hell was tomorrow?

Oksana's eyes flashed wide and she nodded with full meaning at something behind Annie. She turned and looked at her wedding dress hanging from the decorative trellis beside the living room door. She did a quick scan of the room as she turned back to Oksana. There were bridal magazines everywhere, photos of possible hairstyles spread on the coffee table. And her copy of the fucking seating chart was on the couch. Annie had left it there a few days ago. Megan had called before work to tell Annie that Shane's stepmom had decided to bring a date after all. Oksana was looking over every detail of her wedding. Of course they would still have plans for Saturday morning.

"Our session. Right!" Annie's stomach turned.

"It's okay." Oksana patted her shoulder in understanding, which only made things worse.

Be mad at me, Annie thought. *Be something; just don't leave…* But she kept her mouth shut.

Oksana walked to the end table near the couch. When she came back to the front door, she bent low and forced Annie to look her in the eye. There was no animosity. No regret. Any smidge of hopefulness was gone as well. It was all in direct contrast and a perfect complement to the cool metal Oksana softly pressed into the palm of Annie's hand.

"Really. It's okay" Annie opened her hand and numbly stared at her engagement ring. With the tip of her finger, Oksana caressed the round diamond as she murmured softly, "Now you won't be wondering anymore. You'll *know.*"

Annie did know, but she didn't know how to say it or even what to say. She had to straighten things out with Jeff first, but clear determination in Oksana's eyes told her that she wasn't willing to wait.

Oksana didn't hang around for the weak good-bye that slipped through Annie's lips. She was already down the front steps and climbing into a rugged looking Charger when Annie found the skill to breathe.

The loud engine purred its way down the street, and when it was silent again, Annie slumped against the door. And she stared at her dress, wishing for the life of her that Oksana had never seen it.

Scooter didn't ask any questions, just handed Oksana a sweatshirt and turned the radio up. She slumped in her seat and pulled the worn hoodie over her head. That's why she called him. Scooter was no bullshit. That, and Ronnie would never come out to Venice at six in the morning, and if she did Oksana would never hear the end of it. She was already prepared for a thorough ragging from Ronnie and full-on verbal assault from her grandmother. For now, she needed silence or the best of Lynyrd Skynyrd. Anything but facing the truth.

When they pulled up to the big house twenty minutes later, she kissed Scooter on his stubbled cheek.

"I'm working all weekend, but I want to see you next week," he rasped out. He'd been working long hours and partying even harder afterward. He glanced at her quickly, his eyes telling her everything she needed to know. Even though he had no clue who Annie was, he understood that Oksana had gotten herself into another sketchy situation. But he wouldn't judge, and most importantly, if she needed him, he would continue to be there.

"Okay," she said with a weak smile. She hopped out of his Charger and waved as he drove away. She took one step up the driveway before Baba Inna came out on the porch, Vasily's leash in hand. Oksana could outrun the old lady for sure, but she couldn't avoid the third degree forever. Not if she wanted to enjoy her grandmother's cooking again. Or see her sister.

Baba ambled down the stairs and stopped in front of Oksana.

"Same girl?" she asked.

"Yes," Oksana replied. Baba glared at her, one eye squeezing almost shut and then the other. That was how she squinted before she came to a decision.

"One more time and I meet her." She held up her hand as Oksana began to assert that there was no way in hell there would be another time. *"One more time and you bring her home. I meet her. Ekaterina meets her, and we settle this. No more games."* She pressed her hand above Oksana's heart. *"No more games."*

Baba Inna didn't wait for an answer. She took their dog and headed off down the street.

Oksana made it all the way back to the little house before she started to cry.

CHAPTER FIVE

THE FACING OF FACTS OVER AN OVERPRICED SALAD

Oksana walked into Travar Salon and waited by the front counter. She only set foot in Beverly Hills for two reasons: clients and Ronnie.

"We'll roll in a sec," Ronnie called from the sinks near the back. Jan, the owner, didn't appreciate it when Ronnie yelled, but Ronnie was the best stylist they had, and Jan just had to deal with all parts of Ronnie if she wanted to keep the majority of her clientele.

Ronnie appeared a moment later and wrapped a silk shawl around her shoulders. She and Oksana were the perfect pair, both tatted and pierced with mouths like sailors, but always dressed fresh and professionally. Even though she was in the middle of her sessions, Oksana had on her most fashionable spandex and matching jacket. They threw people off and it was funny.

Oksana followed Ronnie next door to a small cafe. They ordered their lunches, both salads. Ronnie did so because she was a natural size sixteen and maintaining a size ten took some effort, and Oksana because in a little over an hour she had to run a client up to the Griffith Observatory. Puking up a burger and fries, or even a pesto panini on the trail wouldn't be a good look for Oksana or Elite Fitness.

They slid into a small table by the window and Oksana forced herself to eat.

"You look like shit," Ronnie said with an eyebrow raised. She was right. Sleeping fitfully for four hours, upright, was not rectified by forty-five perfect minutes of sleep wrapped in Annie's arms. God, she missed her already.

"I feel like shit."

"It all adds up then. Well, dish. Another night of earth-shattering sex? Actually…" Ronnie got serious for a second. "Start from the beginning." Oksana never got to tell Ronnie how she'd ended up sleeping with Annie in the first place, so she started back with Annie's initial idea. Ronnie agreed that she wouldn't have passed up that sort of one-night stand either, and they both agreed the texting and the parking lot lip-lock was where she went wrong in terms of the follow-up, but when it came to the incident at The Maypole, Ronnie threw Oksana a real curve.

"How do you feel about her?" Ronnie asked. "And don't lie. I'm gonna give you shit either way."

Oksana sighed and pushed her chickpeas around. "I really like her."

"Beyond the sex?"

"Yeah. I liked her before the sex, before she even brought it up. She's refreshing. It's weird. She's so upbeat and open." Among a million other things. Oksana couldn't shake Annie's face out of her head. Her smile, her skin, her amazing chest, the way her eyes closed when she came, the way she felt pressed against Oksana's back. It didn't matter how hard she tried. All morning long, all she could think of was Annie.

"I'm not trying to freak you out here, but on the surface, from what I saw and from what you've said, she sounds a little like Vivian," Ronnie said. She sat back in her chair like she expected Oksana to punch her in the mouth for making such an insulting comparison.

"What?"

"I mean in the beginning. Remember? Vivian was like that. All cheery all the time and bouncing off the walls. She was the poster child for positivity."

"No, Annie's different."

"How do you know that?" Ronnie asked.

"I..." She didn't. Vivian had been like no one she'd ever met before. She made Oksana feel more alive. Oksana had shared everything with her, secrets she'd never shared with anyone. She'd shared her life, and one day Vivian had literally disappeared. No note. No text. No phone call. Annie would never do something that heartless.

"She's not like Vivian. She's honest, for one."

"Well, that's a plus."

"I'm serious. This whole thing is fucked. I won't pretend it isn't, but she has told me everything from the start." Oksana smiled to herself, thinking of Annie trying to weigh her gayness. "Even the embarrassing stuff. She could have lied to me about what she wanted, about her fiancé, but she didn't. Vivian just told me what I wanted to hear. She was a yes-man."

"Now that shit is true." Ronnie shuddered, sharing Oksana's disgust. "Man, she was psycho. Anyway, you gonna hit it again?" Ronnie laughed.

"God, no. Baba was up when I got home this morning and she gave me this whole ultimatum."

"Really?"

"Yeah. If I see Annie again outside of our workouts, I have to bring her home so Baba can meet her. She thinks I'm playing games with her."

"You are."

"No, I'm—"

"You are. You've slept with her twice in three days, and if you keep sleeping with her, *you're* going to get hurt. If you like her."

Oksana knew Ronnie was right. Annie had a wedding, a fucking husband waiting for her on the other side of their tryst. Oksana saw the proof of it all over her living room. She'd briefly held it in her hand. Great sex was not enough to end an engagement over. Once Annie was done with her, Oksana had a new client and an endless number of lonely nights ahead of her, but she didn't see how she was the one playing games. Annie was engaged, not her. She explained that to Ronnie, but still they didn't agree.

"You're putting up with this, Sana. Sex is fun, but you've never been the type to sleep around. You're a relationship person. But since you like her, you're taking what you can get. It's not as bad as Captain Abandon, but it's pretty close." Oksana fought like crazy not to cry, but her lip still trembled. How had she let herself get wrapped up in such a shitty situation? Where was the fun she'd been looking for? The easy opening into a new phase in her love life?

Ronnie reached across the table and took her hand, rubbing the ridge of her knuckles. She wasn't much on friend PDA, but she knew when Oksana needed it.

"Hey." Oksana looked up into Ronnie's eyes. "I'm not trying to make you upset, I just want you to look at the red flags. If they're there, you can't ignore them. You deserve better. You are worth more."

And hadn't that been the mantra? It took some serious personal analysis, but Oksana was finally able to admit to herself that her crappy relationship with her parents left her feeling, in some ways, unworthy. That shitty feeling had only been compounded by Vivian's swift exit. She'd had her breakthrough moment and Oksana was able to see that she couldn't weigh her personal value against the people who felt they were too good to be a part of her life.

"What if she has genuine feelings for you?" Ronnie asked as if she could feel Oksana's mood really starting to plummet.

"Yeah, right" Oksana wiped her eyes. "And what if she weren't getting married and what if—"

"I'm serious. Let's forget Vivian for a moment because we both *know* she's crazy. This new chick was drunk, but she was pumped to see you. That much was real. She went down on you?"

"Like it was her last supper."

Ronnie frowned for a moment. She was really thinking this over, which bothered Oksana a little. She loved that Ronnie cared, but there was nothing to think about. Things with Annie were over and done with. Period. The gorgeous A-line gown hanging in her den was proof of that.

"I can't speak on her feelings for her man, but I think she likes you. What would you do if she did?"

"I'd date her, if—*if*—she wasn't engaged."

"Which she is."

"Which. She. Is."

"Sucks, comrade. What's the non-hypothetical plan?"

"I haven't heard from her today, so I'm guessing we're still on for our hike tomorrow. We'll see how it goes. If she's willing to end our hot, steamy affair, I'll stick with her schedule. She's paid up through July."

"Jesus. Can you do that?" Oksana shrugged. "And if you can't?"

"Hopefully, she'll go with another trainer without any drama."

"Hmm. Good luck."

"Thanks." Oksana made a real effort to finish her lunch then. She had to get over Annie. There was no hope for them, and the sooner Annie was out of her life in every sense, the sooner she could try at love again. With a normal, single, gay woman. With absolutely no baggage or sociopathic disorders. If a woman like that even existed.

"So how'd you get home?" Ronnie eventually asked.

"Scooter."

"Ha." Ronnie laughed. Of course he would come through. "Our man Scoot."

❖

Annie shifted in her flip-flops and glanced at her phone. The line in Greens and Beans was ridiculous. Luckily, the studio was paying for lunch. Well, Sergio at least. She'd been praying that Megan would somehow forget that Annie's wedding was around the corner and subsequently forget all her maid of honor duties. No such luck. Her text came at ten that morning.

Coming over the hill for the afternoon. Meet me for lunch?

Annie wanted to text her a rain check, but Megan knew Annie could take a two-hour lunch and no one in her office would care. Still, that wasn't the point. She had to talk to Jeff before she came clean to her friends, so for the next three weeks she had to act natural. She packed up her stuff and left the office, but not before her executive producer got a good look at her.

"You look like shit, Collins. Here, lunch is on me." Sergio had handed her a few twenties, which she snatched without a word. She wanted to shove the bills into his mouth, but she loved her job so she pocketed the money with a half-hearted thank you and drove the whole mile to the restaurant of Megan's choosing.

Back in the horrible present, Megan placed her order for an extravagant salad with everything on the side, then moved forward, checking her BlackBerry while Annie ordered the most fattening salad Greens and Beans served, with extra dressing.

While they waited, she stared at Megan's ass. Annie worked hard, but her bestie was the only one in the group who had a real adult day job and she was the only person Annie knew who still wore anything remotely formal to work. Her tight pencil skirt hugged her hips. Annie had been attracted to her the summer after ninth grade when Megan really got boobs. She dreamed about feeling her up and fingering her, but Megan was so confident and so clearly straight Annie knew she couldn't be talked or seduced into any sort of experimentation.

Doesn't matter now, does it? Annie thought. It didn't.

Annie paid a small fortune for their lunches and they headed to a small booth in the back.

After a few minutes, Megan put down her phone. "Sorry. Where were we?"

"You asked me to lunch. We haven't gotten much further than that," Annie grumbled as she played with her food.

"Whoa! Take it easy. David just needed me to send some e-mails. No more BlackBerry. I promise." Megan put her phone down next to her plate for easy access.

"Yeah, sorry." Annie sighed and leaned back in her seat. "Work is kicking my ass. I got no sleep last night."

"You look exhausted. Where's your ring?"

Annie none too subtly dropped her hand into her lap. Megan was the fourth person to ask about her missing ring that day.

The ring was a lie now.

Important things had changed in those early morning hours after Oksana drove away with her friend. Once Annie pulled herself away from the door, the ring went right back in the box Jeff had given her and that box went right into her nightstand. Next the dress was zipped back in its garment bag and shoved deep into her closet. Photos and that fucking seating chart were stacked and shoved in the dining room chest.

Annie was officially having doubts about Jeff. She tried to be objective in her thinking, not wanting to lay the decision to break up at Oksana's feet, but realizing that Oksana had been the cause. Either way, her feelings for Jeff had changed, and whether she had a future with Oksana or not, she wasn't so sure she could marry someone she was having such blatant second thoughts about. Thinking of what the hell she was going to say to Jeff, her family, *his* family, and her friends was bad enough; Annie didn't want to spend the next three weeks looking at reminders of the nuptials that were now up in the air, but Megan didn't need to know that.

She rubbed her palm against her jeans. "I'm getting it cleaned."

"Hmm. Any word from lover boy?"

Annie smiled down at her salad. Megan hated Jeff. She thought he was boring and didn't appreciate his small sense of humor. In his defense, Annie always claimed that he was just quiet. He was funny; he simply didn't feel the need to entertain people all the time. Megan didn't care. She'd kept her feelings about their engagement to herself. Megan was single with no aspirations to mingle. Her career came first. Though helping Annie plan her wedding gave Megan the perfect distraction when work was slowly killing her soul. She let the less than perfect choice in a fiancé slide.

If she only knew the truth.

"He e-mailed this morning," Annie said. The first one since he left. Annie had broken out in a cold sweat when the e-mail popped up on her phone while she was waiting in traffic. Even though he just e-mailed to tell her he and the boys were moving on from Dublin and that he'd gotten her a T-shirt, she was convinced somehow he knew about Oksana. "He's enjoying himself."

"I'm sure he is. So…" Megan picked up her phone again and clicked a few buttons before holding her screen up for Annie to see. "I think this is the hair."

Annie took the phone and looked at the impressive double twist that led to a blond ponytail down the model's back. The style was gorgeous.

"And look…" Megan took her phone back and pressed another button, showing Annie the front of the woman's hairdo. "You wouldn't have to grow out your bangs."

Annie stared at the photo and suddenly the sound of the whole Pacific Ocean felt like it was pounding in her ears. The tides and currents had been rolling through her all morning, tousling her back and forth against the rocky shore of where she was, miles away from where she wanted to be.

"I'm having an affair."

Megan froze, her fork halfway to her mouth. "You what?"

"I'm having sex with someone who isn't Jeff."

"Are you fucking joking?" Megan yelled. Like actually yelled. Everyone in the restaurant turned and looked at them. Annie lowered her voice hoping Megan would respond at a reasonable volume.

"I'm having an affair with my trainer. Well, it might be over now, but for the past few days we've been sleeping with each other."

With disturbing precision, Megan placed her fork on the lip of her large salad bowl. She lifted her napkin from her lap and settled against the booth once the linen square was on the table. She was not pleased. "How did this happen?"

Annie told her everything she could, skipping the play-by-play of what had actually happened in bed. "I don't know. It just started off as this silly, stupid idea, and now I…I don't know what to do."

"What do you mean? Are you gay now? Bi?"

"I'm definitely, bi, but I…I thought I could sleep with her, I mean we had an agreement. I thought I could sleep with her just that one time and it would be fine. It would be my last hoorah, but we just kept talking and then I kissed her outside the gym the other night *and then* we fucked again last night and all I want to do right now is call her or text her, but she knows about Jeff. She doesn't want to deal with all of my bullshit." Annie tossed her napkin on the table in frustration. Megan watched her, working her tongue behind her teeth. "Say something."

"I'm pissed and I'm not," Megan said. "If you had just told me you wanted to fuck some woman instead of having a bachelorette party, we could have bought you a hooker. David knows plenty and that would have saved you all this emotional drama and I wouldn't have this sick sense that the months and months of work I've put into your wedding is about to be flushed down the shitter."

"Wait. I didn't say anything—" Megan cut her off with a deadly glare.

"On the other hand, the part of me who absolutely hates your boyfriend is just a little relieved. He sucks for you."

Annie was suddenly annoyed. Sure, she knew Megan wasn't a huge fan, but she hadn't said that Jeff was wrong for her. She hadn't said a single thing about them getting married.

"If you hate him so much why didn't you tell me?"

"If you love him so much why are you fucking someone else?" Annie swallowed and shifted in the booth. That one stung. "I did tell you. Feather's birthday party, when you and Jeff first started dating? Remember he showed up with that stupid flask? And we were at a bar."

"You make him sound like he's a complete douche," Annie said. Jeff wasn't perfect, but the trouble in their paradise was all Annie's invention, not his.

"If the flask fits, honey," Megan said, cocking her head defiantly for a second before she relaxed. "Listen, I know he's nice to you and I know he's not a bad guy. I just don't like him and I don't like him for you. I'm sorry if I'm late, but I'm saying it now. You need someone kinder, someone more nurturing who likes your soft and gooey sides. I feel like Jeff keeps you around because you're hot, but when you need him to let loose and have fun with you, he's always so fucking uptight and serious. In plain terms, you're too nice for him. He needs someone more Hollywood and more heartless."

"You felt all this and you were going to let me marry him," Annie almost whispered to herself. Everything Megan had pointed out was true, but along the way, those were all parts of Jeff she figured she would just have to accept. That's what you do in a relationship; you love the person as they are and accept what you can't change. Or do you? Megan seemed to have a clear understanding of how relationships were supposed to work and she hadn't said a word. "Why didn't you say anything?"

"How old are you? I'm serious. This isn't about me. I told you one time exactly how I felt and you told me that's just how he is, it's fine. He's nice. He's this. He's that. After that it wasn't my job to tell you he sucks."

"He doesn't suck, but I see what you mean."

"The question is do you want to be with Jeff when you're seventy, eighty, one hundred and twelve? And better yet, *why* did you want to sleep with someone else?"

Annie didn't have a good answer. Her mind was in After-Oksana mode. She couldn't remember her reasoning before they'd had sex. All she could remember was how good that sex had been and all she could think about was doing it again.

"Tell me about her," Megan said. Annie pulled out her phone and dug up a picture of Oksana from the Elite Fitness website. She handed her cell over to Megan.

"That's her. Her name is Oksana."

"Wow. She's gorgeous. God, I want to fuck her."

"I know." Annie sighed. "She's beautiful and she's funny and her body is killer. She lives with her grandmother too. How sweet is that? I don't know what the hell I'm going to do. It's just sex, right? Tell me I'm just getting cold feet and this is the guy in me who needs to sow his wild oats before he takes the plunge."

"No. You tell me how you feel about her. Be honest. Don't think about Jeff. If you were single, what would you do right now?"

"I'd...I'd try to be with her." Annie dropped her head forward, exhausted from thinking. "I'd want to see where it goes."

"I should meet her."

"What? No way."

"Yes way. I'm an excellent judge of character and you know it. It doesn't have to be anything super formal, but if I can just meet her

I can tell you, objectively, if you're just thinking with your crotch. Either way, you should dump Jeff."

"Oh, just like that?"

"Yeah, just like that. And don't think you're not going to owe me like seven hundred favors for dealing with Taum on these wedding arrangements. You *know* I hate your mom." Her mother was a little over the top. From her false pleasantries to her weird insistence that everyone, including Annie's childhood friends call her by her first name.

"Ugh, I'm sorry. Should I tell Shane and Feather?"

"Not yet. Let me meet her first and then we can finagle something." Megan's cell phone sang and rattled on the table. "Fuck, hold on. It's David."

Annie ate silently while Megan and her boss had some conversation about contracts. She wanted to feel better, having passed some of this burden on to Megan, but somehow she felt worse. Jeff was going to get hurt. Bad. And Annie couldn't help but wonder how far the fallout would wash her out to sea.

CHAPTER SIX

THE LAST TRIP TO THE PARK

The next morning, Annie waited patiently near the entrance to Griffith Park. Every Saturday, she met Oksana near one of the very bottom trails. They stretched and then hiked to the observatory near the top, or they ran higher up one of the peak trails, depending on how much complaining Annie was doing. A steep, two-mile run would actually do some good to burn off some of the nervous energy that had her leg shaking as she sat on the picnic table.

Megan had already texted her, begging for more girl time that afternoon. Annie understood her need to unwind, especially after she handed off the whole wedding to her, but Annie hadn't replied to that text. She'd think about Megan and the rest of the wedding party later, after she talked to Oksana.

Annie faced the woods, but she could hear Oksana approach. Her steps crunched over the dirt and dried twigs that surrounded the rest area. Years of foot traffic and low rainfall had obliterated the grass in that part of the park even though the trees overhead had thick, full leaves. This was the perfect place to talk.

Oksana came around the picnic table cautiously. Annie realized then that Oksana looked just as good in her street clothes as she did in workout apparel. She gave herself a few seconds to admire Oksana in her black, calf-length spandex and fitted Dodgers T-shirt.

Lines around her eyes made Annie realize she wasn't the only one who'd had a sleepless night.

"Hey," Oksana said. "Are you okay?"

Annie sat up and slipped her phone into the pocket of her thin running jacket.

"I have to say this."

"Okay…"

"I want to tell you everything. And I know how it's going to sound, but please just hear me out and then, I don't know. You get the floor to rebut."

"Okay." Oksana's scowl didn't help with Annie's confidence issue, but they'd crossed the bridge of too late days ago. She had to say this.

"I'm not sure if I'm going to marry Jeff."

"Why?" Oksana asked hesitantly.

"Because…I think I have feelings for you."

Oksana's reaction was immediate.

"Oh! Come on, Annie!" she yelled, throwing her hands in the air. "Don't do this!"

"Oksana, I have to. Can we please just talk about it?"

"Why? Because we had sex?" Oksana groaned. "I don't want you to do this. I should have—this was a bad idea. We shouldn't have slept together. You had your plan or whatever, but it's clear it didn't work out, Annie."

"Yeah, because of you."

"What do you mean 'because of me'? *You* told *me* it was no strings. You told me it was your freebie, your pre-wedding, my fiancé doesn't care fling."

"It was and then things changed. You seemed fine with it when I kept texting you, and you seemed more than fine with it when my fingers were in your pussy. You didn't stop me from kissing you, and you weren't complaining in my bed yesterday morning either." The truth wasn't pretty, but Annie couldn't let her twist certain truths between them.

Oksana took a stunned step back and gritted her teeth, her cheeks flushing with a small hint of pink. Seeing how pissed she already was, Annie dug the hole a little deeper.

"I'm not saying this is about you. It is and isn't. I knew Thursday wasn't ladies' night. I looked it up before I went out, but I went anyway."

"Why?" Oksana asked, seeming genuinely confused.

"Because I had to get out of my house. Because I wanted to be with you!"

Oksana's face fell. Annie couldn't understand why this was making her so angry, but she let her speak.

"Great. Well, I'm glad you could use me to scratch your itch. I'm glad I slipped up and fell into your bed again, right when you wanted me to."

Annie's mouth gaped open. "That's not it at all. I've always liked you."

"Bullshit."

"It's true. I'm just not a big fan of pushing myself on someone who isn't interested at all. If you were straight, I figured you'd be lacking that certain interest in me, but then you offered. You agreed to be a part of this. With me."

"So why did you lie about ladies' night?"

"Because that was my initial intention. I wanted to see if it was you or women in general, but I knew it was you I wanted to be with. The thought of being with someone else just…I don't know. I went out and tried to drown my sorrows in mint and liquor and then I…"

"What?" Oksana said.

"I shouldn't have thrown myself on you like that." Annie heard herself getting louder and louder, but she didn't reel in the momentum. "I know. I'm sorry. I couldn't help myself. I was already horny just thinking about you before you got to the bar, and then I was so relieved when I saw you. I mean how often are you just praying to see someone and they come walking up to you? And you looked so hot. I wasn't thinking."

"Okay. So you had your time to think and now you're questioning your relationship with Jeff because we fucked twice. You wanted your one night of freedom and you got two. Why the change in plans?"

"I'm questioning things with Jeff because right now I care more about how *you* feel than how Jeff feels. It's messed up, Oksana. I know. I have been thinking about you non-stop since the first time we slept together. I can't be sure about marrying someone else when they aren't the most important person on my mind."

Oksana spun around and Annie watched her back as she wrapped her arms around her ribs. This was not going well. She knew Oksana wouldn't be excited to hear that she'd had a part in ending her engagement to Jeff, but she had to come clean. She never considered she'd be hurting Oksana in the process.

Annie wanted to cross the short distance between them and hold Oksana until she somehow magically understood what Annie was feeling, but she'd made that mistake once, letting what she wanted rule the moment. She couldn't push right now.

A deep breath trembled over Oksana's shoulders and then she turned back.

"I don't want this," she said quietly.

"I…understand." She did, but it didn't stop her stomach from dropping to the dirt below the picnic table.

"No, you don't." Oksana was suddenly furious. Annie stared at her, afraid to make any sudden movements. "You really thought you were just going to tell me that you're confused about Jeff and I was going to jump for joy and run away with you? I had a good time with you. I won't deny it. You're great in bed, okay? But I'm not a fucking home wrecker. You told me it was no big deal and now it is, and I don't want to be the person who gets blamed for your wedding ultimately going to shit."

"Who's going to blame you? Jeff won't—"

"Right. He sounds great, but what about your friends and your parents, people who've already shelled out money for dresses and hotels and plane tickets. I've been in a wedding before, Annie. That shit ain't cheap. So when all those people get your, 'Oops, sorry. I'm a lesbian now,' phone call or text message or however you plan to break it to them, guess who they are going to blame? Your new fag girlfriend who corrupted you away from Jeff."

Oksana's words had set off an emotional bomb right there in the park. Annie couldn't hear the birds or the traffic from the street. Just her own strangled breathing and stuttered heartbeat.

Annie closed her eyes, swallowing the pain in her throat.

"I don't think I can marry him," she replied before she looked back at Oksana's exasperated expression. "I've thought about everything you just said. My mother is going to kill me if I do this. I know it, and I know some of my friends will probably never speak to me again, but again, that's just whatever. It's—I know how I feel about you, but this part of it, with me and him, that's not about you, Oksana. Even before we had sex, I was excited for him to leave because I knew I was getting a chance to be with someone else."

She shocked herself with those words, but they were true. From the moment Oksana had agreed to sleep with her, she'd been counting down the days until Jeff left town.

"I don't think about him beyond what I'm going to say when he comes back. I don't miss him. Who doesn't miss their fiancé? I know he's sleeping with other women while he's away and I don't care. I should be furious or jealous or something, but I'm not.

"I wasn't moping about when he was coming back or wondering why he wasn't writing me more. These past few days all I could think about was making things right with *you*. If I could, I would undo the way we got here, but I wouldn't change the way I feel. I really like you, Oksana. I just wanted to tell you. I should thank you. You've given me even more to think about."

"Do I get the floor now?"

"Do you want it?" Annie said, defeated. Oksana rolled her eyes at Annie's dramatics.

"The way I feel about you doesn't matter because we can't undo anything. You are my client. I should have never slept with you. Period. And I should have never slept with someone who was in a relationship because that is wrong. It doesn't matter how you slice it."

"Oh, fuck you," Annie nearly shouted. "I get you're upset with me, but stop painting me like the evil bitch here and tell me why *you* did it if it was so wrong. You let me fuck you and then stayed. You didn't drop me off and leave. You didn't cut and run for the door after I kissed you. You let me take your clothes off and you spent the night. When does your guilt come into play?"

And then they were just arguing.

"I fucked you because I've wanted to since the day I met you."

"So you're attracted to me. Do you have feelings for me?"

"Of course I do. If I didn't I wouldn't have gone to you at the club."

"So besides not wanting to feel like a home wrecker, what's the problem? If you like me and I like you..." Annie brought her hands together in front of her chest in that meshing motion.

"Annie, you don't even know me," Oksana said.

"And you don't really know me either. What's your point?"

"That *is* my point." Oksana didn't skip a beat before she confessed, "I've been down this road before." That stopped Annie's sarcasm in her tracks. Her mouth flapped open. She didn't want to believe that Oksana had broken up a couple before, but Oksana went on before her mind could ask the question. "Not this exact situation, but I was with someone a little like you. She was perfect and I loved her so much, but it turned out she wasn't so sure either."

Annie reached out her hand, but Oksana stayed put. Annie pulled her hand back and shook her head. "You cannot put that on me. I'm not your ex."

"I know, but you're just as dangerous. I have rules for myself. This..." Oksana pulled up the left side of her shirt and revealed the large Cyrillic letters that ran the height of her ribs. Annie had no clue what it said, but she was transfixed as Oksana pointed right to the K. "I got this to cover up her name. I branded myself with her name because I thought we would be together forever and she did everything in her power to make me believe that. I thought she loved me, I thought she loved my family, but she didn't. Me, *we* were something she was unsure about.

"After that I promised myself I wouldn't ignore warning signs anymore. Not with friends, not with my career, and I've stuck to that. I fucked up by sleeping with you, but you're not at risk of a DUI now and I'm thinking more clearly. I can't willingly walk into a relationship that starts like this, Annie. I don't want you to marry someone you're unsure about either. But I can't take a chance on someone who is showing me every sign that they aren't thinking clearly. You really think you're just going to call the wedding off and everyone's going to be all 'Oh, okay. Whatever'?"

Annie snickered and shook her head at the face Oksana made, but she had a point.

"No. I don't."

"*I* want something better for myself. I need someone I know I can trust. I need someone who is one hundred percent sure about me. That's not asking too much, is it?"

"No," Annie huffed indignantly.

"And can't you see how this sounds to me? You're still engaged and telling me you have feelings for me. How do I know you're not going to turn around in two months or a year and tell me you're actually straight or that you'd rather be with someone who can father your children, because that I can't do."

"That's not fair," Annie grumbled.

"Why isn't it fair? It is and you're just mad because it's not what you want to hear."

"So what if we gave this a try and you decided you didn't want me? Then what?"

"I don't know. I have to think about my grandma and I have to think about Kat."

"I want you to. I want to fit into *your* life. I'm not asking you to change just see if you can work me in."

"And what about your friends? You think they'll warm up to me when they find out the truth?"

"My best friend wants to meet you, actually."

"You told her?"

"Yes. I needed to talk to someone. My other friends…"

"Your other friends and your family will hate me."

"At first they might, but I don't care about what they think."

"Yeah, you say that now."

"Well, what do we do?" *Because I'm falling for you even harder,* Annie wanted to say. *Plus, I kinda want to know if you're wearing any underwear under those spandex.*

"I don't know."

Annie's ragged breath propelled her off the picnic table. She felt Oksana's eyes on her as she paced in the dirt.

"Jeff comes back in three weeks and then I think I'm ending it."

"And you hoped we'd hang out in the meantime."

Annie turned on her with a glare. Oksana glared back until Annie relented.

"What should we do about this whole workout thing?" Annie asked with a sigh.

"I need to blow off some steam so I'm going to run up to the top. You're welcome to join me. When you break things to your mother, we'll refund her for the rest of this month."

"No. I'll pay for it. Just let me know how much." Her mom really was going to kill her. "In three weeks—Jesus. In three weeks, can I call you?"

"No." Oksana straightened her shoulders and focused those beautiful dark green eyes right on Annie. "When it all blows over, when you know, not when you think, not when you're a little confused. When you *know,* then you call me."

"Fine."

For some reason, at that moment Oksana's ex popped into her mind. Annie said, "I don't know who she is, of course, but I'm sorry about what she—"

Oksana held up a hand, knowing exactly what Annie was about to say. She'd probably heard it so many times before. "Don't. It was a long time ago and it's over. And whatever she did is definitely not your fault. I just have to watch my own ass."

Annie just nodded slightly, not knowing what else to say.

Oksana jerked her head to the mouth of the trail. "Let's go."

They walked the first few inclines slowly, silently. Annie had more to think about than she realized. Soon their walk turned into a brisk jog and then a full-on run after they passed the observatory and a full out race to the next peak. Annie knew her feelings weren't going to change.

She'd never felt this way for Jeff. They loved each other and she cared about him deeply, but she never ached to touch him, never dreaded the idea of them spending time apart. Never once did she wish that he would call. He traveled all the time for his photography, and Annie never minded watching him go. But as they came back down the mountain, she hated the idea of Oksana walking away. It could take a fucking year for all of this wedding shit to go away, even longer to be forgiven by all the disappointed relatives and put out friends. Annie couldn't wait that long.

She looked at Oksana, dripping with sweat from the crown of her head, her own look of concentration on her face as they neared the rest area at the bottom. Annie fought the urge to wipe Oksana's brow. That touch would lead to more, and Oksana had made it clear that now was the time for less. Distracting herself with her partial clean up, she watched Oksana use the short sleeve of her shirt to do the job instead. She took a bottle of water Oksana had stashed in the trunk of her SUV. They chugged in silence and Annie smiled to herself when she realized Oksana's Tahoe was the same metallic gray as her gunmetal nipple rings.

The nipple rings you'll never see again, she reminded herself.

There was an awkward good-bye, no promise of a phone call, and Annie lumbered on weak legs over to her car. She waited and she knew there were still things unsaid or things undone that would make this time apart even more miserable.

After a moment she realized she hadn't heard a car pull away. There were pebbles all over the road leading in and out of the park. Even her Prius bumped and rattled when she'd pulled in. She turned around and saw Oksana's Tahoe still parked twenty or so yards away.

Selfishly, as was the way with Annie Collins, she walked toward the SUV. Oksana was around the other side, leaning her forehead against the driver's side window, her keys hanging limply in her hand.

"Sana..." She hadn't meant for her voice to sound so breathy and desperate. Dropping the "Ok" just came naturally.

Oksana turned in her direction, and the look on her face told Annie everything she'd been wanting to hear. The hesitation and the fear were there, but the yearning was too. She may have brought up some pretty valid arguments as to why they shouldn't be together, but with just that look Annie knew Oksana didn't want her to go either.

Annie stepped closer with sudden determination, their height difference exaggerated as she looked up into her sad, searching eyes. They swallowed at the same time, nervously. Annie didn't want to pressure her. She wanted Oksana to come to her at will, but there was just something about Oksana and her light cocoa skin that blushed pink, the same shade of her warm lips. Annie had to kiss her one last time before she could really say good-bye.

She watched as Oksana's tongue quickly wet her bottom lip, and she was done in. Annie's arms went around Oksana's waist, pressing the damp T-shirt into the small of her back.

"I'm all gross," Oksana breathed.

"So am I." Annie wasn't going to let a little sweat get in the way. She could feel the tight tips of Oksana's nipples and the balls of their tiny barbells through the fabric of her jacket. She needed more. Taking a slight dip of Oksana's head as her sudden consent, Annie leaned up and took those full lips with her own. Oksana didn't resist or argue.

"Annie," Oksana said one last time. "We can't." But her arms draped over Annie's shoulders and she pulled her closer.

Their kiss was slow at first, sweet and salty, and as fresh as the cool water that had just passed through both their mouths. Ignoring that they were in the middle of a public parking lot, in broad daylight, Annie savored every passing stroke, letting her hands wander along Oksana's back.

Her attention was returned with equal care and gentleness, but Oksana pushed it over into frenzy, sucking Annie's bottom lip between her own. Annie whimpered and shoved her thigh between Oksana's legs. Oksana let her weight drop and Annie caught her, grinding her leg more firmly against Oksana's scorching hot body. Her clit surged at the contact. Her pussy was already wet, but was now throbbing as they started rubbing against each other.

Somewhere in the distance she heard the single beep of the car locks. Oksana shoved away and opened the rear door.

"Get in."

❖

Annie jumped in the backseat of the SUV, kicking her running shoes to the floor as she flopped on her back. Oksana followed, climbing over her, and closed them in the roomy cabin of the car. Green types all around town loved giving her shit for driving the monster SUV, but they could never pull this off in the backseat of Annie's Prius. She watched as Annie braced one knee on the seat and another knee on the floor. Their thighs were intertwined again, and moments later so were their lips, wrestling together in a salty-sweet push and pull, a delicious suck and tug. Suddenly she felt Annie's hands roughly palming her ass pulling her closer. Oksana groaned, glad that she'd skipped wearing underwear.

"Where's your ring?" she murmured into Annie mouth. She'd noticed the huge diamond was still missing. She sat up so Annie could unzip her jacket.

"I never put it back on," Annie replied as she threw her jacket over the front seat. Her shirt was right behind it.

Oksana followed her lead, ditching her shirt and her sports bra. "No one noticed?"

Oksana fought the urge to snap her fingers in front of Annie's face. She wasn't paying attention to a word Oksana was saying. Her eyes were focused on Oksana's nipples. Oksana leaned forward, at first pushing hard with her hips, sliding her slit harder against Annie's thigh, but keeping her tits just out of reach. She pictured her juices seeping through her spandex, and wanted to leave a mark on Annie's yoga pants, on her skin. The thought made her whimper. She had to get Annie completely naked. She had to go down on her again.

"Did they?" Oksana said, trying to bring Annie back to reality, which was just as good, if not better, than her own fantasies.

"No, they did. I just didn't care," she said, arching into the kisses Oksana laved along her neck.

"Mhmm."

"I said it was getting cleaned…You, up."

Oksana sat up and Annie went right for her nipples, cupping her breast in her hand and squeezing gently. Oksana freaked, her back going instantly rigid.

She loved how fascinated Annie was with the tiny pieces of metal. She would never know how good it felt to have a warm tongue sliding against her piercings. Annie had no idea how hard the slightest suction and the right amount of pressure could make her come. But Annie seemed to understand how to treat her sensitive nipples. Oksana had gotten the piercings on a whim. It was the day she turned eighteen and the day of her first legal tattoo. Once they healed, she became fascinated with touching them. Still nothing topped a hot mouth closing over her nipple as it puckered harder than she thought possible around the surgical steel. Oksana rocked against her as Annie adored both barbells, just as their kissing had started out. Slowly at first, so slowly Oksana could feel every small motion, Annie traced the smallest textures of her skin, the tiniest bumps and grooves and then over the metal itself.

Oksana pitched and strained, whimpered Annie's name, but this time "Anne, Anne" as she trembled above her. Beyond the contact of their legs and thighs, their bodies were barely touching. The careful sucking continued as Oksana fought through her orgasm.

Eventually, Annie let go, dropping gentle kisses across Oksana's chest, along the tattoo she surprisingly hadn't asked about yet. Oksana sighed, settling her weight back on Annie's thigh as Annie gently stroked her neck and the back of her head. Now she could feel the soaking heat between her legs spreading through the fabric of her pants. She wanted more.

Annie kissed the corner of her lips. "Did you just come?"

"Yeah," Oksana panted bashfully. The whole park had probably heard her. "I told you they were sensitive."

"No. I remember," she murmured. "That is so hot." Annie lowered her mouth again and slowly stroked over the other nipple, making Oksana arch and shudder some more. Oksana shoved her hand between their bodies, and when she started massaging Annie's pussy through her yoga pants, Annie let her nipple go and did some arching of her own.

Soon Oksana's hand slipped away and their bodies made the contact she'd been wanting all along, even through the layers of their clothes. She shifted off the edge of the seat and let Annie's pussy press flush against her. Annie cried out. Oksana nodded in numb agreement at the sensation on her clit. The cotton that separated them made them both push harder, grind more fiercely toward their finish as they panted each other's names and came together.

"Anne."

"Sana."

Oksana collapsed on Annie's chest, finally sliding both knees to the floor. Annie let her fingers trail down the smooth length of Oksana's bare back, the soothing motions bringing them both down from their highs.

"A month," Oksana breathed. "Call me in a month and we'll see how it goes." The flags, they were bright red and everywhere Oksana looked. They waved in gale force winds with every word Annie said, but something deep inside, a strong niggling in her heart told her to hold on. She couldn't let Annie disappear from her life completely. Something told her to be patient and eventually, maybe in a month those signs of caution would fade to a different color. Somehow red would morph to green.

They lay for a while on the now damp upholstery. Oksana noticed the seat belt was digging into the side of her knee, but she was too content to move. Eventually, they had to.

Suffocating in the backseat of her Tahoe was not the end Oksana had in mind. Annie agreed. They peeled themselves apart and did their best to appear decent before they climbed out and shoved back into their sneakers.

"One month?" Annie asked, the hopeful tone in her voice suggested she would settle for something in the ballpark of one week.

Oksana leaned down and kissed her. "One month." She watched Annie walk back to her car. Annie paused once, looking over her shoulder with a lustful yet forlorn look in her eye. Oksana felt like she was doing the right thing. Annie wanted to spend time with her, not just fuck her at every opportunity. Annie wanted a chance, but thankfully, she didn't argue with Oksana's terms.

As she drove out of the park, refusing to look back at the Prius that stayed behind her until she reached Sunset, Oksana knew this was going to be the longest month of her life. Or maybe it would pass too quickly, before she had enough time to really think.

When she reached the little house, she showered and ate an exotic parfait Baba had been nice enough to leave in the fridge for her. Her session with Stewart was pleasant and quick. A nice trip to another place with someone who wasn't complicated, someone who wanted her professional guidance and her trust, not a piece of her heart.

She watched a horrible TV movie with Kat and did her best to relax. Sometime after dinner though, she caved. She needed to talk to Annie. Bring the emotions and speculations down and talk to her about the possibility of what they could have. She wasn't ready for a relationship, but she needed to talk, with calm words and rational thinking, and not in public. They exchanged a few texts, and once it was confirmed that Annie had no plans Oksana asked, *Can I come over?*

Yes was Annie's reply.

Baba didn't ask where she was going when she snatched her keys from the counter. Something told Oksana she already knew.

CHAPTER SEVEN

THE BEGINNING OR THE END,
DEPENDING ON WHOM YOU ASK

Oksana climbed out of her Tahoe and took a deep breath. She adjusted her shirt and her Adidas jacket over the top of her jeans as she came around the front of her car. Annie was standing on the front steps in her pajamas.

"Hi," she said with the most adorable, dimpled grin. "Are you hungry? I have pizza."

Oksana couldn't fight her smile as she walked up the steps. "What kind?"

"Pepperoni and sausage. I have ice cream too," Annie replied, standing up on her tiptoes, lips pursed for a kiss. Oksana gave in and gently took Annie's lips with her own. She'd come to Venice to talk, not to fuck or make out, but something in Oksana's heart had already latched on to Annie, claimed her as someone worth kissing on sight.

Annie fell back on her heels and grabbed Oksana's hand. "Come inside." She followed Annie to the couch, noticing immediately that every trace of her wedding had vanished from the room. She kept her mouth shut about the missing dress and the fact that *Runaway Bride* was playing on Annie's TV.

They collapsed on the couch facing each other. Oksana was suddenly at a loss for words. Now what?

She watched her…Ex-client? Lover? Annie looked down at her fingers and continued to chip away at the leftover nail polish on her left hand. Thank God the ring hadn't made a return.

Oksana waited. Annie took a deep breath then looked her in the eye. "I've done a lot more thinking today, but tell me how you're feeling."

Oksana reconsidered what she'd been planning to say. This was the first time since before their little romp that they'd had a real conversation that hadn't started off with the spark of a heavy emotional charge. For some reason, she hadn't expected Annie to be so considerate. She wasn't used to considerate.

"I'm nervous about what you want," Oksana admitted.

"What do you mean?"

"This is a lot." Oksana gestured between them. "You want to start a relationship before you end one, *and* you are new to being with women. I don't know anything about your relationship with Jeff. I don't know that you're not running from something bigger."

Annie nodded, but twisted her lip with uncertainty. "I get it. That's fair."

"Are you looking for something new?" Oksana said. That cute face had gotten away with murder all week. "Are you trying to break from some mold you feel trapped in? I just can't be the person to help you figure that out. If you're even remotely unsure about me then I should leave."

"No. I was happy with Jeff, but there's something I feel for you that I don't feel for him. That I've never felt for anyone. He and I, we melded together. We met, and after so long without any drama, I thought why not get married. But when I first met you, I was excited. You remember, I gushed over you for like three sessions."

Oksana did remember. Annie had told her how beautiful she thought she was. She had gone on and on about how glad she was that she actually liked her and that she hadn't gotten stuck with some weird health nut. It was part of the reason Oksana found it so hard to fight her attraction to Annie. She always had the nagging feeling that Annie might have gone for her under different circumstances.

"I know how it looks and sounds. I know I'm coming off as a complete flake, but I have to tell you, I'm not impulsive."

Oksana snorted in laughter. Annie smiled back, nudging her leg. "I'm serious. I'd been planning our affair for months, well *the* affair, for months. I did plan on going to The Maypole to see if any other woman caught my eye, but this whole time I've been thinking about you. I want to be with you and see where that goes, but I want to know what I can give you to make *you* think it's worth giving me that chance. Besides, I know we just slept together this week, but we met three months ago. That is something."

Annie had a very valid point. This part of their relationship was new, but their connection wasn't. Oksana gave that thought its footing. Still, there was more to straighten out.

"I'd also like to know the last time you were tested."

That sobered Annie right up. "Oh, ah…right before Jeff left, just in case he brought any surprises back from his trip. I'm good to go. I'm also not pregnant. *You*?" She smiled again, lightening the question.

"I got tested right after my ex and I split. I haven't been with anyone since."

Oksana let that hang in the air, giving Annie a moment to ask what she could tell was on the tip of her tongue.

"How long has it been?" Annie said quietly. Oksana wanted to believe that Annie was full of shit, that Annie was going to take her down in a blaze of selfish glory, but this tone was sincere. It wasn't about Annie getting what she wanted. It was about Annie showing she actually cared.

"Three, almost four years. I know it sounds like a long time, but really, it was good for me. I needed that time to grow up a little. Though I haven't been acting all that mature lately. I am clean." She took a deep breath and pushed the ghost of Vivian off the couch. "I'm not going to ask you about Jeff or your family. I'm staying out of that, but *I* need time. And I need you to be completely honest with me and yourself."

"I can do that." Annie nodded confidently.

"There's a good chance you might lose some friends when you end things with Jeff. I want to be there for you if that happens, but I don't want to take the blame, and I don't want to be hanging on to us if you suddenly realize you should be with him. I don't trust you," Oksana said plainly. She needed Annie to understand.

"But," Oksana leaned forward and kissed Annie on the mouth. As she pulled away she smiled again at the look of shock slowly fading on Annie's face. "I also know that this could turn out to be a good thing. For us both. I like you and I want to spend more, less confusing time with you."

Annie's eyes glistened in the low light as she replied. "I want you to trust me, but I know that will take time. What can I give you tonight? What can I give you this weekend?"

Oksana sighed and finally relaxed into the couch. Annie reached over and softly stroked Oksana's hand.

"My grandma wants to meet you, like tomorrow."

"Really?" Annie smiled as if this was some small triumph.

"Yeah. And that's the other thing. I'm not interested in getting hurt, but I also have a family. My sister is getting older. Still, for the next few years, I technically have a daughter. She's already excited about the idea of us, so I have to keep her in mind."

"Do they know you're here now?"

"Yes. I didn't tell Kat all the details. My grandmother knows everything."

"Everything?" Annie's eyebrows shot up.

"I didn't tell her how good you are at eating pussy, but—"

"I'm good at eating pussy?" Annie's frown flashed to a dirty grin.

"Shut up. In my last relationship, I tried to protect my ex. I made excuses for things she did because at the time I didn't think they were strange. And when we broke up, Baba made me promise I wouldn't lie to her about my life anymore."

"I think that's a good bargain."

"It is, but when I was coming home late or staying out all night this week and checking my phone like crazy, she knew something was up. I told her the whole truth."

"Does she think I'm some sort of whoring trollop?" Annie patted her thigh. "Come on." Oksana wasn't doing a good job at hiding how exhausted she was. She followed Annie's lead as she moved to the far side of the couch and rested her head on Annie's flannel covered thigh and closed her eyes. Annie began stroking her hair. She'd be asleep in no time if she didn't keep talking.

"No. She just doesn't like games."

Annie's thigh flexed under her cheek. "Neither do I."

"Shit, this has been a long week. I just want to relax. Some short girl keeps fucking up my carefully orchestrated yet calm existence."

"I'm sorry." Annie laughed. Her other hand slid under Oksana's jacket and gently stroked her ribs. "I called Paulo this afternoon. I straightened everything out, and he gave me the final amount. He said your job is still safe."

"I know. He's my boy. He told me."

"Good. What are we now?"

"We're becoming friends. Meet my family, break up with Jeff, and then we can be something more." Oksana buried her face deeper into Annie's lap, lifted her tiny T-shirt, and kissed her stomach. Annie giggled.

"Friends who have sleepovers?"

"Are you asking me to sleep over?"

"Yes."

"I'll think about it." On the TV, Richard Gere and Julia Roberts were haggling about her fee for a proper interview. Oksana loved that movie, but thought the bit worked better when Roberts was playing a hooker. She sat up for a moment and peeled off her jacket. "I can't believe you're watching this." She grimaced as she made herself comfortable back in Annie's lap. Annie's hand went right back to her head, fingers massaging deeply around her temple. She'd be drooling in no time.

"I couldn't help it. Plus, it was this or a marathon of *Extreme Wedding Cakes*."

"That sounds terrible." Oksana yawned. Then something else occurred to her.

"Where were you and Jeff planning to live?"

"He's planning to move here. He has a loft studio space in Koreatown, but he was going to rent that out. Hopefully, I can talk him into keeping it."

"And if it's too late for that? I mean, what if he's already found someone to take over the lease or whatever?"

"Then I'll offer to help him find a new place. If he'll let me."

"This is a huge clusterfuck. I hope you know that," Oksana said, snuggling deeper into the couch and closer to Annie's heat.

"I know," Annie said quietly. Her fingers moved to Oksana's temple. "Go to sleep."

Seeing no reason to argue with that suggestion, Oksana dozed for a long time, finally feeling some sort of peace. She wanted to run, get as far away from Annie and her wedding party as possible, but it had been a long time since she'd been touched this way. A longer time since she'd been as happy as she was now. As Annie continued with her gentle petting, Oksana fell fast asleep.

❖

A while later her own snores woke her up.

"Come on." Annie nudged her gently. "Bedtime." Oksana stood, rubbing her eyes like a toddler while Annie began shutting down the house. Once the lights were off and pizza stowed safely away, she followed Annie to her bed.

"You want something to sleep in?" Annie asked, eying her closet.

"I usually sleep naked," Oksana admitted. "I'm in workout gear ninety percent of the time. I like letting my body breathe."

"I'm okay with that."

"Of course you are." Seeing no point in being bashful since Annie had already sampled all the appetizers at Oksana's buffet, she stripped down to her birthday suit, but by the time Oksana stepped out of her boy shorts, Annie was frozen on the other side of the bed. Her mouth was hanging open as she gripped the corner of the covers.

"What?" Oksana asked as she roughly rubbed the underside of her tits. "You've seen me naked before."

"Yeah, but—Never mind. Hop in."

Oksana climbed into bed. Annie turned off the lights and joined her. They both rolled in the darkness, facing each other. In real sleepover fashion, Annie pulled the thin white sheet over both their heads. After a moment Oksana's eyes adjusted to the slanted light coming through the bedroom window. There were no trees in Annie's backyard, and the light pollution from her neighbor's security beams was outstanding.

Annie reached over and touched the sunflowers across her stomach.

"You have to tell me about these."

"All a tribute to Mother Russia." Annie's eyes lit up as Oksana let her accent drawl. That slight reaction was good to know for the future.

Annie's hand drifted higher to the letters stacked up Oksana's side. "What does this say?"

Oksana's skin twitched a little and she licked her lips. "It's my surname."

"Grinkoff?"

"Good God." Oksana shuddered and laughed as Annie flattened every flow-able syllable. When she replied, Oksana let her accent come in fully as she gave Annie her first Russian lesson.

"It's pronounced Gorinkov."

Annie repeated back in the same spine-tingling fashion as before.

"Your accent is horrible."

"My French teacher in high school wanted to kill me. Straight As and I sounded like a stupid American right till the very end," Annie said, smiling.

Oksana leaned forward and kissed her dimpled cheek. "You just—" She gave up, shaking her head into the pillow. "I'll help you if I can."

Annie's eyes softened. "I like this. Being here with you."

"It's not so bad for me either. Take off your shirt."

Annie hesitated for a moment before she sat up and pulled the baby tee over her head. "I thought you needed some time." Her voice came out breathy, a little desperate.

"I do, but I want to touch you while we wait," she said, but Oksana kept her hands on her side of the bed.

Annie scowled and slid a little closer. "Did you do this when you were younger? Have sexy sleepovers with girls in your class and make them take off their shirts so you could feel them up?" Annie was having way too much fun.

Oksana shrugged.

"Tell me."

"You go first." Oksana smiled.

"No, it's boring. All boys. Two in junior high. Three in high school. Two in college. Then..." Yeah, they all knew who came next. Even Baba and Paulo knew who came next. Oksana tried not to let it bother her.

"Ew. Boys are gross."

"Tell me," Annie said.

"There were a few turns in the minor leagues, but I didn't get another girl off until I was sixteen."

"Oh, I feel like a pervert listening to this. Go on."

Oksana thought for a moment, gazing at the dark curves of Annie's tits, their generous size weighing them down toward the mattress, creating the most distracting cleavage. Oksana shifted her legs a bit, rubbing her thighs together. Apparently, it didn't take much from Annie to make her wet.

"Did you two play doctor?" Annie teased her. Oksana forced herself to look her in the eye, but that didn't last long.

Slowly, she drew one finger over the top of Annie's breast and watched the goose bumps pop out along her skin. She hadn't planned on sleeping with Annie again so soon, but now Oksana realized it was too late, especially with them both being topless. She wanted to touch Annie more, play her fingers and mouth along her body. She stared at Annie's chest, the large nipples and puffy round areolas that blended seamlessly with her beach-bronzed skin. Her tongue tingled at the thought and her clit stiffened at the possibility.

"Tell me," Annie breathed as she squirmed in their cocoon of linens.

Oksana moved her fingers lower and captured Annie's nipple. She didn't squeeze, but gently rubbed around the tip. Annie swallowed harshly.

"Her name was Stacy and she was in my homeroom."

"And what happened with Stacy from homeroom?"

"She figured me out. I was shy, but she saw something there worth being corrupted. We went to her house one day after school and I let her touch me."

"Where?"

Oksana remembered everything about her first times with Stacy, the not-so-shy butch in her homeroom, but all she could picture was Annie sprawled out on top of her. The feeling of her wetness soaking her skin. The sound of her sighs. She forgot all about her story, her past, and focused on her future.

"Everywhere. She kissed me. Fingered me. Took my virginity in every way she could think of."

"What happened to Stacy?" Annie whispered, closing her eyes.

"She works for the city, I think."

Then Oksana couldn't take any more of her own teasing. She reached between them and wrapped her arm around Annie's waist, pulling her closer. She ducked her head and took Annie's nipple in her mouth, curving her lips to take it in deep. She sucked and pulled with a teasing pressure, drew her tongue over the tip again and again. Annie squirmed more, forcing her tit further into Oksana's mouth. Her teeth lightly caught the wet skin, and Annie moaned.

They both tore at the sheet to free themselves. Oksana slid on her back, pulling Annie with her. She wanted more of her breasts, more of her full nipples, and that's what she took. Cupping Annie's ass and leading her into a slow grind along her stomach, Oksana continued to lick and suck. She risked a glance above and was struck dumb by the sight of Annie. Her hands braced against the wall. Her head lolling back, moving from side to side as her hips drove hard and lower on Oksana's hips.

Annie leaned back and made a small noise of pleasure when Oksana followed, keeping her mouth latched to her breasts. Oksana's tender skin twitched, hot and wet under Annie's fingers as she explored her slit. She moaned with Annie in her mouth as she stroked her clit for a few agonizing minutes before drawing her fingers lower. One digit sank in with ease, Oksana's juices slicking a smooth entrance. Annie added two more fingers with no pretext, driving deep into her pussy. Oksana's uncontrollable whimpers pitched higher.

"You like this?"

Oksana let her nipple drop from her mouth. Her hips surged as she caught sight of the trail of moisture that led from Annie's nipple to her mouth. "Yes. Yes," she panted under Annie's driving thrusts. Annie flipped over and speared Oksana with her tongue.

"Oh God!" Oksana cried. She grabbed on to Annie's hips to steady herself. She rode out her first orgasm, hips bucking in the sheets. Annie wouldn't let up. Oksana had never known anyone to go down with such enthusiasm, but who was she to stop her?

She reached up and parted the pert cheeks in front of her and stroked Annie's swollen, wet lips. She rubbed Annie with her thumb, back and forth over and along her clit. Annie's shoulders shot up and she rocked back onto Oksana's hand.

Annie moaned unintelligibly and slid back even further.

"Move back," Oksana groaned as she grabbed Annie by the waist and pulled her all the way up.

Annie followed her cues and gave Oksana better access to what she was after. She worshiped Annie with her mouth and her fingers, distantly aware of Annie's constant caresses between her legs. Soon Annie came, her whole body frozen and tense before violent tremors shuddered down her back, through her legs.

They righted themselves and settled back beneath Annie's sheets. Oksana kissed her, breathing heavy, sharing their salty-sweet taste.

Oksana fell asleep once more in Annie's arms, fully aware of their undeniable chemistry between them, hoping that the rest, the real friendship, and eventually, the love would follow.

Chapter Eight

The Courtship

"D o you think she'll like me?" Annie asked.

Oksana flashed a teasing smile. "I don't know. She hates most people."

"I'm serious. I think I'm really nervous. I've never—" Oksana looked over at Annie sitting beside her in the SUV. She looked so hot. After a quick shower, Annie had ditched the contacts Oksana had no clue she wore for some black frame glasses that stood out against her blond hair. She'd changed her clothes twice and finally settled on some jeans and a light blue shirt that showed off her boobs. At the last moment, Annie grabbed a zip-up hoodie to cover her cleavage in front of Baba Ina. Oksana thought Annie looked perfect, good enough to take in the backseat again, but she didn't like the scowl on her adorable face.

"What?"

Annie took a deep breath, and Oksana could see she was forcing a smile. "Nothing. I was just thinking that I haven't even met Jeff's grandmother yet." Annie laughed and a genuine smile turned up her lips. "Guess that won't be happening now."

"It still can."

"No," Annie said. "I want *this*." Thank God the light turned green. Oksana forced herself to focus back on the road in front of her and the cars around them and not on the emotions changing on Annie's face.

Oksana wondered how long it would be like this. The awkward mentions of Jeff and Annie's family. She wondered, really, how many months she would have to feel this uncomfortable tension with this situation now that she and Annie were "together." Annie had been clear about what she wanted, and that was Oksana.

She believed that the bride-to-never-be was comfortable in her decision, but Oksana still felt like something was going to go wrong. Something besides Annie's entire family, all her friends, and her fiancé going completely grade-A bananas when they found out that Oksana had come between Annie and Jeff. Since the moment they'd woken up, still cuddled around each other, there was this cloud of doom that Oksana couldn't seem to shake.

How in the fuck did I end up in this situation? She scolded herself for the tenth time as they coasted through Beverly Hills.

There was no excuse for how weak Oksana was when it came to Annie. They'd barely scratched the surface of what Oksana was into sexually, and she was convinced she'd only seen a glimpse of what turned Annie on, she had already given Oksana the best orgasms of her life. It didn't matter that Oksana's undoing was as simple as some gentle attentiveness to her nipples or three fingers thrust deep inside her cunt. She couldn't handle the thought of not sleeping with Annie again, and soon.

But beyond what her body was screaming at her loud and clear, Oksana's insecurities and their new relationship status be damned, she was starting to think that Annie actually had feelings for her. Those three months before they crossed that unforgivable line had meant something. Oksana had been charmed by Annie fully.

As she drove them toward the big house in West Hollywood, it was that realization, the notion that this whole thing has been building, that Annie had picked her over Jeff, which made Oksana stick with their decision to try to work out some sort of a real relationship. It didn't matter how much of a flake she thought Annie could be; no one ended an engagement and declared their sexual orientation as something other than straight without giving it some serious thought. Annie was risking a lot, and Oksana couldn't ignore the fact that Annie stood to lose so much just for a chance to be with her.

Even though Oksana didn't exactly trust the reality of how refreshing Annie's eagerness was, the only obstacle standing in Oksana's way was her own fear of getting hurt. She had to let go and let Annie in. What other choice did she have?

As it got closer to noon, Oksana was forced to pull herself out of Annie's bed and get back to her life. She had a full day of driving Kat around from the MAC Counter to the Sephora showroom in between the weekly errands they ran for Baba. She never thought Annie would want to come along.

Oksana glanced down then over as Annie gently squeezed her thigh. "Are you okay?" she asked sweetly.

No, because I'm totally freaked this is going to end badly. "Yeah. I'm fine. And don't worry about Baba. She'll like you."

"Are you sure she doesn't think I'm a slut?"

Oksana laughed. "Who ever called you a slut?"

"I just know how it looks."

"Well, my grandma cares how *it is*. She could give less of a shit how it looks. Just don't win her over then change your mind. She might have you killed."

Silence from the other side of the car made Oksana glance over again. At the same second, Annie looked up from her lap and leaned over the seat. Oksana swallowed thickly as Annie's lips softly brushed her cheek.

"I'm sorry," Annie muttered. "I'm going to work this out soon. I promise. I'll tell him and that will all be over."

Oksana couldn't understand why, but her stomach started turning. Thinking that comforting Annie might help her own shaky nerves, Oksana wove their fingers together in her lap.

"I know. It's okay. We didn't plan it, but we'll both roll with it. Okay?"

"I like *that* plan." Annie sighed with a light smile, settling closer to Oksana in her seat. "So what does Baba Inna do when she's not kicking ass and taking names the Russian way?"

"She only knows how to do it the Russian way. She owns a store on Curson and three laundry mats."

"Is it the store that gives away free condoms?" Annie giggled.

"Yeah." Oksana smiled to herself, thinking of her grandmother yelling at the high school kids who abused the free samples. Baba hated that convenience store, but she liked working there better than socializing with the other old Russian ladies in West Hollywood. It got her out of the house while Kat was at school and on nights when she didn't feel like sitting on the couch. The rest of the time, her two employees, Fel and Gabe, held down the fort. Oksana didn't care for Fel, but he made nice with all the vendors and came in even on his days off to stock deliveries. Gabe was great with Baba, and that won him massive points.

"Get the fuck out! Does she have bright red dyed hair?"

"Yeah. That's Baba."

"Holy shit." Annie laughed louder. "She's fucking scary."

"No, she isn't." *Okay, she is.* Baba was really a sweetheart, the best grandmother/mother that Oksana could ask for, but to people who weren't immediate family, on the payroll, or Russian, she was a little bristly. "My uncles in Vegas set her up with a little something of her own before they took off so she could take care of me and Kat."

"That doesn't sound shady at all," Annie said, tickling Oksana's palm.

"It's all legal. I swear." At least she told herself it was. Her uncles *were* a little on the shady side. Still, nice guys.

"Hey...where are your parents? I'm sorry, I just—" Annie backpedaled. Oksana hadn't meant to flinch. She tightened her grip on Annie's hand and pulled it closer to her stomach. A sign of trust maybe.

"No, it's okay." Every one of her friends had asked the same thing at some point. She should have guessed Annie would be so forward so soon. "My mom is in Paris and my dad is back and forth between there and Guinea Bissau."

"I remember you said West Africa, but I don't know exactly where that is," Annie admitted, which Oksana liked. Most people just nodded or said something stupid about the benefits of the Panama Canal just to keep the conversation moving.

"It's on the coast. I'll show you on a map sometime."

"What do they do?"

"My dad is in the fishing industry, but I think he traffics drugs," she said bluntly. "And my mom is, well, she used to be a ballerina. They met in London while she was on tour. She had me and then went back to the company to get back in shape. She had to quit when she had Kat though. That huge baby ruined her figure forever. She runs a school now."

"So you were both raised here?"

"No, I lived in Moscow with Baba until I was eleven, and then we followed my uncles here."

"And Kat?"

"Mom flew here to visit, then oops, had a baby on American soil while she was in town." It worked for them all in the end, but Oksana didn't bother to hide her resentment.

"How often do you see her? Or him."

"Once every three years. She comes to visit Kat mostly."

"And him?"

Oksana just shrugged. Her father was a nice man. They always had calm, pleasant conversations whenever they were together or whenever he called. He always gave her a firm hug and kiss and told her to be a good girl for Baba, even when she crossed into her twenties, but they had no relationship to speak of. Her mother called the shots in what they called a marriage, and if she didn't want any children around, he was okay with that. Everyone was better off.

Annie took the hint from her silence and moved on. "These uncles, they are your mom's brothers?"

"Yeah. Yuri and Victor. They're pretty cool. What about your family?" It was Oksana's job to get inside her client's lives, but Annie never talked about her family. They'd spent most of their sessions laughing about silly wedding traditions and creating inside jokes about the noises Annie made the first time she did a squat.

"No brothers and sisters. My dad is in finance, but he might be trafficking drugs too, come to think of it." At that, Oksana laughed. Annie smiled back. "And my mom owns a boutique with her friend."

"What kind of boutique?" Oksana asked, glad to be off her weird family for a moment. She drove into West Hollywood and slid her fingers up Annie's wrist, under the fabric of her pink hoodie.

"Designer accessories for dogs," Annie said. "I wish I was kidding, but I'm not. She's kinda…I don't know. I basically raised myself. She's pretty involved with her social life and the accessories of course. Worked out perfectly though. She couldn't have cared less when I said I wanted to work in movies or that I ended up in reality TV."

"Do you like dogs?" Oksana was so worried about dating an almost married woman she forgot about Baba's stupid mastiff whose size alone scared the shit out of the whole block.

"Yeah. Do you have a dog?"

Oksana didn't answer right away. In a few hundred yards, as soon as they pulled up to Baba's house, Annie would see for herself.

❖

Baba Inna was standing in the driveway with a lit cigarette dangling from her lips and her hand clutching Vasily's leash. He lumbered around in circles looking for something to lick off the sidewalk.

Fuck.

Annie chuckled softly beside her. "This is grandma."

"Yes. At least she's smoking outside today."

"And the dog, is he cool?" Oksana watched Annie's wide eyes as she inspected the dog through the passenger window.

"Yeah. He's a big puppy."

Oksana pulled past her grandmother and put the Tahoe in park. There was no way to prepare Annie for Baba's quirks so Oksana just opened her door and met Annie around the other side. They walked, holding hands, to the end of the drive where Vasily met them, panting and slobbering in hello. Oksana actually relaxed when Annie casually stroked his enormous sandy brown head with her free hand.

Right on cue, Baba Inna started on Oksana in her slow, gravelly Russian.

"Good afternoon, darling," she muttered, patting Oksana on the hip. Oksana fought rolling her eyes. Of course Baba would bring attention to the time.

Yes, Baba. It's almost noon. And yes, I'm wearing the same clothes I left in. I spent the night out. Fucking.

"Annie, this is my grandmother, Inna. Inna, this is Annie Collins." She reached over and scratched their dog under the chin, just enough for him to drool all over her wrist. "This is Vasily," she cooed.

"Hello." Annie smiled at Baba and the dog. Oksana could read the anxious look on her face. Annie probably wondered how the old woman talked with a lit cigarette still in her mouth, and like most people who met her, she probably wondered if Baba spoke any English beyond growling out totals from behind her cash register.

Baba stared at Annie for a moment, her left eye squeezing into her trademark squint. She took her cigarette and dropped it on the pavement, leaving it to nature to extinguish the butt. "Come inside," she drawled to Annie. As soon as she turned her back, Oksana ground the cigarette out with the heel of her Adidas.

Trailing Baba Inna and Vasily up the front steps, Annie turned to Oksana, eyes wide with a closed lipped chuckle. So far so good, but Oksana knew they weren't out of the woods.

They followed Baba into the kitchen that probably looked like a Betty Crocker shrine to Russian folk art to Annie. Russian cookbooks and Siberian kitsch lined every sill and counter. A Soviet soldier popped from the front of the cuckoo clock and startled the fuck out of Annie. The little figurine marched in measured steps as the time chimed off.

Oksana was psyched that the place smelled more like spices and onions than cigarettes. She kept an eye on Annie as she watched Baba shovel some leftover eggs into Vasily's bowl. Once he was fed, Baba turned on them. She looked at Annie more closely as she came around the kitchen table. She took Annie's hand and turned it palm side up. With thick fingers, she got a decent hold. Annie yelped as Baba pinched the skin on her wrist. Baba ignored her protest and looked up at Oksana instead.

"You did this to her," she said.

Oksana rolled her eyes this time. She replied in kind. *"Yes, Baba. Her dress was two sizes too small."*

"Well, now she won't be wearing the dress."

"I don't know that for sure," Oksana said.

"I do."

Oksana knew they were being rude, and she felt awful as Annie glanced between them nervously, but this was Baba's kitchen. Her rules. Baba released Annie's wrist then patted Annie on the cheek, gentler than she'd done Oksana's hip in the driveway, then crossed back to the fridge. Oksana lifted Annie's wrist to get a closer look at the damage.

"I'll live," Annie said with a doe-eyed pout. Oksana wanted to kiss her right on those gorgeous lips.

"I need more lamb," Baba announced in English. Oksana's attention snapped back to her. This was a good sign. Shocking, but good. Casual conversation the guest could understand was always a good thing. Baba pulled the list she started off the fridge and added a few more items. "Don't get that other pepper. It's cheap."

"Okay. Where's Kat?"

"She's upstairs with her little friend," Baba replied, handing her the grocery list. Oksana hoped Annie knew she was in for a full day of family obligations, which included stocking the pantry for Baba.

"Okay." She folded the list then froze when Annie took it from her and slid the piece of paper in the back pocket of her jeans. They looked at each other for a moment. Annie's lips quirked up in a slight smile, her eyes admitting that yes, she was in for the whole day. She gently tugged Oksana's finger.

Without looking at Baba, Oksana said, "We'll be back in twenty minutes. I'm going to go change."

"You stay for dinner."

The sudden invitation snatched their attention.

"Uh…um…" Annie stuttered. "Okay."

"Good. Bye-bye."

That was their official dismissal. Baba Inna all but ignored them as they headed out the back door. When they were a safe distance across the lawn, Annie whispered. "What was she saying?"

"She thinks you're too skinny," she replied honestly.

"She's right. I'm seeing bones I didn't know I had. I might burn that dress."

"Don't do that." Oksana scowled. What the dress stood for made her want to heave all over the stone path to the little house, but it was a beautiful gown. If Annie couldn't return it, she could definitely resell it or at least donate it.

"I'm joking, but it's not like I'll be wearing it. I'm about to get soooo fat."

"That's fine with me. Just don't tell anyone else you were using me as your trainer," Oksana joked with a wide grin. She opened the door to her cottage realizing a moment too late that the door was already unlocked. "Sorry it's a mess. I—"

"Whoa!" Annie gasped. Oksana spun around to find her little sister half naked on the couch, a heavyset girl half naked on top of her.

"Kat!" The two teenagers scrambled for their bras and T-shirts. Oksana blinked in horror. "What the heck are you doing?"

"Nothing." Kat jumped up and gave Annie a nice little frontal before she pulled her shirt over her head. "I wanted to show Erica your sneakers. And borrow your peach shadow." As an afterthought, she shoved her bra in her back pocket.

Oksana sighed and tried not to rub the skin off her forehead. "Annie, I'm sorry. This is my sister, Kat, and this is her girlfriend, Erica."

"Hi." Erica smiled back bashfully. She stood, adjusting her shirt, and hid herself half behind Kat's shoulder. At least she had some sense of modesty.

"We're going to talk about this later," Oksana said. Instead of arguing, Kat made a little grumbling noise and looked at the floor as

she toed her Chucks into the carpet. When she wet her lips, Oksana winced at the sight of her sister's tongue stud.

God, what the hell had happened to my cute, sweet little sister? She eyed the ounces and ounces of thick black eye makeup and the hoop pierced through the right side of her lip. Ronnie was to blame for the face piercing; the rest was all Oksana. She hated to even think about it, but Kat idolized her. The moment Oksana got her first tattoo, Kat made it known that she had the coolest sister in the world. She wanted to be "badass" just like her, right down to dating girls. It was flattering in a way, but this shit, fooling around on Oksana's couch, had to stop before it even started.

Oksana knew there was absolutely no way to curb her teenage hormones, but she was still the parent in this situation. The time for being the cool older sister had ended the moment their mother walked out of the maternity ward without her younger child.

"Take Erica up to the house. To the *den,* and we'll be up there in a few minutes."

"Okay. Can I still show her your sneakers?" The collection was pretty impressive, but Oksana wanted them out of her place, like now.

"Later. Erica, do you want to stay for dinner?"

"Yeah. My mom said it was okay." Of course she'd already asked.

"Okay. Go."

She waited until the door closed before she sank against the TV stand with a heavy sigh.

"I am so sorry about that."

"It's okay." Annie laughed. "How old is she?"

"Fifteen going on whore." Oksana chuckled. "She figured out she was into girls when she was ten and I—seriously, she's brought out half her school. Erica is girlfriend number five this year."

"So she's been busy," Annie said with a stern nod.

"Yeah, you could say that. Make yourself at home. I'll be out in a few minutes." Oksana looked at the defiled couch cushions then pointed at the lounger across the room.

Embarrassed beyond belief, Oksana quickly walked into her room and started shedding her clothes. Her shower was hot and just long enough for a full body lady-scaping. Clean and refreshed, she dove into her closet. She tossed a moss green, short-sleeved blouse with tiny white polka dots and a high ruffled collar on the bed. A pair of trouser jeans landed right beside the top. She bypassed the racks that housed her custom sneaker collection and dug out a pair of moss green ballet flats.

Oksana wasn't sure how many tattoos she was going to get, and she promised Baba she wouldn't pierce her face, but she was pretty sure she'd be shaving her head for a while. She had her own style, but as a concession to some sense of responsibility, she liked to at least dress like an adult when she was out with Kat. The ink and the lack of hair threw people, but her genuine politeness, coupled with her own seasonal Coach bag, put most gawking strangers right back in check. It would be interesting to see the reaction she would get now that she would be on the arm of a preppy, bubbly blonde.

"Sana," the blonde in question called from the living room. Her voice grew louder. "I'm going to grab some water. Do you want me to use the plastic cups—Helloooo."

Oksana watched Annie flop down on the bed. She held up Oksana's dildo, the Commander, the one she'd cleaned but forgotten to put away. She knew Annie wasn't shocked by the length of the toy, but the girth. The black dildo was pretty wide around.

"This yours?" Annie smiled that smile that instantly made Oksana wet. She shifted on the heels of her feet and adjusted her towel. The terrycloth rubbing against her nipples didn't help curb her sudden arousal.

"Yeah." Oksana swallowed.

"It's pretty big. When was the last time you used it?" Okay, Annie licking her lips wasn't helping either.

"Yesterday." *Right after we fucked in my car.*

"Oh really? When?"

"I came back here to change for my afternoon session. After I left the park, I was still pretty worked up."

"And this is the toy of choice?"

And like that, Vivian was in Oksana's ears, bitching and whining. Certain things set those memories off. Just the way Annie said "toy" sent a weird strain up the back of her neck. Annie must have sensed her panic because she was across the room, still clutching the dildo, in a heartbeat.

"What's wrong?" she asked gently.

Oksana swallowed her nerves and shook her head. "Nothing.

Annie cradled her cheek and kissed her softly on the lips. "Tell me. Would you be interested in me using this on you?"

"Yeah," Oksana replied and shifted again. There were two teenagers waiting for them. Now was not the time to bend over the bed and beg.

"I'll have to fuck you with it then, and who knows?" Annie pressed their bodies together, gazing up with those baby blues. "Maybe some time you can put this in my ass."

"What!" Oksana's eyes popped wide. She knew Annie had a little freak in her, but—

"I'm kidding." Annie chuckled. "This would split me in half." She held up the dildo and eyed its broad rises carefully. "But if you slip a finger in my ass and finger my pussy just right, I've been known to squirt. A lot."

"Oh." *Oh, fuck!* "We might have to try that."

Annie tossed the toy behind her and turned back to Oksana after it landed safely in the sheets. "Hurry. We've got some errands to run."

Right. Errands. The last thing on Oksana's mind.

❖

Annie was staring at her.

"What?" Oksana asked, keeping her eyes on the road.

"Nothing. I'm just so used to seeing you in workout clothes. Not that I mind the spandex. You look good."

Oksana could feel the pink rise in her cheeks and she mumbled her thank you. She liked the outfit too, but it was hard to think when Annie looked at her like that, like they should be having sex that very moment. The smile she'd given her back in the cottage reminded her of the love they made the night before, but the glint Annie had in her eyes now reminded her of what they'd done in the park and just how much Oksana would be up for that sort of desperate fucking again. Which they could be doing right now if it weren't for cursed little sisters and Baba Inna's refusal to get a driver's license.

"I like these jeans." Annie's hand slid over her knee, but stopped midway up her thigh. Oksana would have told her to go a little higher if the two in the backseat were doing a better job of focusing on each other. Erica was looking out the window, singing along with the radio, and Kat was probably busy texting girlfriend number six from her phone.

"So, Annie, what do you do?" Kat asked rudely from the backseat.

Oksana scowled at her in the mirror. "Ekaterina."

"What? Can't I just ask what your new girlfriend does? You are her girlfriend, right?"

"I don't know. Am I?" Annie quirked her head to the side.

Oksana scowled. "We're just friends."

"With benefits?" Kat had a serious death wish.

Annie laughed, squeezing Oksana's thigh. "I work in television."

"Doing what?" The kid was worse than a mob father with a pistol.

"I'm a producer on *Single Dad*, *Barbecue Showdown*, and *Just Dance*."

"Oh my God! Do you know Meta?" Erica fucking screamed.

"Damn, Erica," Oksana groaned, rubbing her knuckle in her ear. That was one thing she could appreciate about Kat. She could be obnoxious, but she wasn't loud.

"Sorry."

Kat ignored Erica's outburst and grumbled, "I don't like her."

"I don't exactly know her, but we have met. I mostly make sure she gets paid," Annie told them. Oksana smiled. She liked hearing Annie talk about her job. She was confident in her work.

"Do you get to go to her rehearsals and stuff?" Erica bounced in her seat.

"No. I'm stuck in the production office all day."

"Who does her hair and makeup?" Kat asked. Oksana had never considered it, but one night during a marathon of *The Hills*, Kat assured her that no one, not even reality TV stars, went on camera without makeup.

"She has this woman named Lux who she likes," Annie said, moving her hand closer to the inside of Oksana's thigh. Tricky thing taking advantage of the distraction. Thank God for decent underwear. Oksana's pussy throbbed even more when Annie gave her a gentle pinch.

Oksana coughed. "Kat wants to be a makeup artist."

"I want to do movies, though. Not TV. My school is doing *A Midsummer's Night Dream*, and they are letting me do the makeup for all the fairies. It's not a film, but it'll be good practice."

"That's so cool. I know some great makeup ladies."

"Yeah, I'm good with the makeup, but I still need to get my hair game together. Sana's friend is gonna let me work at her salon this summer if I keep my grades up."

"And if you stop screwing around on my couch." Kat was sorry; Oksana knew it, but she couldn't let her off the hook without one final dig.

"We're sorry, Oksana," Erica said. "It was my fault."

Oksana caught Annie as she quickly faced front and bit her lip to hold in her laugh. She must have been just as horrified stumbling across those two.

Oksana pulled into the parking deck and quickly found a space a million yards away from the Beverly Center's escalators. She hoped Annie or Erica didn't mind the hike. She didn't like squeezing her Tahoe between little cars just to get closer to the stores. Some asshole always dinged her doors then blamed her for driving such a big truck.

"It's okay, Erica. Just, ya know," she said, cutting the ignition.

"It won't happen again." Erica shook her head frantically. Oksana almost believed her.

"Oh look. We're here." Kat flung open her door and booked it for the escalators. Erica was right on her heels, grabbing Kat's hand and shoulder as soon as she caught up. Oksana stared in horror when her sister paused and let Erica jump on her back. The power of puppy love was ripe between the two, and clearly, the intoxication fueled Kat's quad strength.

Oksana and Annie followed at a leisurely pace, both laughing at the ridiculousness of the last hour. For the first time in days, Oksana felt good, relaxed, but as they joined Kat and Erica on the ride down to the lower levels, she couldn't understand the sudden grip on her stomach or the sweat that broke out across her forehead when Annie casually took hold of her hand.

CHAPTER NINE

THE INVITATION

Annie was happy. The feeling was a mix of Christmas morning, the last day of school, and a really good batch of chocolate chip cookies she made once. That contentment and excitement started somewhere in the middle of her chest and sparked up as a silly grin she couldn't seem to shake off her face.

Baba Inna was still a tad frightening, but Annie could feel the love radiating off the elderly woman. Annie loved the no-nonsense reception Oksana's grandmother had given her, and she was a little tickled that for the first time in her life, someone wanted her to gain weight.

And Kat was just awesome. Annie hadn't been around a teenager since she was a teenager herself, but she liked this kid. She was bold, but it was clear she respected Oksana's authority, even if her raging hormones seemed to get in the way. Annie didn't get serious about any sort of professional aspirations until she'd had her butt kicked across several movie sets. The fact that Kat was actively working toward a career at fifteen was amazing. Plus, it was a little precious that Kat was a smaller version of Oksana—with hair.

Still, through all the smoke and mirrors, they weren't fake smiles and hugs. Annie felt truly welcomed by them both. Kat's questioning in the car felt genuine, not suspicious, and something told Annie that Baba's acceptance of Annie's participation in their mundane family Sunday was a big deal. It made Annie happy. Happy and intrigued.

Oksana and her family were magic.

Being an only child had been a lonely existence and Cheryl, the Collins's housekeeper, had done all of the boring errands, like going to the market. She had been nice enough to teach Annie how to bake, but growing up, Annie knew there was a simple warmth missing from her house. Oksana's home oozed warmth.

It had been a while since she'd spent time outside of work with anyone new. The steady rotation of Jeff and her stable of three friends had grown surprisingly monotonous in the past few years. Planning for the wedding had just made it worse. Annie went from human being with thoughts and interests to bride. Annie actually looked forward to the rest of their afternoon and dinner with Baba Inna.

She fought the urge to kiss Oksana every five seconds and settled for holding her hand as they hung near the entrance to the MAC store.

Kat moved around the boutique carefully, quietly sorting through cosmetics with a focus that Annie admired. Kat knew exactly what she was after. Erica followed close behind, eagerly grabbing the eye shadows and blushes that Kat decided on.

"You having fun yet?" Oksana asked. She seemed a little tense, but Annie chalked the sudden tightness in Oksana's shoulders up to the fact that she was watching Kat like a hawk out of the corner of her eye.

"I'm having a blast. And this parenting thing is kind of sexy on you."

"Oh, really?" Oksana glanced down at her and cocked an eyebrow.

Heat flashed to Annie's crotch. Subtly, but not so much, because they were in public, she pressed herself against Oksana. Their legs wove together and Annie's breasts rubbed against her.

"Yes." Annie couldn't look away from those deep green eyes. The timing was off and the location completely inappropriate, but all she wanted to do was make out with Oksana right there in the store. Another romp in the car would be nice, followed immediately by a trip to a bed. Annie wasn't particular about whose bed it was. She glanced at Oksana's lips and figured a little peck wouldn't hurt.

"Here."

Annie almost jumped away from Oksana's thigh. Kat snuck up on them like a ninja, but Oksana must have seen her creep across the store because she didn't so much as blink.

"You need these." Kat handed Annie a few different boxes.

Oksana grabbed an eye shadow from the heap and carefully regarded Kat. "She's not buying makeup for your amusement."

"It's not for my amusement. Your girlfriend has great eyes and I think this"—Kat held up a little tube of eyeliner—"would make her eyes totally pop."

"But I like my eyes inside of my head," Annie said quite seriously.

Kat smiled wide. "That was funny. But seriously. This, this, and this will look awesome on you. And I would think my sister would want her girlfriend to look as awesome as ever."

Annie laughed at the way Oksana glared back at Kat. "Are you paying for it?" Oksana asked.

Kat rolled her eyes, something that ran in the family. "Yeah, I am. I just wanted to show Annie first."

Annie picked out the eye shadow and read the back. "I'm actually running low on 'Electric Tide,'" Annie read off the label.

"See."

But Annie amended, "I'll buy all this other stuff if you promise to practice on me. And if you promise to be nice to your sister."

"Lame," Kat groaned before her face lit up with another wide grin. "Deal." Annie stepped out of the way as Kat wrapped her arms snugly around Oksana's waist and rattled off something in Russian before she darted back to Erica and a rack of eyeliners.

"Hurry up," Oksana said. "I want to get some lunch."

"What did she say?" Annie asked.

"She said I'm the best big sister ever."

Annie had the sneaky suspicion that wasn't all. "And?"

"And she thinks you're really hot."

"Well, as adorable as she is, I prefer the full-grown version." Annie rose up on her tiptoes. She tried not to let it throw her when Oksana hesitated. She kissed her, quick and light instead of the tongue probing suckfest she'd been hoping for.

Oksana sighed and reached for the small pile of makeup in Annie's hand. "Here, let me get that."

"No, I got it." Annie walked over to the counter and tried not to make any horrified faces when the girl behind the register gave her the total. She shrugged it off as an investment in Kat's future and forked over her credit card.

Oksana didn't miss the ridiculous total. She rubbed Annie's arm while she signed her receipt. "Sorry. Makeup is her crack. You shouldn't have to pay for her addiction."

Annie thanked the cashier and took her bag. "It's awesome. At that age *NSYNC was my crack."

"Oh, we are so over." Oksana frowned. "I was Backstreet Boys all the way."

"Blasphemy. Absolutely blasphemy."

They retreated back to the corner and Annie didn't hesitate to slip her arms around Oksana's waist and rest her head against her shoulder. Oksana tensed again but relaxed as Annie gently stroked her side.

"You okay?" Annie asked.

"Yeah. I'm fine."

"Okay. You'll tell me, right?"

Oksana merely nodded.

Maybe it wasn't Kat. A lot had changed between them recently, and Annie had to remember that not everyone had her bull in a china shop approach to things. Maybe Oksana wasn't comfortable with the shift in their relationship. Or all of this PDA Annie insisted on. Instead of pulling away, she held tight, trusting Oksana to open up if there was a problem.

They moved on to Sephora where neon nail polish was purchased, and just as they were heading for the exit, Kat detoured for the escalator.

"Where are you going?" Oksana asked.

"Upstairs," Kat said innocently. "I need jeans."

Annie looked between them as Oksana scowled at Kat.

"Okay. I *want* new jeans. I swear I'll be fast."

"Fine, but seriously hurry. We're going to eat, grab stuff for Baba, and then you have homework."

"I know. I'll be fast," Kat yelled over her shoulder as she sprinted up the escalator, Erica hot on her heels.

Oksana sighed again and stepped on behind Annie. "You ever want to have kids, just remember trips like this are waiting for you fifteen years down the road."

"It's fine. Really. I'm having a good time," Annie said.

By the time they caught up with the girls, they were already darting toward the changing rooms with more than jeans piled in their arms.

"Separate fitting rooms!" Oksana called after them. Kat groaned but walked into a room next to Erica's.

Annie settled in for a long wait at Oksana's side. They had plenty more small talk to catch up on.

"What's you—"

Suddenly, Oksana froze.

"What? What is it?" Annie turned around to see a bouncy woman making a beeline right for them, weaving her way through racks and patrons. She was beautiful; her long black hair was swept up in a thick ponytail, and her bangs were electric blue. A pattern of stars was tattooed down the side of her neck. Annie could only imagine which trajectory it took along her skin, but the design picked up down the length of her arm. Her black skirt was tight and her red shirt cropped high above her diamond-studded belly button. Intense combat boots gave her a good six inches on Annie.

She pounced on Oksana. "Hey, baby!"

"Hey." Oksana hugged her back. "What's up?"

Annie swallowed some bile and shifted anxiously beside them. This was just a friend, she told herself. A super gorgeous friend, and from the look of things—the hair and the tats down her forearm—a friend who was exactly Oksana's type. Annie shifted again, and on instinct slipped her arm around Oksana's back. *Hello, Jealousy. It's been a while.*

The woman didn't miss the gesture. Her eyes lit up, but she didn't say anything about it. "Not much. Just returning some stuff." She turned to Annie then and stuck her hand out.

"Hi, I'm Noelle." Annie took her hand and was pleased with the firm handshake the woman doled out, but she was still on alert, drawing small, possessive circles across Oksana's hip.

"Sorry." Oksana blushed like crazy. "Noelle, this is Annie."

"*Oh*." Noelle nodded. Oh, this couldn't be good.

"Jesus," Oksana moaned. "Noelle's girlfriend, Ronnie, was at The Maypole with me the other night."

"Oh my God." Annie almost smacked herself. "Can you please tell her I'm sorry? I got a little out of control."

"Pshht." Noelle waved her hand between them. "Ronnie doesn't care. She's been laughing about it for the past few days."

"Oh, that's great," Annie said seriously before she matched Noelle's smile. "I'm glad we've all been properly introduced."

Then there was a five-second pause of the purest, most concentrated awkward silence. Annie almost wanted to laugh. Noelle was trying to be cool, but she failed. Her eyes sparkled at Oksana, the ache to pull her aside and drag this gossip right out of her plain as day. Annie had seen that look a thousand times, given it out a thousand times herself, but Noelle was going to have to wait for another time to interrogate Oksana. Thank God for little sisters.

Kat sprang from the dressing room like a jack-in-the-box.

"Noelle." She beamed and skipped toward them. Actually skipped. Annie sensed a little bit of a harmless crush.

"Hey, gorgeous. What are you doing?" Noelle said brightly, giving Kat a big hug.

Kat turned around, showing off the denim that was trying to suffocate her ass. "New jeans."

"Cute! Get those." Noelle swatted Kat on the butt just as Erica poked her head out of the dressing room. Annie caught the daggers Erica stared at Noelle. Kat skipped away oblivious and asked Erica's opinion on the pants.

"That's the new girlfriend," Oksana said.

"Oh. She might knife me," Noelle muttered through gritted teeth. She waved at the girls as they ducked back into their rooms. Annie could have sworn she heard Erica growling. Apparently, Noelle sparked a little jealousy everywhere.

"So." Noelle turned her attention back to Oksana. And Annie. "Since I've been so busy and clearly so have you, why don't you and Annie come to Señor Kim's with us on Wednesday? Scooter wraps his shoot on Tuesday."

"What's Señor Kim's?" Annie asked.

"Mexi-Korean fusion restaurant. With karaoke," Noelle told her.

Annie spun on Oksana, surprising herself with her eagerness. She didn't want to push herself on Oksana's friends like she'd pushed herself on Oksana and Oksana's family, but that combination of cuisine sounded delicious. "Don't make me ask?" she pleaded. She realized she was at it again. Pushing. But she'd already blurted out her interest to Oksana and her friend.

Oksana simply smiled. It seemed genuine. "Sure. We'll be there."

"Good." Noelle sounded almost appeased. "Bring Annie."

"Ha. Funny. I will. Bye." Oksana frowned back playfully.

"Bye, Kat!"

"Bye, Noelle!" Kat yelled over the door.

"Bye, ladies." Noelle strolled back to the register, not even hiding the fact that she whipped out her cell phone as she went. Annie imagined her girlfriend, Ronnie, if she remembered right, would know about their little introduction in three, two…

"Did I just invite myself to dinner?" Annie looked up at Oksana and bit her bottom lip.

"No. Noelle invited you."

"And you?" Annie asked anxiously.

Oksana's eyes dropped to the ground and now the smile, genuine or not, was gone.

"Hey. What's wrong?" It was the third time Annie had asked Oksana today.

When Oksana didn't answer, Annie gently tugged her into a quiet corner between a rack of vests and blouses.

"Talk to me," Annie said, letting her hands rest on Oksana's hips.

Oksana took a deep breath.

Oh, this really *can't be good.* Annie winced internally.

Oksana shut her eyes tightly then opened them. "I thought I was okay with all of this. I feel like the other woman." The confession just exploded out. Oksana was being honest, exactly what Annie wanted, but the truth was like a stab to the gut. It was her turn to stare at the floor.

"Aren't you afraid we might run into someone you know?" Oksana reasoned. "I mean you're still technically engaged, and you're touching me in public."

Annie sighed and shoved her hands in the pockets of her hoodie. She hated to do it. She missed the warmth from Oksana's body immediately. Still, she was smothering.

"I know, I'm sorry. It's just when I'm with you I sort of forget about everyone else." She looked up finally, searching Oksana's eyes for some understanding.

"I get that, but what if your maid of honor came walking in here right now and we were holding hands. You wouldn't care if she started asking questions?" Megan knew something was going on between them, but that wasn't Oksana's point. This was bigger than the two of them, bigger than what she had spilled to Megan over lunch.

"Should we stop seeing each other?" Annie asked, struggling to keep her tone neutral. She was frustrated with the timing and the situation. She was frustrated with herself and a little bit with Jeff. The truth was it didn't matter how she felt about Oksana. She'd created a nightmare scenario.

"No! No. I—"

"Sana, listen." Annie held up her fingers to start counting. "One, Shane is out of town this weekend. Two, Feather lives out in Topanga Canyon. She and her boyfriend are spending the next week living in the near-authentic tipi they've just erected on his property. And my best friend-slash-maid of honor"—she did the slash through the air—"Megan wants to meet you, so we're in the clear."

"So you're just out with me because it's safe?"

Okay, that explanation came out all wrong. "No. I'm out with you because I love spending time with you. And if we ran into my friends, I would tell them the truth and I would have to deal with Jeff however that came. I would just prefer it if he heard it from me first."

"And Jeff's friends?"

"His close buddies are with him on his trip, and the other ones wouldn't be caught dead in the mall." Annie dialed down the emotion and put a gentle hand back on Oksana's hip. "I want to spend time with *you.*"

"I…" Oksana paused. "How can you be so calm about this?"

"Because I really like you. I mean it. I want to be with you." Annie couldn't think of another way to put it. Her heart skipped when Oksana smiled.

"I should believe you, shouldn't I?"

"Yes."

"I'm into you too, if that wasn't obvious last week and yesterday in the park. And last night at your place. And this morning." Oksana sighed again then finally got to the heart of what was bothering her. "I'm just not ready for labels yet. It's one thing with Kat and Baba because they'll know everything basically. With other people, I don't know. After Jeff gets back, okay?"

"Okay. So until then we're just friends? That's the official report? No touching. No kissing. In public."

"You don't mind?"

Of course I do, Annie wanted to say, but she held that back because Oksana had a point. Being caught by her friends or any members of the wedding party would be awkward as hell, and even though Annie was slightly terrified about how things would ultimately go down once everyone knew the truth, she knew the fallout was her problem to deal with, not Oksana's. Nothing would have ruined their first day out together more than running into Shane or Feather while Annie was busy palming Oksana's ass.

If the tables were turned, Annie wouldn't want to be the other woman. Add in Oksana's romantic past, and the last thing Annie should do was pressure her further, no matter how happy Oksana made her or how sure she was about her decision. She'd promised Oksana time and patience, and that's what Oksana would get.

"No. I don't mind. Even though I really want to kiss you right now, but I get it."

"Are you sure?" Oksana frowned.

"Yes," Annie asserted with a smile. There was nothing to be upset about. "I want you to be comfortable with everything, and if you're not comfortable with the kissing and holding hands for now, then those things are out. And I'll lay off in front of your friends."

"Well…" Oksana shrugged. That put Annie at ease. At least there was some hope.

She squeezed Oksana's hand in a friendly way. "We'll play that by ear, and in three weeks I'm going to enjoy making out with you in front of everybody."

"Who's making out with who?" Kat asked. Oksana spun around to find Kat and Erica waiting with their arms filled with clothes.

"No one."

❖

As the afternoon stretched on, Annie learned quickly just how hard it was to keep her hands to herself when Oksana was around. As they ran Baba Inna's errands, all Annie wanted to do was sneak little touches here and there and perhaps a kiss or two, but she kept her word to Oksana. There were the looks though. Annie saw the glimmer of lust in Oksana's eyes. She felt the humming electricity between them as they helped put the groceries away. She felt the same tug while they took Vasily for a walk around the neighborhood.

By the time dinner was ready, all the magic was back. The cozy feelings that had taken flight during their awkward conversation in the mall had returned. It wasn't just the warmth, Annie realized. It was a true unconditional love that radiated through the house. Baba Inna served dinner with a kiss and a pat on the butt for each girl, Annie and Erica included. She spoke English, even asking Annie polite questions about her job and telling Erica not to talk with her mouth full.

It was a type of attention Annie had never experienced growing up, and it was only made more surreal by the notion that this wasn't an act they were putting on to be polite to their guests. This was the real deal, every night. Oksana wasn't kidding; her family really mattered.

Annie's engagement to Jeff was the first time her mother had shown an ounce of interest in anything Annie did. Her dad still didn't care. Baba cared that the girls ate a full meal. She cared that homework was done. There was no fanfare, no sugar coating. That old woman cared.

Annie could live with that, she realized as they put away the last of the dinner dishes. She could be with Oksana and easily share her life with a dyed and pierced fifteen-year-old and a chain smoker. Not to mention the dog. Vasily had spent most of the evening curled up between Oksana's and Annie's feet. Her mom had a toy poodle named The Duchess who tried to bite Annie every time she went home.

The grandmother, the sister, the dog, and even Erica had their certain charm, and Annie wanted to be a part of it.

❖

Oksana pulled into Annie's driveway. She didn't park on the street. Good sign she could stay for a little while. She probably had more Mom duties to tend to in the morning. For now, though, they were friends with benefits. As they walked up Annie's back steps, Annie wondered who would be the first to instigate a good night kiss or a last-minute good night screw. Annie was in favor of the latter. The tension had been building between them all day. It had been confusing, to say the least, but it was the growing pains of what Annie wanted to build together. She would happily put up with awkward tension and blurring of certain lines and titles for a while if it meant that she and Oksana could be together in the long run.

When they reached the back door to her house and Annie was absolutely positive no one from her wedding party would jump out of the bushes, she slid her fingers into Oksana's palm. The moment they touched, Annie's heart rate picked up.

There was this shy air between them that Annie didn't want to shake. It was that feeling that told her this new thing with Oksana was right. It made her stomach turn in a flurry and made her tongue clumsy in her mouth. This was another feeling she never had with Jeff, the moments of anticipation where she was dying to see what would happen next between them. Oksana's body made Annie's pussy wet; there was no question about that, but it was her sweet personality, the way she cared for Inna and Kat, and her fierce code of ethics that made Annie's heart soar in the cheesiest of ways

"You shouldn't leave your garage door open like that," Oksana told her, her voice a little strained.

Annie peeked around her shoulder at the streetlight reflecting off the Prius's rear window. She didn't expect to be out so late, but the dishes took a while, Oksana got some laundry started, and then Erica needed a ride home. Annie loved the way Oksana helped her home run smoothly, and she loved the fact that Oksana cared about the garage door.

"I know. It's broken. I keep forgetting to call someone to come fix it."

"I can have Scooter come look at it. He's handy with all of that crap," Oksana said, licking her lips. Annie's eyes trailed from her mouth down to her chest and back up to her lips again. Oksana let out a shallow breath. Annie caught the sweet scent of the hot cinnamon lattes Baba had made while they took care of the dishes. Annie's head began to swim. She needed some sex with Oksana. Soon. She wanted that taste in her mouth.

She blinked and focused back on Oksana's deep gaze. "Yeah, that would be great. Am I going to meet this Scooter on Wednesday? I love that you have a friend named Scooter."

"I can't believe you have a friend named Feather." She gently tucked Annie's hair behind her glasses. Annie did her best not to shiver. It didn't work. She licked her own lips, swallowing to clear her mouth.

"Yeah. I can't believe that either." *Why aren't we kissing?*

"Scooter will be there," Oksana said. "I want you to come to dinner. My friends will like you."

"Good. I think I owe your friend Ronnie a drink. Maybe I'll bring Megan, make the group thing a little more balanced." Annie lifted her head and gently pressed their lips together. If Oksana had to go, this could be the start of their good-bye, but not a full good night. Not yet.

Oksana must have keyed into that idea because she held back. No tongue, just soft, wet brushes in the opposite directions. "Has it been three weeks yet?" she murmured once Annie pulled away.

"What time is your first session?" Annie asked breathlessly.

"Not till late. What time do you have to be at work?" Oksana murmured back.

"By nine thirty. Would you like to maybe spend the night?"

"You want me to? Even though I was being—"

"A flake?" Annie laughed as Oksana rolled her eyes. "Well, I figure since I can't feel you up in the mall, it would be nice to wake up next to you in the morning."

"That would be nice."

Annie unlocked the door to the mudroom and let Oksana walk ahead of her. "I'm too short to carry you inside. Otherwise, this would be way more romantic."

"I don't know. Did you see Kat pick up Erica?"

They walked into the living room, and Annie flicked on the small overhead light. "Holy shit. I know. Have you been making her do her squats before school?" she asked.

Oksana's burst of laughter and the way her eyes looked in the soft golden light made Annie's cheeks strain with a smile. So far, things *had* been a little weird between them, but she loved the little moments like this. She loved seeing Oksana happy.

"No. She's just strong."

"I love your family." Annie had to tell her.

"You do?"

"Yeah. You're right, and Baba isn't as scary as she looks. She can cook." Now Annie knew why Oksana worked out so much. Baba Inna wasn't skimming on the butter or the cream or the sugar or any of God's other sweet, fattening goodness when she cooked. The stroganoff was mouthwatering and the fresh bread and cheeses—

Annie would be back to her winter weight in no time if she kept eating over there. Hopefully, she'd be invited back.

"I'm glad you like them, and I'm glad you came over today. Don't worry. My grandmother thinks everyone is too thin, even me. Her worst nightmare is me becoming all Hollywood skinny."

Annie lazily eyed Oksana's long frame. She would look sexy as hell with more padding, but Baba had a point. Annie would hate to see those curves go.

"Do me a favor?" Annie said.

"Sure."

"Take off your clothes. All of them."

Oksana blinked, but nodded. "Okay." She swallowed thickly.

"I'll be right back." With that, Annie left Oksana so she could gather a few things to spice up the night.

She wanted to show Oksana just how well she could behave not only in public, but just how well she could treat Oksana in the bedroom, or on the living room couch. Deep in the back of her closet, ugh, right under her wedding dress, she found a gag gift Shane had given her for her birthday. The dildo was easily over nine inches long, a light tan rubber with thick veins running all the way down to a ridiculous set of plastic balls. It was still in its original packaging, but after a quick look Annie figured it was about the same size around as Oksana's dildo at home.

Annie ripped the plastic open, then ducked into the bathroom to give the toy a quick scrub. Before she went back to Oksana, she threw a thick towel over her shoulder then she grabbed a bottle of water from the kitchen.

She tried to act casual when she stepped back into the living room, but then again how could anyone act casual with such a gorgeous ass staring them in the face?

Oksana whipped around on the balls of her bare feet. Her eyes sprang wide once she got a load of the stuff in Annie's hands.

God, she looked so fucking beautiful, nervously crossing her hands over her waist so her arms just barely covered her nipples.

"You cold?" Annie asked, eying Oksana's piercings.

"No, just, ya know…naked."

Annie ran her tongue over her teeth. "I know. I like it. Here." She placed the water and the dildo on the coffee table, then snapped the towel out over the couch. "We might make a little mess." If Annie had it her way. "Have a seat."

Oksana crossed to the couch and perched on the edge, right in the center of the towel. Annie pulled a cushion off the loveseat and smiled at Oksana as she quickly caught on and opened her legs. The large pillow flopped between her feet. Annie came right behind it and dropped to her knees.

"You seemed a little stressed out today, so I thought I could help you relax."

"By getting me naked?"

"And making you come like crazy." Annie reached behind her for the rubber cock. Then she leaned forward. Oksana followed, her elbows on her knees, but Annie stopped just before their lips met.

"Listen, from what I've seen today, you're a great mom. I know you're a great trainer. I just feel like it's been a while since you've had someone take care of you. And *no*, I don't count Baba's cooking for you. I don't have a big ole strap-on, but I have this." She ran the rubber between her fingers. "And my mouth."

"Well, I'm ready for that mouth."

Annie sat back and gently opened Oksana's legs, getting a perfect look at the moisture glistening on the bare cocoa-pink skin.

"Yes, you are."

CHAPTER TEN

THE SHIFT

Oksana reached inside Annie's shirt and pulled out her tits. Her top was cut just low enough for the luscious orbs to spill over the scoop cut collar. Annie's nipples were already hard, but they were instantly harder the moment the AC hit their full tips. It was difficult to keep her mouth to herself, but Oksana held back. She liked the direction Annie was taking things. First, though, she kissed her.

It had been a long day, but every odd, uncomfortable moment leading up to this point had been worth it. Oksana tasted Annie's lips, her pussy growing more and more wet as Annie whimpered against her mouth. It was nice to know she wasn't the only one practically crazed with lust. More than once, Oksana wanted to push Kat and Erica off on Baba so she could drag Annie to the little house, if just for a few minutes.

Yes, she did feel like the other woman, and she was afraid of running into Annie's friends, among other things, but she did want Annie. When she took the time to ignore her fears, Oksana noticed her skin tingled every time they touched. When she noticed just how far she'd come, what she stood to gain from trusting the right person, her heart felt like it would burst. Oksana was happy.

Annie had fit in perfectly with her family. She deserved a prize for sitting through Erica's constant yammering, but what Oksana loved the most was the way Annie had treated Kat. At first glance, the kid screamed delinquent, but Annie saw right through the makeup and the piercings and encouraged her. Her friends were great with Kat, but no girlfriend or lover, especially not Vivian, had taken an interest in her or treated her with real respect. That meant a lot, and Annie didn't have to do it.

She regretted the request she'd made in the mall. Oksana and Annie were a good match, but in the long run, Jeff had to be dealt with. She was game for all of this, for all of Annie. There had to be real closure, before her fears truly faded away. Fears she was willing to ignore at the moment.

She drew her fingers across Annie's chest, fondling her breasts like she had the night before. Maybe she was developing a fetish.

Oksana slid further to the edge of the couch and deepened their kiss.

She loved being with Annie, she loved talking to Annie, loved sitting with her around the big house. She had real feelings for Annie, and as the hours passed and those feelings grew stronger, she was starting to think Annie felt the same way, beyond wanting to see where things could go between them. The question was, would she have the balls to ask, to say the words herself?

Annie pulled away from their kiss.

"I'm starting to get that U-haul joke," Annie whispered, her eyes glazing over as Oksana kept on with her breasts.

"There's no way I'm moving to Venice," Oksana said before she leaned in to take Annie's mouth again.

"I wouldn't dream of taking you away from West Hollywood, but I'd love to spend more nights with you." Oksana sat back a little as Annie sat up and began licking her way down her neck. Oksana turned her head slightly and got a whiff of Annie's shampoo. She smelled like oranges and sunshine.

"Bring a change of clothes with you to work tomorrow. Dinner is at seven," Oksana moaned as she pinched Annie's nipples.

"I'll be there. Now stop with the boobs. I want to fuck you."

Oksana gave in and sat against the couch. Annie bit her lips as she gazed over Oksana's body. Oksana thought it was sexy as hell, fucking adorable when Annie's cheek twitched, causing her dimple to jump.

"Try to relax," Annie said with a smile as she cupped her left tit. Oksana groaned quietly as soon as she realized what Annie planned to do.

Slowly, she drew her nipple up the length of her cunt. They shuddered together. Oksana couldn't believe what she was seeing. The honey brown areola now tucked between her lips, the tip caressing her clit, the full underside pressing against her opening. So soft, but so good.

"You like my boobs don't you?" Annie breathed with the hint of a grin.

"Oh, you couldn't tell?" Oksana groaned, then gave in to the urge to roll her cunt against Annie's chest. It was so hot to see her wetness spreading out across Annie's chest.

"I could do this for hours." Oksana looked down just in time to see Annie's eyes roll back slightly. "You smell so good. My pussy aches." Oksana felt her own muscle contract against the soft skin spreading her slit.

"How does that feel?" Annie breathed.

Oksana stared into her eyes a moment longer, watching the motion of Annie's hand guiding her tits. Her nipple was covered with her juices, all around, above, and below the broadly puckered tip.

"I-I'm going to come," Oksana grunted. She climaxed, her legs shaking on the couch, her eyes squeezing shut. It was the best and the worst kind of orgasm. Great, but not nearly enough when Annie was still in the room. Thank God for that length of cock she'd scrounged up.

Annie kissed her thighs, making Oksana's whole body tremble. She licked at her pussy a few times for good measure before she sat back on her heels and rubbed the sunflowers inked across her belly. The room was a little cool, but it was Annie's touch that sent goose bumps all over Oksana's body. She shivered from the pleasure.

"Good, baby?" Annie chuckled lightly.

"Yes," Oksana sighed. "Very, very good." The baby part made it even better.

"Let's try this." Annie grabbed the plastic cock, examining Oksana's pussy with clinical interest.

Oksana saw the doubt in Annie's eyes and welcomed the challenge. She said a silent amen to her years of yoga and Pilates instruction then grabbed her ankles. With her feet firmly planted on the couch beside her ass, she shifted closer to the edge of the towel. The towel was a great idea.

Oksana liked a big cock, always had. Even Vivian came to terms with a plastic dick being a part of their sex life. Oksana liked the feeling of her pussy being stretched. She'd come to love a deep thrust, slow or fast. She was impressed with the way her body reacted when it was pleased the right way. Adding Annie as the vessel for that pleasure made her cunt weep before the firm tip of the dildo brushed her sensitive labia.

If Annie did what Oksana hoped she was about to do, Oksana would come enough to make the towel necessary.

Annie spurted with laughter.

Oksana glared back at her playfully. "I know you're new to this whole lesbian thing, but laughing while your head is between a woman's legs is a bad idea."

"No, no," Annie snorted. "I just thought how horrible it would be if I told you to open wide."

"You're a fool." Oksana shook her head.

"I know." Annie laughed even harder then sat up and gave Oksana a juicy kiss. After a moment they were both giggling. But Oksana's smile faded as Annie's fingers found her pussy again. Another warm-up, as if she needed one. Annie let her hand lazily pet up and down her wet lips.

When it was clear that Oksana was more than ready for the main event, Annie bent between them again and grabbed the toy. She glanced at the girth again.

"You're sure it's not too big? It was a gag gift."

"Yes. I'm sure." Oksana's hips rose just a fraction on the couch and Annie watched fascinated as the muscles around Oksana's pussy contracted. "I'm ready."

At first, Annie teased.

The first brush was cold, but Oksana shuddered for other reasons. For so long she had been wanting this, not the synthetic cock, but someone who cared enough to give her pleasure, someone who didn't have to be persuaded. Someone whose pleasure she wanted to return. Things had been so fucked after Vivian. It hurt that she was still realizing that fact after all this time. Vivian had ruined every joy for her, simple and complicated, but now with Annie, she was getting those things back.

"Okay?"

"Yeah," Oksana replied eagerly. "Go ahead."

❖

Annie pushed against Oksana's body. Her pussy bloomed automatically, taking what Annie was offering. The unnaturally smooth head slid in. Annie imagined how good the cock felt as it probed the edge of her sensitive gland.

"You can go deep," she said, almost begging. "I can take it."

"Tell me when," Annie answered, pushing in further. She stopped when she knew she'd hit the limit. She felt the natural resistance, and when Oksana didn't ask for more she withdrew just as slowly.

In and out, again and again, she drove the plastic cock, soon faster and faster at Oksana's command. With a sudden joy, Annie realized she would never have to measure up to this toy. She almost laughed. It must really suck to be a guy.

Soon Oksana was shaking, but Annie knew there was more. Keeping her focus with her hands, she lunged for Oksana's right piercing, sucking lightly as she kept up her thrusts. Oksana screamed.

"You thought I forgot about these?" Annie murmured, switching to the other breast.

"No. Fuck. Fuck," Oksana chanted in desperation. "I-I..." Oksana started coming. Annie kept sucking until Oksana's body was twitching helplessly. Then she stepped on the gas.

She drove the toy hard and fast, tilting the angle up just slightly, still fascinated at the way the wet, delicate skin, the flushed pink flesh seemed to gobble up every inch. Suddenly Oksana forced the cock out. Her cunt convulsed, along with the rest of her body, and soaked the towel and Annie's chest. Annie's reflexes kicked in then and she replaced her fingers where the dildo had just been, milking Oksana until she was limp and panting on the couch.

"Annie. Shit," she moaned.

Once Oksana's body stopped pumping and spasming, Annie pulled out her fingers and licked the moisture from her hand. "Watching you come, the noises you make are so fucking hot," Annie panted. "You have no idea. Have you ever squirted like that before?"

"I've only ejaculated a few times," Oksana managed to say. Her feet sagged to the floor.

Annie grinned in satisfaction. "Heavenly, isn't it?"

"You've done it before?" Oksana asked.

"Oh, yeah." Annie jazz hands-ed her fingers in the air. "On my own, of course. I'll have to show you sometime." She set down the dildo then and took another look at Oksana's pussy.

"I've never tried to take something that big before. What's it like?" Annie asked as she gently traced her thumb around Oksana's opening and softly kissed her thigh.

"Stand up."

Annie followed Oksana's command and stood between her legs, holding perfectly still as Oksana unzipped her jeans then pulled them down her legs.

"I'll show you sometime."

Oksana leaned forward, taking the slit of Annie's cunt in her mouth, wet panties and all. It was only a matter of seconds before Annie's own orgasm crippled her.

❖

Annie was totally late for work. She'd woken up to an empty bed, but after she followed the most delicious smell, she found a barely dressed Oksana; a homemade bacon, egg, and cheese bagel sandwich; and an iced coffee waiting for her in the kitchen. Some kisses came with her gorgeous chef and some harmless groping.

After they ate, Annie dragged Oksana to the shower. They didn't just have sex. They made out under the hot water for at least twenty minutes, feeling each other up like teenagers before they got down to the real business. Business that migrated back to Annie's bed.

Annie was late by the time they finally got dressed. Forget the drive across town. And the seven minutes or so they spent saying good-bye to each other in Annie's driveway.

"You want to take this?" Annie glanced down at her oversized tote bag.

"Insurance policy?" Oksana asked, but took the bag anyway and put it in the backseat of the Tahoe.

"Yes. My favorite underwear is in there. I'll be slipping them on tomorrow morning. After I spend the night. At your adorable cottage."

Oksana turned and slipped her arms over Annie's shoulders. Annie's hands went to Oksana's waist just as easily.

"I'll give Venice one thing. I found good bagels," she said.

"That you did," Annie replied.

Right then she almost said it. Annie almost dropped the L-bomb. It was right on the tip of her tongue. She looked up at Oksana and couldn't think of any reason not to say those words. Other than the fact that they'd been together for a whole day. It took her almost two years to share the sentiment with Jeff, and in the moment, she had simply returned his declaration. It felt like the right thing to do at the time, but *this time* was different. This time there was heat and energy and weightlessness. Annie knew for sure now that she had fallen in love with Oksana, and she was even more sure that telling her those words almost guaranteed that Oksana would go running to the hills, never to return.

But Oksana surprised her. "I'm starting to have certain feelings for you," she said cautiously.

Annie held in a gasp. "I think I already have certain feelings for you." Then she waited while Oksana stared in deep concentration at the small space between them. This is good, Annie told herself. *This is really good. She's not running. Just give her some time.*

"I want to say it, but then I don't," she admitted.

"Say it when you're ready, and in the meantime, know that I feel the same way."

Oksana stared at her for a moment, one eye slowly squinting, then the other. "Do you really?"

Annie took a huge breath and threw herself off the ledge. "I know it's kinda soon, but I do." She wondered then how many times Oksana had heard those words and how many times they had turned into a lie. She wanted Oksana to believe her, painfully so, but the situation was still a little screwed up for all the fairy tale pieces to come together. "Do you see that?"

"I do. I feel—" Tears gathered in the corners of Oksana's eyes, though her expression barely changed. Annie gently wiped the tears away. Oksana gathered herself, swallowing thickly, and spoke again. "Part of this feels wrong because I wasn't expecting this between us."

"The giggly butterflies?" Annie knew exactly what she meant. That was the warmth. The Christmas cookies. Plus the sex was off the charts amazing. The awesomest. Oksana nodded. "I wasn't expecting it either.

"I want it to work, but I didn't think it would. Now I feel really good about us, but I am scared."

There was nothing Annie could say, so she just hugged Oksana. It was the first time they'd actually hugged as a couple. It was a weird thing for Annie to notice, but she did. She and Jeff never held each other like this. He was a fan of the one-armed side hug thing, and any "real" hugs were reserved for special occasions.

She held Oksana tighter, hating the idea of spending the day apart. Finally, she stepped back and kissed her softly on the lips.

"What is your day like today?" Annie asked.

"I have some cleaning to do. Session at eleven, Pilates class at one, then I have another session at five. I'll pick Kat up from school too."

"There you go with that sexy Mom shit again."

A lighter smile returned to Oksana's face. "I know. Carpooling is fucking hot."

In Annie's purse, her cell phone started going off. She looked at the display and groaned. Her executive producer probably got to the office and had a stroke when Annie wasn't there to remind him that Esther's name wasn't Emma. "That's Sergio. I have to go. See you at seven?"

Oksana smiled again and kissed Annie lightly. "Seven."

❖

By the time Annie got to work, Sergio had completely forgotten what he wanted. She retreated to her office before he had a chance to remember. She was in a perfectly good mood, and a conversation with Sergio about anything would ruin her high. Esther noticed immediately that she was in a better mood, but thankfully, she didn't ask why, or attribute her happiness to Jeff.

The rest of the morning was full but ran smoothly. All the not so glamorous tasks that go into making reality shows run. After lunch, she was on guard duty. With most of her work for the day done, she sat in her office waiting for any news from her crews and Esther's drafts of the next day's call sheets. She busied herself for a little while, organizing and throwing out some unnecessary paperwork. She prayed this cycle of shows was well received. They were on the verge of getting a new office space, which she desperately craved. She didn't mind sharing an office with Esther, but she'd like a bigger one, possibly with a window and room for more than one piece of art on the wall. Art from Jeff.

She thought of Oksana of course. It was impossible not to, but soon her mind turned back to Jeff. Annie had opened her other e-mail account reserved for semi-important e-mails she didn't want cluttering up her work account. Plenty of spam from fake contests and credit card approvals was mixed in among comment notices for their wedding website, itheewed.com. Against her better judgment, Annie opened the first e-mail and clicked through the first link.

Under a black and white picture of her and Jeff on the beach were at least fourteen comments. They'd been building over the last few months. The most recent one was from Jeff's sister, Farrah.

You two are so gross ;)

Annie and Farrah weren't very close. Neither were Farrah and Jeff. Megan had put the Web page together for them ages ago, and as far as Annie knew, this was the first sign that Farrah had bothered to look at it. Annie didn't care.

Somewhere in the back of her mind it dawned on Annie that Jeff's family wouldn't actually be that upset about their breakup. They lived in San Diego. They had no flights to cancel. Annie's father was paying for the whole thing. He would be mad about the money and Taum would be insane with rage about how Annie's seemingly sudden shift in sexuality would make her look. She'd be annoyed about dealing with the vendors, but there would be no tears shed for their relationship when it came to either of their families. Unless Jeff actually cried once they talked.

Annie closed her eyes and sank down in her chair. Their relationship had never included their families, but he did love her. She would give anything to avoid the inevitable conversation with Jeff. Anything to keep from hurting him, anything to keep him from thinking this was all his fault. It was Annie's mistake for not being more proactive in her own life. Hopefully, he wouldn't hate her too much.

Annie's BlackBerry jumped on her desk. It was Megan.

"Hey."

"Okay, so you dump this on me on Friday and I haven't heard from you since. Tell me you ditched Jeff and spent all weekend screwing this hot trainer of yours," Megan said in one breath.

Annie glanced up at Esther. "No to the first, yes, and then some to the second. I met the family."

"Oh? What are they like?"

Annie thought of her answer for a moment. "Good. You have plans on Wednesday?"

"No, why? Can I meet her then?"

"Yeah. I think a bunch of us are going to go out. You can be my—"

"Wing woman?"

"I think we're past that point. Just come and you can see for yourself."

"So, the family was good and I'm guessing the sex continues to be great."

"You have no—"

A loud bang broke Annie out of her mental dissection of the future. She and Esther both froze and side-eyed the hallway.

"I don't care! Where is Sergio? I want that bitch fired," Meta's voice screeched through the office. Annie glanced at Esther, then jumped up from her desk.

"Hey, let me call you back," she told Megan as she jogged down the hall. She reached Sergio's office just as Lauren, their field producer, came flying through the front door.

"Meta," Lauren called after the spoiled diva. "Do not do this."

Sergio hung up his phone and glanced between their star and poor Lauren. "Good afternoon, Meta. To what do I owe the pleasure?"

"This is not my fault," Lauren quickly explained. It was a childish claim, but she'd been putting up with Meta's mood swings all season, and finally, something had snapped.

"Where are the guys?" Annie asked her.

"Pace and Justin are downstairs with Beth. Johnny, Brad, and Dre are back in the studio. She walked out in the middle of makeup."

"Here." Annie handed Lauren fifty bucks. "Take them to get some coffee and snacks or whatever. We'll handle this."

"Fine. Sergio, you can reach me on my cell."

"Yeah, whatever. Go." Sergio waved Lauren out the door. She sighed and disappeared toward the exit. "Now what's the problem?"

"Lauren promised me I would not be embarrassed," Meta said, all sour-faced.

"Who embarrassed you?" Sergio asked. "All I've seen is hours and hours and hours of you dancing, hanging out with your friends, and talking on the phone." He left out the blatant flirting with anything that breathed and the constant arguments she had with her assistant that kept the viewers coming back. Meta didn't see those degrading screaming matches as a mark on her character though. Making her assistant feel like crap was part of the business, how she paid her dues. Annie really hated Meta.

Their star straightened and adjusted her cut-off sweatshirt. She had the whole *Flashdance* wardrobe down. "I fell the other night at The Maypole, and Lauren told me you were going to air it."

"And?" Sergio had seen the footage, but he wasn't about to tell Meta that he'd laughed at it himself for a good hour.

"And if you do, I quit."

"I thought you wanted Lauren fired."

Meta's mouth opened, but she didn't have a response.

Sergio leaned over and dug through his filing cabinet, then thumbed open what must have been a copy of Meta's contract.

"We have promised to not film you while you're taking a piss. While you're having sex, which is a huge concession. Trust me. We'd be making more money off you if there was sex, but the drinking, the partying, you falling on your face is fair game."

"My life is my style and my coordination. I can't have footage of me drunk and falling on my face on television for everyone to see," Meta fumed.

"I must say your timing is perfect. We're holding casting right next door. I'm sure all the teen girls and their mothers are already texting about the crazy woman screaming in the hallway. Maybe I can have Jewel go over and whisper the identity of the screamer."

Meta turned fire engine red. She needed her target audience to dislike her a little. Genuine hate did not go a long way.

"Annie, you'd say our rigs are fairly big, and Brad had to mic you before you went into the club."

Annie shrugged. "Yes."

"It's not like the crew snuck up on you," Sergio went on, giving Meta that "so what the hell do you want from us" look.

Realizing she wasn't going to win, Meta settled down and pouted. "She promised me, Sergio."

"This show is not about your life, Meta. It's about the life we want to show. Three years ago, you were a backup dancer for a shitty pop star no one remembers. Your life was instant noodles and praying you booked another gig to pay your rent. Your words, not mine. But the truth is we looked at six other girls. Lauren got you on TV, not your mad dancing skill. You can walk, but we'll sue you.

Your show's worth more than your paycheck. I don't care how you feel right now, but Annie's a nice gal. Annie, how can we spin this?"

Moments like that kept Annie in this line of work. She did not enjoy being around Sergio, but she loved this company, and Sergio knew exactly how to keep this place running when it mattered. Even though they disagreed on a lot of things, Meta getting her ass back over to the dance studio so they could start shooting was not one of them.

"You saw the footage?" Meta asked Annie.

"Yes."

"What the fuck, Sergio? Who hasn't seen it?"

"I have an idea," Annie told her. "Meta, do your interview and play the fall off. Everyone can relate to getting wasted and taking a spill. If you laugh about it, people will forget it sooner." Annie could relate to getting wasted and molesting a woman who at the time wasn't hers to molest. She could definitely identify with Meta's pain on that level. Still. "You make it an issue, you delay the episode, it goes to the tabloids—"

"And that footage will totally get leaked. Then you fell, you lost your show, and you got sued. See? You say you got silly, you fell. No big deal. You're human. People love humans."

Meta and Annie both stared at Sergio for a second.

Annie shook off his last remark and turned back to Meta. "Meta. It'll work. Trust me. And maybe we can split the fall with tomorrow night's performance. People see your accident and then spend the next four minutes watching you prep and rocking an awesome show."

Meta calmed down for a moment, thinking this new plan over, but Sergio didn't want to give her much more time to contemplate.

"Go back to the studio, finish makeup, and let's try and save the hour of daylight you've just wasted."

"Fine. I'm still not speaking to Lauren."

"Okay. Great. We'll see you soon."

Meta stormed out of his office.

"Nice save, Collins." Sergio leaned back in his chair and flipped Meta's contract closed. On closer examination, Annie saw that he'd actually been looking at a copy of the crew list. She'd wondered. The contracts were in her office.

"You threatened her. I didn't save anything," she replied honestly.

"I hate that bitch. Call Lauren and have them meet Meta back at the studio."

"No problem." Annie whipped out her phone and started texting Lauren.

"You're looking better today," Sergio said. Sometimes he was sincere.

"Thanks. I stopped with the blow."

"Oh." Sergio frowned for a moment before his expression brightened. "You have a guy?"

Annie rolled her eyes and walked out the door. "I'll be in my office."

Her phone buzzed with a reply from Lauren before she made it halfway down the hall, except when Annie looked at her phone, the text she read wasn't from her field producer. It was a text from Oksana.

I miss you already. What did you do to me?

I didn't tell you. I'm a witch, versed in the magic of seduction, Annie texted back.

You're ridiculous is what you are.

Miss you too, she replied one more time, then skipped back to her desk.

❖

Oksana flipped through her copy of *The Angels of Prairie Run*. Typically, she didn't care about the material's details when she was training someone for a project, but she didn't want to miss some change in the narrative that might change the actor's appearance drastically mid-film. Paulo was almost done with his last session and then they'd talk about the next step for these particular clients.

She stretched and rubbed her head. It was time for another shave. Maybe something she and Annie could do together.

She sighed lightly and flopped sideways against Paulo's couch. She couldn't believe she told Annie she missed her. Desperate much.

You like her, stupid. And she likes you. It's okay to say it, she reminded herself. It was true. She was allowed to like someone new and she was allowed to express it. Annie was being patient without making Oksana feel like she was waiting for something. Annie was awesome.

Annie, she sighed to herself. She was acting more pathetic than Kat was over Erica.

Annie.

Oksana could not stop smiling. All day, her clients and her students had noticed how happy she seemed. And she was usually pretty fucking upbeat at the gym. Kat had called attention to her perkiness too. Kat liked Annie a lot and she made it perfectly clear during their family meeting of two over breakfast, she and Baba Inna agreed that Annie was welcomed into the Gorinkov Organization.

Paulo's door opened and Oksana sprang upright.

"Give me two seconds, chica, and we'll talk," Paulo said as he walked into his private bathroom. They could have talked the next day, but the truth was Oksana was killing time before Annie came over. She knew if she went home she'd be pacing in the driveway waiting for Annie to show up just so they could make out for a few minutes before dinner.

A moment after the toilet flushed, Paulo popped out of the bathroom and flopped down at his desk. "So. You're dating again." His fake accent was firmly in place.

"I'm not sure we're dating exactly. More like hanging out."

"But you're happy?"

Oksana grinned like a fool. "Yes."

"She was really nice on the phone. Still good in bed?"

Oksana nodded gravely.

"Well," Paulo said. "That's good because now you won't be tempted to screw your new addition."

"Oh, we have a name?" Oksana thought the script was a courtesy from the studio. The leads were still up in the air, she thought.

"We do. Are you ready for this? Are you ready? Are you?"

"Paulo, shut up and tell me." She chuckled.

Paul leaned forward in his chair and smiled. "Are you ready?"

"I'm going to kill you. Who is it?"

"Willow Cruz."

Oksana blinked in shock.

"I know, right. Willow Cruz."

Okay, Oksana had not expected that name to come from Paulo's mouth. Willow Cruz wasn't A-list. Willow Cruz was beyond the A-list. The out-lesbian in her early forties had won her first Oscar at age nine. Two more followed. She was a notorious character actor Oksana had drooled over in countless films. She was beautiful, the definition of. She had dark features and light eyes and an amazing body. She'd actually gained thirty or so pounds for her most recent role in *The Gatekeeper* where she starred as a British madam in post-war London, but the weight gain just made her look more voluptuous. She was also part Russian.

There had been rumors that she was an intelligent, consummate professional and perfectionist. A flirt and a little bit of a womanizer. Just a little bit. Any woman who could tie her down had truly been gifted a golden ticket.

Thank fucking God she was "hanging out" with Annie. Willow was just the kind of woman to seduce Oksana and leave her looking like a puppy-loving fool. She was far from a star fucker. Most actors drove her crazy, but Willow was on her Celebrity Three list. She was in the number one slot.

Thank God for Annie.

Oksana sat back and tossed the script aside. "Gee. No pressure there. Who's playing Clem?"

"Did you read the script already?" Paulo looked surprised. He'd given it to her a whole two hours ago.

"No. I told you I read the book."

"Oh. Ryan Perry."

"Okay, he is hot. You're going to have fun with him."

"It'll be hard not to let him blow me, but I'll manage." They both laughed.

"When do we start?"

A light knock on the door frame interrupted their conversation. "Excuse me."

Oksana and Paulo looked toward the pleasant female voice coming from the door. There standing right inside Elite Fitness was Willow Cruz. Oksana was actually nervous. She'd never been starstruck before, but this was Willow Cruz. Come on, she was on the list.

Paulo hopped up and rushed to kiss her cheeks.

Oksana followed and shook Willow's hand as Paulo went through introductions. Willow had a firm handshake, a trait Oksana loved.

Too bad Annie's hugs are better. She smiled to herself. Luckily, Willow thought the smile was for her and not for a woman a few miles down Santa Monica Boulevard.

"Sorry. I know I'm about four days early, but I wanted to drop this off for Oksana?" Willow glanced between Oksana and Paulo then handed a folder to Oksana. She quickly flipped it open and got a glimpse at Willow's medical history. Perfectionist, right.

Willow caught on to her amazement. "I had to go through a nutritionist to put this all on. I wanted you to be in the loop before we took it all off. And then some," she added, smiling just short of winking at Oksana. Paulo noticed too.

"I'll let you two get to know each other," he said with feeling before he closed the door behind him.

"Sorry he's—"

"He's not Italian, is he?"

"No." Oksana laughed. There was no point in lying. "He's not."

After making themselves comfortable on the couch, they talked for a while. Willow had been very helpful in bringing her information by. Some clients, especially famous, arrogant ones, loved lying about their health, usually to cover up some drug habit or some eating disorder. Oksana could tell from the get-go that Willow didn't have either. They would have to get her below her normal weight from the look of things, but that wouldn't be a problem.

Oksana was able to get a lot of information out of Willow to help in their workouts without coming across as being all business. Willow seemed to appreciate her approach. Oksana tried to ignore the fact that her new client was indeed flirting. The flirting was having the opposite of its intended effect. Willow was attractive, there was no doubt about that, but as the clock on Paulo's desk continued to tick off the minutes, all she wanted was to get back to the big house. And Annie. Willow represented what drew people to Los Angeles, the glamour and the fame, but Annie was real.

Finally, after an hour, Willow seemed pleased with the initial ideas Oksana had to shed her excess pounds. Oksana humored her with a few more minutes of small talk, and as soon as Willow was out the door, Oksana booked it home.

Annie's Prius was parked on the street.

She found Annie in the living room, sitting on the couch. Kat sat on the coffee table in front of her, her makeup kits spread out on all the available surfaces.

"Hey." Annie beamed the moment she caught Oksana out of the corner of her eye. "Kat's practicing for the play."

"I'm almost done." Kat added one more stroke. "Perfect."

"How do I look?" Annie stood and gave Oksana a full view of the blue and green designs that swirled around Annie's left eye and cheek. Kat had some serious talent, but at the moment all Oksana could think about was getting a kiss.

Annie bit her lip knowingly and stood on her tiptoes. "My butterflies are going crazy. I think they missed you too," she whispered just as their lips met.

CHAPTER ELEVEN

THE FINAL SEAL OF APPROVAL

After their adult sleepover on Monday night went so well, Oksana and Annie decided it would be a good idea if Annie stayed over on Tuesday night too. The little house was much closer to Annie's office than her place. With the rising costs in fuel, it only made sense, even if Annie drove a hybrid.

Tuesday night was so much fun, Wednesday morning, they overslept again. This time Oksana was late for her first session and Kat was late for school. She came banging on the little house door fifteen minutes after she was due in homeroom.

"Where's Baba?" Oksana asked as she scrambled around for her clothes.

"She already went down to the store."

"Shit."

"Do you need a ride?" Annie asked as she zipped up her jeans.

"Uh, yeah."

"I'll take her," Annie said.

Oksana paused mid shoe tie. "Are you sure?"

"Yeah, you're late. Even if I drop her off, I'll be early for work. I'll get some paperwork done."

"Great," Kat answered. "I'll go get my bag."

"I'd love to argue that it's too soon for me to be pushing off the kid-carting on you, but I'm real fucking late." Oksana kissed

Annie before she grabbed her bag. "Spare key is under the rock by the door. Bye."

Ten minutes later, Annie was behind the wheel of her Prius, Kat at her side. There was no unease in the air, an impromptu pit stop for McGriddles killed any chance of that, but Annie didn't want to say anything to make things awkward between them. She took the casual, let's focus on you without trying to pry, approach.

"You hanging out with Erica after school?" she asked just after Kat directed her to take the next left. Annie knew of one high school on this side of town and Kat didn't go there.

"Yeah. She's going to come to play practice with me." Kat inhaled the last bite of her breakfast sandwich then crumpled her trash into the bag. She was quiet for half of an ABBA classic before Annie felt Kat's gaze on her.

"I don't want to be that annoying little sibling. I'm not naïve. I know how these things work, but do you really like my sister?"

"I do."

"For more than just her body?"

"Yes."

"A lot of people like her for her body," Kat said frankly.

Soon Annie saw Kat's school just ahead. She stopped at the front curb.

"I can imagine. How do you feel about us?" she asked, turning to Kat. Her green bangs were out of her face, but tons and tons of black makeup surrounded her eyes. Annie realized in the three days she'd been hanging around, she'd never seen Kat with her makeup off. She had the same green eyes as her sister. A gorgeous girl, but Annie imagined she gave people the wrong impression of her every day. Annie stopped herself from smiling. She knew with Baba Inna and Oksana at her back, Kat probably never cared what those impressions were. The stud of her tongue ring darted out across her bottom lip before she answered.

"You're still kinda engaged, right?"

"Yeah." Annie winced. There were no secrets, but it was a little odd hearing that sort of thing from someone other than Oksana.

"I think you'll really leave him. It sounds shitty, but I want you to. Did she tell you about her last girlfriend?"

"Some, but no details."

"She was crazy. You're much better."

"I hope so." Annie laughed.

"No, I mean she was nice in the beginning," Kat went on. "She tried really hard to butter me up in front of Sana, but she seemed so fake. You seem like you just want to be around, not like you want to control everything. I don't know. I like you and I like you for my sister."

An instant smile broke out across Annie's face. She needed Baba Inna's approval, but after spending more and more time with the Gorinkov clan, she knew Kat's approval was just as important. They were a unit, these three special ladies, and Annie knew wolfing down Baba's cooking and helping with the dishes wasn't enough. She had to get to know Oksana's family and they had to get to know her. Annie loved their magic, and apparently, they had seen that Annie had her own something special to bring to the table.

"Thanks, Kat. That means a lot." Annie let out deep breath. "I don't really have much of a family so it's nice just being around."

Kat reached across the seat and hugged her. Annie was shocked at first, but she gave the hug right back and then did her best not to choke up like a baby. She cared about Kat. Not that she wouldn't, but she never realized that she would. With all the effort she'd put into getting Oksana to give her a chance, she didn't give much thought to what would happen if things worked out. But things were working out, and Annie was starting to love the whole family.

Kat sat back and reached for her backpack. "You'll be home for dinner?"

"I think we're going out to eat, but I'll be over before we go."

"Can I do your hair? I'd ask my sister, but…"

"The bald thing. Sure."

"Cool." Kat smiled. "See ya."

She jumped out of the car as Annie said her good-bye. She also realized then that she wouldn't mind driving Kat to school every day.

❖

The night was warm, and as they stepped out of the little house, Annie was starting to see the perks of staying on this side of town. It was minutes from the office, twenty yards from Baba's butter infused cooking, and just a short city light and moonlit walk to Señor Kim's. Her hair looked fabulous, but after Kat had finished with the rockabilly do she called victory rolls, a style Annie had drooled over before with no label to attach to it, she wished she'd packed more than the T-shirt and jeans Oksana insisted would be more than enough for a night out with her friends.

Annie wore her glasses, per Oksana's subtle, yet adorable request, and let Kat try out the eye shadow they'd picked out on Sunday. She thought she looked pretty decent, but Oksana looked better.

Annie had never really noticed, well, she'd never had the opportunity to notice, but where Annie looked like a sad, shriveled troll at the end of her workout even after she showered and hydrated, Oksana looked like some sort of Egyptian queen with her heat-blushed skin and exotic eyes. She wore a skirt like the pleated one she'd worn to The Maypole that night. This one was purple. Her plain T-shirt was white, and Annie couldn't decide for a moment whether her nipple piercings showing through the fabric bothered her or not. She decided it didn't. It did make her horny though, and gave her something more to look forward to after dinner.

"Your friend's meeting us there?" Oksana asked. Megan had called to confirm that she'd be working a little late, but she was not passing on this chance to meet the one person to shake up Annie's life.

"Yeah. She's a little intense, but she means well. I think you'll like her."

"I better or we are so over."

"Not funny," Annie grumbled playfully.

She was strangely excited to meet Oksana's friends. She'd been too out of it to get any real impression of Ronnie, but Noelle seemed really cool once Annie realized she wasn't coming on to

Oksana. There hadn't been much talk about Scooter or his buddy Neil, but Annie imagined if they were important to Oksana, they had to be pretty good guys. Annie had it in mind to tease her about them a little as they walked, but not before she told Oksana about her day.

"I've been doing my research," Annie said as they walked through Oksana's neighborhood. This part of the city was quiet at the moment. Just the sounds of traffic on the main street a few blocks away.

"On what?" Oksana took her hand when they reached a crosswalk.

"Your tattoos."

"And what mysteries did you unfold?"

"You were telling the truth about your tribute to Russia. The sunflower is the national flower. The birch is the nation's official tree," Annie said. "The pattern across your shoulder is a street map of Moscow, and the birds around your heart tattoo aren't to show your American patriotism. I've learned that the Russians also value the eagle."

"I'm impressed."

"You should be. Wikipedia is made for people like me who paid absolutely no attention during world history," Annie said proudly.

"Well, I'm kind of a closet history nerd. I can share more of my infinite knowledge with you any time you like."

"Do you have a favorite?" Oksana looked down as Annie stroked her forearm.

"This one." She pointed to the silhouette just under Annie's fingertips. "Bears are misunderstood. We're big, but really, we just like cuddles and honey."

"I thought you would say the heart."

"No, that was therapy and a reminder." Oksana shook her head casually. "The bear is my spirit animal."

"And another national symbol of Russia. I don't think I have a spirit animal."

"You're a chickadee because they're little and they never shut up," Oksana said.

"Stop with this fitness thing. You're a natural-born comedian."

"I know. I'm funny." Oksana paused just before they passed out of the residential streets and stepped into Annie's arms. "Thanks for doing your research. It shows that you care and that you can read." She kissed Annie sweetly on the mouth. For a minute, they stood there in the shadows, breath mixing, hearts beating. When they pulled apart, Oksana's eyes were still closed as she sighed. Annie broke out in a smile.

"I'm giving you the giggly butterflies again, aren't I?"

"Yes."

"I'm glad." Annie stepped forward and kissed her again. "So what's so special about Scooter and Neil? I didn't know lesbians hung out with men."

"Typically, we don't, but Scooter pays us to make him look cool in public."

"Wait, I can get paid?"

They continued walking on to Hollywood Boulevard. Annie knew then exactly where Señor Kim's was. She'd passed it dozens of times on random field trips to the post house. Just a few more blocks up, between a lingerie store and a tattoo shop.

"I met Scooter when I was in high school."

"What about Neil?" Annie asked.

"He and Scooter are part of the same package. You'll see."

This time Annie stopped Oksana with a slight tug of her hand.

"Should I go home tonight?" she asked. Annie was having a great time, but the days were starting to blend together. She knew if she didn't take a second to at least check in with Oksana, Wednesday would easily turn into Sunday without Annie so much as setting foot in her house for more than grabbing another set of clothes.

"If by home you mean my crotch, then yes," Oksana said with a frown.

"I'm serious. I've been basically living at your house, driving your sister to school. I just don't want to crowd you or whatever," Annie said, trying to end on a casual note.

"I'll let you know when I'm feeling crowded," Oksana said while she caressed a curl hanging off Annie's shoulder.

"I believe you," Annie said. She took a step closer, walking Oksana back toward a closed storefront. "So are you feeling crowded now?"

"No."

"How about now?" Annie stepped closer so their bodies were touching.

"Nope." Oksana's breath came a little shorter.

"And now?"

"If you don't stop I'm going to fuck your crowding ass right here on the sidewalk."

Annie looked at the puddle of runoff beside them. "If there wasn't a near certainty that we would both get the plague, I would tell you to go for it." As payback for her joking, Annie kissed Oksana. This time she got a little grabby, sliding her hands up under Oksana's shirt.

Oksana shuddered. "I'll take you to the floor when we get home."

"Sounds like a date."

They walked the rest of the way in silence, hands still together, trying to rein in their physical cravings. When a tall blond guy covered wrist to chin in tattoos came around the corner, Oksana let go.

"Scootie!" Oksana lit up and skipped toward him.

"Hey, girl," he replied, scooping her up in his arms. This was probably one of the few guys in L.A. who was taller than Oksana, by almost a foot. Scooter was handsome. His hair was spiked up into a stylish faux hawk, and a stubbly brown and blond beard covered his face. There was a huge scar going across his forehead stopping just above his eye.

"What happened?" Oksana asked in the same tone she used with Kat.

"We had to roll a few cars yesterday."

"Yeah, cars. Not your forehead. Jesus." Oksana examined the cut further. It did look pretty bad, like it should be stitched up, but something about Scooter told Annie he only went to the ER if a body part was hanging off. At least the gash wasn't bleeding.

"I'm fine. Neosporin fixes everything," he said, letting Oksana turn his head the other way. "You want to introduce me to your friend?"

"Annie, this is Scooter. Who loves taking his life into his own hands at every possible opportunity." Oksana scowled. Annie chuckled at her motherly display.

"Chris 'Scooter' Skogstad. Stunt driver for hire."

"Ah. Explains the busted forehead."

"And the fucked up knee and back and ankle," Oksana added.

"Annie Collins, glorified production accountant. It's nice to meet you." She held out her hand for Scooter to shake it.

"No. No. None of that shit. Get in here." Before she could protest, Scooter grabbed Annie's arm and yanked her into a tight hug. She barely came up to his ribs, he was so tall. She melted into the hug. He smelled nice, and there was something about him that was very familiar, but Annie couldn't place it.

"Where's Neil?" Oksana asked when he finally let Annie go. She stepped back to Oksana's side, warmed all over when she took Annie's hand again. At least PDA in front of the friends was okay.

"He's parking." Scooter pulled a cigarette from behind his ear and lit it.

"Hey, can you do me a favor?" Oksana asked him.

"Sure, what's up?"

"Annie's garage door is busted. Can you take a look at it?"

"Sure. Carlos has my tools," he told Annie. "But I'll get them back and we can figure out a time for me to swing by. Sound good?"

"Uh, yeah," Annie replied. "Thanks." A commotion interrupted Scooter before he could reply.

"Bullshit. This is bullshit, man!" A homeless man came darting across the street. Annie had seen him before. A black man in his forties or so. He'd been on the streets a while, but he was functioning.

"Cap'n Stan. What's got you down, brother?" Scooter said like they were old friends. Maybe they were.

"My man, Scoot." He gave Scooter a low five then settled in for some conversation with his hands on his hips. Annie snorted quietly to herself, shaking her head when Oksana looked at her. Feather would feed her own hand to a hyena before she touched someone without a lease to his name. "Nothing got me down. Just the same old bullshit. Give me a cigarette."

Scooter patted his pockets. "I'm out, man. This is my last one."

"Here." Annie dug through her bag and pulled out the cigarettes she'd been saving for the crew.

She handed the unopened menthols to Cap'n Stan. "Take the pack." She felt Oksana's curious gaze on her. "I get them for our camera guys. A little morale boost."

"Thanks, pretty lady. I like your style. This your woman, Scoot?"

"Can't say that she is, Cap'n Stan." Scooter laughed out a puff of smoke.

"I'm her woman," Annie said, sidling closer to Oksana.

"Oh ho ho. You gonna let him watch?" Cap'n Stan asked. He was serious.

"Fuck that. Are they going to let me participate?" Scooter joked. Annie hoped. He was handsome, but no.

"No. You fucking pig." Oksana groaned, slapping Scooter on the shoulder.

"What did this dick do now?" Annie peered around Scooter and Stan and saw…well, a little person coming up the sidewalk.

"Nothing," Oksana said, rolling her eyes. "Hey, Neil." She leaned over to give the man a hug. His goatee was neatly trimmed. He was dressed in gray slacks and a light blue polo shirt with the sleeves rolled up. His forearms were covered in tattoos and he had small gold hoops in each ear. Annie was starting to notice a theme.

"Hey, gorgeous," he said, patting Oksana's hip as she straightened up. It was a friendly gesture, but for some reason it made Annie feel like a real outsider. Oksana had years of history with these guys, years of comfort built up. She and Oksana were comfortable with kissing and sleeping together. Still, Annie couldn't wait until they got to the point where simple touches like a pat on the hip were second nature between them. She couldn't wait for that kind of history.

Oksana quickly introduced them while Scooter chatted up Cap'n Stan about some weird street gossip. Neil was formal, taking Annie's hand and politely greeting her with a smile.

"Finally, someone my height," he said.

"Well, at least I have someone who understands the short jokes." Annie grinned.

"True. Let's go," Neil said, nodding toward the door. "Ron said they already got us a table."

"Scooter, get me some tacos!" Cap'n Stan called after them.

"We're gonna be a while."

"And where you think I'm going? My summer home?"

"Tacos! Coming up."

Inside the dark restaurant, lit only by neon lights and signs along the walls and around a stage near the back, they followed Neil as he barreled his way across the floor to a large booth right near the stage. A girl around their age was in the middle of an interesting rendition of some Journey song Annie couldn't remember the name of.

Annie recognized Noelle immediately. She was wearing a Princeton lacrosse sweatshirt, sitting next to a gorgeous Latin woman in a white v-neck who Annie vaguely remembered as Ronnie. A hoop ran through the middle of her bottom lip, and she had a diamond Monroe piercing in her cheek, one Annie had actually considered once upon a time. She was glad she'd trusted Oksana on the wardrobe choice. The dress she'd had in mind might have been a little much. Ronnie's right arm was ink free, but the left arm had bright, intricate designs down to her hand. Annie was really starting to feel left out.

Noelle jumped up and hugged everyone, saving Annie for last. "I'm so glad you came. Your hair looks awesome."

"Thanks. Kat did it."

"Turn around," Ronnie instructed her. Annie did as she asked, bending her neck to give a full view of the style. "Kat's getting good," she said to Oksana.

"I know. She might not need your help," she replied.

"Everyone needs my help. Annie, it's nice to meet you officially."

"Likewise. Sorry about our first meeting."

"Don't worry about it. Looks like things have worked out just fine."

The waitress came back to the table and they all ordered. Annie followed Oksana's recommendations and they decided to split a little bit of everything on the basic menu. A bunch of tacos and a burrito stuffed with Korean barbecued beef and Asian spices, with plenty to cover Megan when she showed up. Scooter filled them in on all the details of the cut on his head and the actors he'd taken the beating for.

Just as Annie took her first sip from her Coke, Noelle turned to her.

"So…" She nearly bounced in her seat. Annie was starting to like her and her energy. "Tell us about you."

Well, I'm engaged to this guy, but I'm falling for your friend. "I am a line producer for Blink Media." Annie told them about the three shows that kept her busy, without boring them to death with the mundane details.

"Meta gave our receptionist crabs," Ronnie said bluntly.

Annie's mouth dropped open. "And you expect me not to tell my whole crew, why?"

"I like her," Noelle said to Oksana who just smiled.

Ronnie kept on. "No, please. Tell everyone. Shit, tell Meta. She wouldn't take poor Cheyenne's phone calls for a month. Anyone on your crew hook up with her?"

"I don't think so, but ew. Thanks for the heads-up." Annie laughed, silently reminding herself to have a conversation with Sergio first thing in the morning. Nothing fucks up the chemistry between a crew like crabs.

The food and beers came quickly and they all dug in, table manners tossed to the side.

"So, Scooter," Annie asked after her second taco. "Oksana says there's a great love story between you and Neil. Can I hear it?"

"Dickhead farted on my face." Neil took a casual sip of his beer just as she choked on her soda.

"Excuse me?"

"Few years ago I was at Coachella, and from behind, Neil looks just like my buddy Little Fred," Scooter explained.

"This piece of shit runs up to me, spins me around, blams one right on my forehead."

"Yes, I know two black midgets." Clearly, Scooter and Neil were past being PC with each other.

"This is how you treat Little Fred?" Annie asked with a grin.

"Fred is an asshole." Scooter smiled back.

"What did you do?" she asked Neil.

"I punched him in the dick and then when he fell over I started beating the fuck out of him."

"Once he stopped kicking me, I told him who I thought he was. He actually knows Little Fred and how much of an asshole he is. We've been boys ever since," Scooter finished.

Annie couldn't help but laugh. "That is sweet." Beside her, Oksana slid her free hand into Annie's lap. Annie turned to her. Amid the chatter and the music and the general noise, everything faded away.

Annie slid closer and kissed her on the cheek. "Hi."

"Hi. Are you having fun?" Oksana asked just for the two of them to hear.

"I am."

"Of course she is. Scoot, go sing," Noelle said.

"Annie, you karaoke?" he asked.

"Not unless she's wasted." Annie turned around to find Megan walking up to the booth.

"Hey. Guys, this is my friend Megan."

"Sorry. David needed me to tie his shoes," she said.

"Your boss?" Ronnie asked. She quickly introduced herself and Noelle.

"Yup. I can't wait to press him for a raise." Megan continued with the hand-shaking rounds, taking care to be extra polite to Oksana, which Annie appreciated. Annie also noticed that Megan did a double take when she got to Scooter. She'd seen that look before. Megan was interested. *Scooter's* eyes looked like they were going to pop out of his head when Megan slid into the booth directly across from him and ordered a whiskey neat. Annie looked to Oksana to see if she'd noticed their fireworks. Oksana nodded back.

"What did I miss?" Megan asked.

"Scooter, I thought you were going to go sing," Noelle said.

"I will. I'm just getting to know our new friends here."

"I'll be here all night, Scoot," Megan said as she thanked the waitress for her drink. "Why don't you treat us to a song?"

"Ladies, if you'll excuse us." Scooter slid out of the booth after Neil. "You are in for a bit of a show."

"You're in for it all right. They usually close the place. The owner loves it," Oksana told them. Scooter and Neil walked over to the bar. Neil hoisted himself up on a stool and ordered a bottle—not a shot—but a bottle of Patrón. They waited, passing the bottle between them as an older Asian gentlemen started in on a frighteningly on-key version of Whitney Houston's "Shoop Shoop" song from *Waiting to Exhale*. At the table, Megan settled in and caught Oksana and the other women up on her work life. She asked Oksana all she could about herself without being too forward or pushy. Annie paid for her next drink.

"Oh, Sana, I forgot to tell you. I sold the last painting from my March show," Noelle broke in.

"You did? That's awesome. Noelle's an artist," Oksana told Annie and Megan.

"Really? Would I have seen your work?" Annie knew jackshit about painting; that was Jeff's thing, but she knew when she liked a piece of art. He was always dragging her to openings and shows. She pretended to be interested in the pompous talk until Jeff forgot she was there. Then she would wander around to look for pieces she liked. She'd never purchased; that was also Jeff's thing, but she did end up falling in love with a work or two along the way.

"Look up Noe Crane," Ronnie said.

"Wait. You're Noe Crane?" Annie asked, surprised that she actually knew who Ronnie was referring to.

"Yup."

"I have your *Struggles of a Junior Accountant* hanging in my office. My—I got it as a gift." From Jeff on a non-birthday weekend.

Noe Crane had done a series of paintings featuring children struggling with adult occupations. Annie never bothered to think of the artist's true motivation for the theme, but every time she looked at the little blonde, behind the enormous desk stacked with papers, staring hopelessly at an adding machine, Annie felt that little girl knew her workday pain.

Jeff had gone on and on about how the artist never kept a single dollar from the sales of her work. Apparently, she had a primary source of income and donated every dime to charities around the city. Jeff had explained that the subjects of each portrait in the particular show he had attended had come from low-incomes families. He'd paid a nice little chunk for the painting and her family had been given every cent.

The best part of it all was the donations were a secret from the public. Noe Crane used Hollywood connections and the need to be seen to get her shows filled. Any information of where the money went wasn't listed on her website, and Noelle took no credit for the good she had done. Jeff had heard the rumor and only found out the truth when he'd met one of Noelle's subjects.

"I've seen that painting," Megan said. "You're fucking amazing."

"So you're both fans?" Noelle asked.

"Everyone who's seen your work is a fan, baby," Ronnie assured her.

"Thanks, lover." Annie looked at Oksana as Noelle and Ronnie started sealing their affections with a kiss, a little heavy on the tongue. Not that it was a struggle to watch an attractive couple sucking face, but every second Annie watched was another second she wanted to pounce on Oksana.

"They do that a lot," Oksana whispered before she kissed Annie on the neck.

"I don't blame them," Megan said under her breath, but her eyes were on Scooter.

"You know, Megan, he's single," Oksana said.

Megan turned to Oksana with a smile. "I'll take that under advisement." Annie was elated that they were getting along.

Suddenly, Noelle was back in the conversation. "I had another show in March and I was trying to unload this final piece."

"She painted an injured Iraq vet's initial wounds as he described them to her," Oksana added.

"Whoa." Annie grimaced, for all sorts of reasons.

"It finally sold though," Noelle said.

"And he'll get the money? Sorry, I didn't..." Annie said when Noelle ducked her head a bit, blushing.

"No, it's okay. People are weird when they hear where the money is going. Out here, it's like they'd rather feed a hip artist than a broken family."

"Oh, I know what you mean," Annie said. Megan saluted with her empty glass in agreement. They'd both met plenty of the sort. Worked with a few of them. Annie was raised by one in particular. Her mother would much rather go to a charity ball for some trivial cause than donate any real time or money to people who really needed it. It made Annie sick to think about.

"Right when Ryan got out of the hospital they found out his daughter has leukemia. He said he was going to use the money to help with her medical bills," Noelle said.

Annie couldn't help but feel a twinge of upper class guilt. She couldn't imagine serving in the military, and men and women like Ryan made it so she would never have to. She was grateful that people like Ryan *and* Noelle existed.

"Ronnie, what pays your bills?" she asked to take some of the heat off Noelle.

"My parents, but I do hair to keep myself entertained." Annie liked the honesty in her admission. Most people in their thirties wouldn't admit to living off their parents, especially if they were dating someone as selfless as Noelle. Annie hated when her parents offered to give her anything, money included. Even a wedding...

"See." Oksana's lip twitched as she tried not to smile. "We have our very own Ivy League trust fund babies."

"So you didn't get the sweatshirt at Goodwill?" Annie grinned, nodding at Noelle's sweatshirt.

"No." Noelle chuckled as Ronnie began stroking her neck with her fingertips. "We were roommates freshman year."

"Yeah, Noe here gayed up my college experience. And three months after we moved here Sana tried to pick me up at Baba's store," Ronnie said.

"Like hell I did. She started talking to me about my tats while I was stocking shelves. And then she introduced me to Vivian."

"Don't start. I said I was sorry. Besides, she's long gone now and you've moved on to better women." Annie couldn't tell exactly how serious Ronnie was, but beside her, Oksana flinched. She rubbed Oksana's thigh then took her hand.

"And from what I hear, I've definitely made up for it this week," Ronnie continued.

"What happened?" Annie asked.

"I got Oksana on as Willow Cruz's trainer for her new movie."

"She did?" Annie turned to Oksana. Willow Cruz was a huge star. "Why didn't you tell me?"

"I just found out a few days ago. She's just another client."

"Yeah, who could get you Bob and Jillian money," Ronnie said.

"I don't want Bob and Jillian money. I don't want my own weight loss show. She's made it pretty clear that she wants to sleep with me. So what I *want* is to train her and send her off to set."

Before Annie got to ask any more questions, Scooter and Neil took the stage. Megan gulped down the rest of her whiskey and leaned forward out of the booth.

"This song goes out to the lovely ladies right over at table four," Scooter oozed into the mic.

"Blow me, Scoot!" Ronnie yelled.

"I intend to, Veronica. I intend to."

Neil hopped on a stool beside him just before "The Stroke" by Billy Squier started blaring out over the cheap speakers.

Annie burst out laughing as Neil and Scooter started singing together. Four songs later, they came back to the table, sweating and reeking of tequila. They let two other people have their turns before they jumped back up and launched into several 70s and 80s R&B

ballads that Neil took the lead on. His tastes seem to center around Bobby Brown and the Commodores.

Eventually, Noelle turned to Ronnie. "I'm ready," she said.

Annie looked away as they started kissing again. She was having a fun time, but she could definitely go for some alone time with Oksana. Ronnie stood and waved to Scooter before she nodded toward the door. He nodded back, not skipping a word of "Easy Lover."

"They'll be here long after we're asleep," Oksana told Annie. "You want to go?"

"Yes," Annie replied, trying not to sound desperate. "Will they be okay to drive?"

"Probably not, but they'll call a cab," Oksana said.

"Megan, where are you parked?" Annie asked.

"Don't worry about me," Megan replied. "I'll give them a lift."

"Are you sure? This is like a two on the rowdy meter for them," Oksana said.

"Don't worry. I got 'em. I'll call you tomorrow," Megan told Annie.

Annie and Oksana hugged Megan, then waved to the boys as they headed toward the door, Noelle and Ronnie close behind. They said their good-byes. Annie agreed to go shopping with Noelle as soon as she could rationalize spending any of her available time away from Oksana.

As Ronnie hugged Annie good-bye, she whispered in her ear.

"Don't hurt her," Ronnie said. This wasn't a threat. It was a genuine plea. One Annie heard loud and clear. She wondered if Megan had left any messages with Oksana when they'd embraced.

Annie pulled back and looked Ronnie right in the eye. "I got it." Oksana was too important. She cared for her too much to risk hurting her. Annie wanted Oksana long-term. Their own kids, their own house, and over-sized slobbering mutt long-term. It was a scary conclusion, but it was the truth.

They walked home a little faster than they'd walked to the restaurant.

"How was it?" Oksana asked.

"Your friends are great. So is your family. What the hell? Why do you have the monopoly on kick-ass people?"

"Just lucky. I like Megan."

"Good. She likes you too, though not as much as she likes Scooter."

"I'm not shocked. He's a straight lady magnet. It's the beard." Oksana sighed, but laced her fingers tighter with Annie's. "I didn't tell you about Willow because I saw how you looked at Noelle in the mall and I didn't want you to freak out."

"I get it. I've never been jealous before. I can see myself being jealous over you. I mean, I *was* jealous, but I know that actor type and I don't think that's your type."

"You're right. She's too tall anyway."

They entered the yard of the big house and Annie followed Oksana as she did a quick check to make sure all the doors were locked, not that an intruder would stand a chance against Vasily.

After that, they headed to the little house. Oksana led them inside but pulled Annie to her before they could make it to the bedroom. Annie looked up into those searching eyes, eyes that were focused on Annie's chest.

"I've learned my lesson from sleeping with clients," Oksana said quietly. "And I think I've already used up my heartbreaks, which means you have to date me forever. Like forever."

Annie reached up, softly cupping the side of her neck. "I'm not going anywhere, but I am wondering. Do I have to get a full sleeve to keep hanging out with you guys?"

"No." Oksana bent until their lips barely touched. "Just be you."

As she promised, she made love to Annie. Right there on the living room floor.

CHAPTER TWELVE

THE BROWN BEAR AND THE BIRD

Thursday, in the interest of preventing Annie's house from being burgled, they decided to spend the night apart. Annie went into work that morning already feeling a sense of separation. She was on edge, antsy as hell as the day went on. She missed Oksana and she was dying to hear Megan's impressions of their own night out. When Esther took off to run some errands, Annie texted Megan. *Call me when you're free.*

A few seconds later, her cell rang.

"Okay. I want to hear it," Annie said. She quickly closed the door to her office.

"Scooter's dick is huge."

Annie froze halfway across the room. "What?"

"We dropped Neil off and then we went back to his place. He's the best lay I've had in years."

"Well...good. Congratulations?"

"Thanks. And I don't know if I'm going to see him again, but I gave him my number."

"Okay..." Annie had no idea what to say. This conversation had taken a bizarre, slightly unnerving turn.

"Of course I liked her," Megan said. "She's awesome. Noelle is awesome. Ronnie is awesome. Neil has a voice like a dark, chocolate angel. They are all hot as hell and funny. Just call Jeff now and dump him. I'll pay for the international minutes."

"No." Annie let out a dry laugh. "I can't do that."

"Listen. I think your mom is going to shit. Like there's no way she's going to be cool with this, but there is something about Oksana. You're right. She's exactly what you need. She laughs for one. Haven't seen Jeff do that." Jeff had laughed plenty of times in front of Megan, but she was on to something. Oksana was warmer, more inviting. Sweeter. She made Annie happy, not just comfortable. This wasn't pre-wedding jitters. This was a chance at the life Annie really wanted with someone she was starting to love.

"You should see her with her sister. She's a great mom too."

"I don't even know why we're having this conversation. Even if you and Oksana don't live happily after, can't you see now? There is someone better out there for you. Jeff isn't it."

Annie let out a hefty sigh and slouched on the end of her desk. How the hell was she going to break this to him?

"But I think the real test will come when he's back. You have to see how you feel when you see him again."

"You think I'll still marry him?" A flash of anger warmed Annie's face. The thought of staying with Jeff felt like such a gross betrayal to Oksana. God, how the tables had turned.

"No, but I think you might screw this up if you're not careful."

"Gee, thanks."

"Annie, you don't like hurting people. Even though I'm pretty sure he's a soulless automaton, I do think Jeff loves you in his own robotic way and you're going to have a hard time cutting him loose."

"I know."

"But you'll do it or I'll strangle you."

"Trust me, it's happening. What should I do about Shane and Feather? They still want to go out, and I've kind of been avoiding Shane altogether these last few days."

"I'll handle them. Just act natural if they call you, and then after Jeff knows you can tell them. I'll back you up. You just worry about telling Taum."

Annie pictured her mother and all the various things she could possibly say or do. Best-case scenario, she surprised Annie with some miraculous level of understanding and accepted Oksana as the new person in her life. Worst case scenario? She'd only seen her mother really angry a few times in her life. It wasn't a pretty sight.

"You have two some odd weeks to enjoy spending time with her, so enjoy it," Megan said.

"And what will you be doing in the meantime?"

"Probably Scooter. I have to go. David's meeting is over." Megan hung up before she could say good-bye. Annie paced across the four available feet in her office. Inside her chest the happiness and the peace she felt with Oksana was warring with fear of having to deal with her family. She thought of the way Oksana had giggled as Annie kissed her stomach the night before. The happiness and the peace took another round in this game, as with all the rounds before. Annie smiled to herself and sent Oksana another text, just to see how her day was going.

❖

"What are you watching?" Annie asked.

Oksana stretched then settled her feet back under Annie's thigh.

"It's this show about the art the Nazis stole during the War. Stop talking to me. This is interesting," Oksana said, waving her off without blinking. If makeup was Kat's crack, PBS was hers. Despite what Annie claimed were the perks of Wikipedia, history had always been her favorite subject. She liked it in-depth and accurate.

"Would you date me if I was a history teacher?" she asked, half listening for an answer. A British professor was talking about the move to preserve Italy's art during the bombing.

"Yes." Annie laughed. "I'd date you no matter what you did. Do you want to be a history teacher?"

"I don't know. Sometimes."

"Well, what do you like about training?"

Oksana paused the TV and settled back for a moment, thinking of her answer. "I have this client. Old Hollywood money.

Hollywoodland money. He's enjoying his fortune, writing sitcoms in the 80s just because he can, and then his partner dies."

"When was this?"

"I think ninety-five, around there. Afterward, he becomes a complete shut-in. Quits the show, doesn't leave his house for years. Literally. Has an assistant living his life for him, and while all this is happening, he puts on two hundred pounds."

"Jesus!"

"Yeah. One day his assistant doesn't show up because he's sick, but Stewart doesn't believe him. He gets so pissed that he drags himself to the garage just to drive down the hill to catch his assistant sunbathing or waiting in line at Disneyland, whatever he thought he was really doing. He walks outside and sees that his neighbors have added a tower to a wing of their house that is a total eyesore. He completely forgets about his assistant and starts off for his neighbors to curse them out. He made it like a hundred feet before he gave up, but he realized how bad things had gotten. I deal with a lot of difficult people, and Stewart is difficult, but he doesn't see me so he can look good for some silly reason."

"Like a wedding."

Oksana nudged Annie's leg. "A wedding is a perfectly good reason. I mean like true vanity or revenge. Stewart wants his life back and I love being a part of that." Oksana smiled, thinking of how much Stewart had opened up to her and how much he would probably like Annie.

"What were you doing before?" Annie asked.

Oksana motioned for Annie's laptop. She handed it over and Oksana pulled up the official website for InkLadies.com. Her profile was still up, but the videos were long gone to make room for the new girls. She found her pictures and handed the computer back to Annie.

"It was a glamorous way to make a living."

Annie squinted at the monitor before her eyes sprang wide. "Holy shit! This is you. Oksie Cocktail?"

"I'd done some modeling during high school, but the agency wanted me to travel, and I didn't want to leave home. A friend of

Scooter's ran this website, and Scooter would come to shoots with me." She sat up and looked at which images Annie was clicking on. It was porn, not art, the way some of the girls claimed it to be. Porn for people who liked girls with tattoos and girls who liked other girls.

Annie clicked on a set of photos Oksie had taken with a girl who went by the name Lucy Boots. There were a couple dozen pictures of them stripping each other and eventually having sex in the backseat of a vintage Chevy.

Annie's face was bright red. "What did Inna have to say about this nakedness?"

Oksana laughed. "She told me to enjoy my perky tits while they last. She didn't care, and contrary to what you saw with her and Erica, Kat's really shy about being in a bathing suit. She wouldn't follow in those footsteps."

Annie frowned and stared at one of the more porny photos.

"Do you think less of me now?" Oksana asked.

"Wha-what!" Annie did a double take. "No, not at all. I was just thinking about how different you look with hair. Jesus, Sana." Annie squirmed a little. "These pictures are really hot. I would never have the guts to get naked like that."

"It was pretty fun for a while."

"What made you stop?"

"My ex."

"Oh, you were dating while this was going on?"

"Yeah, but it's not what you think. She was all for this type of modeling."

"Really?"

"Yeah, I think..." Oksana didn't want to tell Annie what Vivian had really been like, but hiding the truth was pointless. "I think I made her feel stronger, more independent."

"What do you mean?" Annie asked.

"You know how I said Stewart came from old Hollywood money? Well, Vivian came from old oil tycoon money." Oksana saw the recognition on Annie's face. She knew Annie understood the kind of legacy Oksana was talking about. "I don't know how much of this is true, but from what Ronnie and I were able to piece together, Vivian had been lying about her life, her family, everything ever since she entered prep school."

Annie laughed. "Like *The Prince and the Pauper*?"

"Exactly!" Oksana said. "I don't know why, but I guess she didn't want people to know how rich she was and exactly what her family name meant, so she came up with this elaborate scheme to be someone else. She gave all of us a fake last name, came up with this whole other life, and when Ronnie and Noelle decided to move out here after Princeton, she came with them."

"Ah, I see. She was looking for an adventure and you were something very exotic and different to her."

"I guess." Oksana took a deep breath. She hadn't actually talked about her breakup with Vivian in years. "The thing is I really don't know why she did what she did. I don't know if she was hiding or she was taking a break from the pressure or if she was just playing make believe. We were living together in Beverly Hills. I came home one night after a shoot and she was gone. Like completely gone. Her stuff, our furniture, even the TV. All of my things were piled in one corner of the living room with an eviction notice from Vivian's father. He owned the house."

Annie's mouth hung open in shock. It was an appropriate reaction. "What did it say?"

"I had fifteen days to vacate, but what was I going to do? Sleep on the floor?"

"What *did* you do?"

"I called Ronnie to see if she had any idea what was going on and she and Noelle came over and helped me load up my things."

"And what happened to Vivian?"

"Well, the Internet was able to tell us her real last name was Vonburn, but now that she's married it's Mainer." Oksana let Annie process that information for a moment seeing another light bulb go off in her eyes.

"You mean Vonburn as in Vonburn Center?" Oksana nodded. "Holy shit. Her family *invented* money."

"And they pioneered the railroad and the oil industry among other things."

"What did she tell you they did?"

"She said her dad was a lawyer and her mom was a teacher and she'd gotten into Princeton on a scholarship. There's a building at Princeton named after her grandfather."

"Jesus. So—"

"So I never heard from her again. I called her and her phone was cut off. She never responded to my e-mails. After a while, the account started bouncing the e-mails back." And like that, the woman she thought was the love of her life vanished and Oksana was left with years of wondering why she'd been a part of Vivian's sick game.

"This"—Oksana pointed to the images of her naked body on the laptop—"was just another part of her escape, I think. She could never pose nude or even get a tattoo without serious repercussions. She lived that life through me."

"Do you think it would have worked if she had told you the truth?"

"I don't know. She gave me everything I wanted in our relationship. We never fought, she always said yes, but after she was gone I could see that she was going out of her way to make me too happy, as if she knew she wouldn't stay and she wanted me to be as happy as possible when we were together. There were little things though. We all saw them, like she never had a bad day ever. No one is in a good mood all the time. Once, though, when I brought my toys for the first time, she hesitated."

"Wasn't a big fan of your monster dildos?"

"I don't think so. She wouldn't admit to it, but I could tell she didn't want to use them with me in bed. She did anyway. I just wish she had told me something. Noelle comes from the same kind of money too, not as old, but just as blue and plenty of it. Her family hates Ronnie, but she doesn't care. They made it work."

"Oh, Sana."

"It's not like I want her back or anything, but you understand now why I was a little hesitant to get involved with a girl from

Laguna who was already engaged. You see why I want you to be sure about us."

"Yeah, sort of. So how did you end up at the gym?"

"Once I realized Vivian really wasn't coming back, I had a bit of a breakdown. Okay, it was a full-on crazyfest. Noelle thought yoga might help me find my center or something. It didn't. It just gave me more quiet time to think about killing Vivian, but I became really tight with the instructor. I told her I was looking to try something new and she told me about a gym that was doing fitness certifications. She'd started training after a breakup herself so I figured why not."

"And it stuck."

"Meeting new people helped me get my mind off Vivian and the exercise helped me focus on myself. After I finished my certification, Ronnie introduced me to Paulo. He hired me at Elite and the rest is...the present?"

"And now you're stuck with me."

"Anne?" Oksana asked cautiously. Annie was the honest sort, and a little voice told Oksana that the truth would be something she didn't want to hear. "Are you going to leave him?"

"Yes. Yes, I am. I can't imagine being without you. Jeff..." Annie puffed out a sad breath. "He isn't right for me. He and I, we're friends. We're not in love. He doesn't give me the honey bear giggly butterflies. He doesn't make me feel good about gaining five pounds in a week."

"It all went to your tits. I'm sure of it."

"No." Annie grinned. "It went to my stomach and face, but whatever. I am counting down the days until Jeff gets back so I can end things once and for all. I compare the two of you. I compare your family and friends to mine. I think it's natural when you see what you're missing."

Oksana moved Annie's computer to the coffee table then slid to the floor between her legs. She felt Annie's eyes on her as she spread her thighs and shuffled closer.

"Are you nervous about talking to him?" Oksana asked.

"No. I'm anxious. I want to get it over with and put it behind me so we can move on. What are you doing? We're talking about our feelings." Oksana had unzipped her jeans and was now in the process of taking off her own shirt and her bra.

"Keep talking." She leaned forward and settled her chin on her crossed arms in Annie's lap. "You were saying?"

"You play dirty." Annie sighed before she stroked Oksana's trimmed hair. "I used to ignore my feelings a lot, as recently as a few weeks ago. What I needed from friends. What I wanted in bed. I don't have to do that with you. I was miserable planning the wedding, but how could I tell people that? Jeff is perfectly nice. He cares about me, and I mean, who else was there?"

"You didn't want more?"

Annie hated that the question was even necessary, but it was.

"You know, I did. When I met you, I started smiling in a way I hadn't before. I *wanted* to go to the gym. The most exciting part about getting married was seeing you twice a week. I wasn't worried about being bi or gay. I'm not now. I've never cared about that sort of thing. If I did, I'd still be in Laguna with fake even bigger boobs. I would be a trophy wife, like—" Annie stopped, then frowned.

"Like who?"

"Like my mom. She has no sense of self-worth. What Noelle said about *those* people, my mom *is* one of those people. She used to be my dad's mistress." Annie closed her eyes and pictured Taum.

"His first wife died and she swooped in and nabbed that brass ring. I overheard her once bragging about snagging the wealthiest man in town under fifty. When I was Kat's age, she told me that my boobs would be my ticket to a rich husband. The only reason she's on board with Jeff is because he did this amazing spread for *Vogue* last year and she was able to brag about it to her faux-friends." She'd never told anyone that before, not even Megan, who might have enjoyed that piece of information.

"I think our moms would be best buddies. She said my hair used to be my glory. Vivian loved it too. It felt so good to shave it off," Oksana said.

Annie leaned down so their foreheads were touching. "You have to put your shirt back on."

Oksana tilted her head up so their lips were touching. "Why?"

"Because we're having a serious conversation and you're making my butterflies horny."

"That's the point," Oksana whispered.

Annie looked at her a few moments longer. She wanted to talk more, but there was something irresistible about being near Oksana, and if she started stripping, it was hard to focus on much else. It was still early in the afternoon and Annie had to come up with a budget for a possible production trip to Paris.

Oksana leaned up a bit further and drew her tongue across Annie's bottom lip. "Let's go to bed."

"I have something to tell you first." A simple truth that Annie didn't think would matter until now. Oksana sat back, a wary look on her face. "My parents pay for my place too. I'm almost thirty. I have a good job and all I really pay for are my clothes and my food."

"That doesn't bother me," Oksana said. "I don't pay rent at Baba's."

"I know, but—"

"Annie, the cost of real estate in Southern California is outrageous. At best, I thought you rented this place at a deal. I never thought you were paying a mortgage on a house this size in Venice. I know reality TV doesn't pay that much."

"Oh." Annie hadn't anticipated Oksana to be so keen to that aspect of her situation.

"If things go south, like way south, just don't shut me out. Okay? Tell me what's going on. Tell me what to expect. That's what I couldn't stand about Vivian. It wasn't that her life wasn't a perfect fit for me. She never cared about me enough to let me in. She didn't give enough of a shit about me to just leave me alone."

"Or maybe she never cared about herself enough to go after what she really wanted," Annie said.

"Maybe." Oksana nodded toward the bedroom one more time. "I don't want to talk anymore. Let's go."

Annie stood and led the way down the hall, walking a bit slower when she felt Oksana's hand on her waist. Oksana undressed Annie as they made their way to her bedroom, leaving a trail of clothing in their wake.

Naked, Annie slid on top of the covers and waited for Oksana to follow. Annie rubbed her breasts as Oksana shucked out of her jeans, pinching her thick nipples to a peak.

"Are those for me?" Oksana asked as she crawled over Annie. She didn't wait for an answer. Instead, she went straight for Annie's lips.

They kissed slowly as Annie stretched out on her back. She let go of her chest and starting pawing along Oksana's skin. Their legs tangled together, a sweet pressure building in Annie's clit and nipples.

Oksana's fingers found Annie's pussy. She was wet, but not as wet as she wanted to be. Oksana was patient, caressing Annie's entrance, massaging her wetness out of her. She moved down Annie's body, licking and kissing her neck until she reached her breasts. She kissed along the top, licked in between the ripe curves. Annie's moans filled the room.

Annie could feel the temperature rising between her legs. Her heart was thumping. There was no need for comparisons anymore. There was no room for it. There was only Oksana.

Oksana pushed a finger inside and then another. Annie reached for her breast and held it up for Oksana to suck. Oksana traced the tip with her tongue, sucked it between her lips until Annie arched and moaned again. It took a while, longer than Annie anticipated for her to come, but she enjoyed the ride. Oksana had the perfect touch. Her kisses were still electric, but Annie couldn't seem to turn her mind off. She couldn't focus on her pleasure. All her senses were tuned to Oksana. The feel of *her* skin and the skill of her tongue. Annie wasn't chasing an orgasm, just more time with Oksana. She didn't want the afternoon to end.

It doesn't have to, she realized. They could be together. This wasn't part of the fantasy. They were together now, and all the wishes and dreams she'd had about Oksana had come true and doubled over into a rightness that couldn't be matched. There was nothing keeping them apart anymore.

Annie came, trembling beneath Oksana. Before she settled, she added her own fingers to the mix. She watched Oksana's eyes as she stroked her clit.

"Fuck me some more," Annie whispered.

Oksana obliged. She pulled her fingers out, just for a moment and traced Annie's swollen lips below her clit. She was soaked now, her juices coating her pussy and her ass. Annie sighed as Oksana plunged her fingers back in, deeper, twisting against and stroking the right spots. Annie couldn't hold her orgasm back this time. She came quickly and hard and nearly blacked out as Oksana drew her cum out of her. She squirted, just a little, but enough to make her jerk and cry out on the sheets.

It was ages before she opened her eyes. Oksana was still touching her with gentle strokes up and down her thighs with her other arm wrapped around her waist.

"Do you want me to get a strap-on?"

"No. Why?" Annie panted.

"I didn't know if you missed being fucked that way."

"I like your fingers just fine. Come here." Annie gripped Oksana's hips and motioned for her to move up the bed. She didn't stop until her knees were on either side of Annie's head. Annie latched on to Oksana's pussy with her mouth, drawing her wet lips in. She scraped her with her teeth, teased her with her tongue until Oksana started to move. Annie held on to her hips as Oksana rode her face. Her motions were fierce and jerking and some of the sexiest undulations Annie had ever experienced. She encouraged her. Annie cupped Oksana's ass, rocking her back and forth, probing her hole with the sweetness that was spread all around. She devoured every inch, hoping in the back of her mind that at some point she would be enough to heal what Vivian had done. Would anything be enough for that sort of repair?

Oksana spent into Annie's mouth and she swallowed every available drop. She orgasmed again, rolling her forehead against the wall as she screamed Annie's name. "Anne. Anne."

When her thighs couldn't take much more, Oksana collapsed beside Annie on the bed, breathless and blinking. She slid close to Oksana's still trembling body and stroked her hair.

"I think about you all the time," Annie whispered. She didn't know where the confession came from, but she wanted Oksana to know.

"I think about your dimples." Oksana touched her face as she smiled. A second later, she drifted off.

Annie left Oksana sleeping and snuck to the living room to grab her computer and her phone. There were two missed calls and a text. All from Shane.

❖

Two days later, Annie still hadn't answered Shane.

Annie stared at the texts—*Hey, where are you? I want to bowl. Call me. Call me bitch. Don't make me come over. Are you dead? Don't text me back if you are*—and didn't know how to respond. She wanted to tell Shane *and* Feather the truth, but in a spiteful way. She wanted Shane and her mother off her back. She wanted them to know the truth so they could get a head start on accepting the new person Annie had become, the person she was meant to be, and the person she was meant to be with. Annie had been avoiding Shane for over a week now, but she had to reply before Shane did something foolish like showing up at her house while Oksana was there.

"I'm sending Jewel to get Thai for lunch. You want anything?" Esther asked.

"Uh, yeah," Annie replied. Esther wrote down her order then glanced back up.

"I must say you are pretty ballsy, or you must have some serious faith in your trainer."

Annie froze with her hand on a stack of time sheets. "What do you mean?"

"I couldn't eat chicken Pad Thai and not have it go straight to my thighs. If Pace and I were getting married, I wouldn't eat for a year beforehand."

"Oh yeah. I'm not really worried about it. Oksana's a genius in the gym."

"Obviously." Esther chuckled as she walked out of their office.

Annie felt terrible. When she and Oksana were together, the rest of the world didn't exist. Annie was still happy, happier than when they first agreed to give each other a chance, but she was so tired of pretending her wedding was still going to happen.

She had to tell Shane and Feather the truth and her parents, but Jeff had to know first. Annie hadn't heard from him in a while. She expected she might not hear from him again until he got home. Clearly, he was having a blast. Annie couldn't decide whether that made things better or worse. Would Jeff remember this trip as the reason his engagement fell apart? If he hadn't taken the trip, Annie might never have been with Oksana. Would he blame himself for that? There was no way for Annie to know until they talked, and that conversation was still days away.

Annie couldn't avoid Shane that whole time. She dialed her number.

"Oh, hey. Finally taking calls, are you?" Shane said. She was pissed.

"Hey. Sorry, it's been kind of crazy at work. I was trying to catch up on sleep this weekend." Which was sort of true. She'd brought her computer back to bed, but as soon as she laid eyes on Oksana, she decided a cuddle nap was a better idea than working on a budget. They'd slept all afternoon, ordered pizza for dinner, then watched a documentary on the history of Africans in Latin America. Annie was starting to understand Oksana's love of history. It was pretty cool learning things about the world you never even considered before.

"Feather came out of the tipi. I took her for some real food and we went to the movies. You should have come. We decided what shoes we're going to wear and constructed a whole plot to kidnap you for your bachelorette party." Right, the shoes. Megan had mentioned they were all going to wear different shoes during the ceremony.

"I know. I'm sorry. What are you up to this weekend?" Annie cursed herself as soon as the words left her mouth. She already had plans this weekend.

"Nothing yet. You want to hang out?"

"Uh, yeah. Sergio got this new pilot green lit, so let me just make sure I don't have to be on set, but if not, it's me and you."

"And Megan and Feather. They miss you too. Let's do something before Jeff gets back."

"Yeah, okay. I'll let you know."

Shane seemed okay with that.

❖

A couple days later, Annie met Shane near her office. It was awkward and forced, but Shane was so busy chatting about the wedding she didn't seem to notice.

On Friday night, Annie told Shane she was sick.

On Saturday, she ignored her calls.

CHAPTER THIRTEEN

THE TRUTH

The doorbell rang, but that didn't stop Annie's pacing. She was ready. She hated to hurt Jeff. It still made her sick to think of breaking his heart, but things between them were over, and Annie had to tell him the whole truth.

Jeff had flown in that afternoon. He and the boys took a shuttle from the airport. Beyond getting back to his house and washing the Europe off his face, Jeff hadn't tried to make any official plans. He wanted to come over so they could catch up. He had stories, according to his last e-mail. The only other e-mail he'd sent during his trip, but Annie wasn't bothered by the lack of communication.

The last few weeks had been exceptionally good for her and Oksana. There were moments of awkwardness when the elephant in the room would make a strange noise and draw them both out of the haze of their deepening relationship. A call from Shane, Feather, or worse, Annie's mom, while they lounged on Baba's couch. A simple question from Kat about Annie's wedding dress.

When the beast was silent, though, Annie felt herself settling into this new life, a new partnership with Oksana that felt perfectly right. She had a new family of sorts in Kat and Baba Inna, who now included Annie in everything, and she'd grown closer to Noelle and Ronnie in that time too. She even had Megan's continued reassurance that she was doing the right thing when it came to

Oksana. Annie knew where she belonged, and now that Jeff had returned, she could close the door on that part of her life and start fresh. He didn't deserve to be disregarded, but Annie deserved to be happy, and that happiness came in a very specific form.

She would have to deal with the aftermath of any regular breakup and the questions that came once people discovered you were seeing someone else. There would be questions about Oksana, and the extremely annoying questions about what happened with her and Jeff. Annie refused to go into detail about either. But she would defend what she had with Oksana and defend what used to be with Jeff. It wasn't his fault; they simply weren't meant to be.

The back bell rang again. Annie had to answer it.

Oksana had offered her services in any way she could, but all Annie needed her to do was wait. Oksana hesitantly agreed, and for now, she was on standby for a call or a text from Annie that begged her to come and console. Hopefully, it wouldn't get to that.

By the time she made it to the backdoor, Annie was shaking. Her stomach was in a sour knot. If she'd had enough nerves to eat anything at work, she would definitely throw it up.

He knocked loudly, just as Annie reached for the knob.

"Hey," she said with a weak smile.

Jeff frowned at her for a moment. "Hey."

He stepped inside and wrapped his arms around her. The embrace was strange. He wasn't a hugger, but Jeff pulled Annie tightly against his chest, as if he were trying to memorize her frame. He smelled different. Not bad, but not good. Like unfamiliar cologne and spices. Summer was late and the breeze from the ocean made his odor somehow stronger. Annie wrinkled her nose to shake the scent as he pulled away, grateful he hadn't gone in for a kiss.

"Come on in." She looked him over as he walked into the mudroom. He looked like shit, exhausted. His hair was wet, but he was anything but refreshed. Dark bags shadowed under his eyes and his beard had gone from scruffy-chic to scraggly.

"You look different," Jeff said, still frowning.

"The glasses maybe?" She'd been wearing them a lot lately.

"No, it's something else." He touched her face. Annie did her best not to jerk her head away. It didn't feel right having anyone besides Oksana touch her like that anymore. "You look healthier."

"Oh. I put on some weight."

"That's probably it." Annie tensed as Jeff leaned in, but he planted a kiss on her forehead instead of her lips. At least his breath smelled fresh.

"Come on," Annie said. "Come sit down."

Jeff accompanied her to the living room, his arm loosely draped over her shoulder. She swallowed, praying he was too tired for any more affection.

As they sat, Jeff sighed and stretched out with his feet on the coffee table. His black boots looked new.

"How was your trip?" Annie slid back to the arm of the couch, just out of his reach. She shoved her hands in the pockets of her sweatshirt and turned the black ring box around. Annie thought about putting the engagement ring on the table, but that was a bit dramatic.

"It was good. Took lots of pictures. I got you some stuff, but it's over at my place. I'll bring it by later." Jeff looked her in the eye, and that's where Annie found her courage. She didn't feel the same about those brown eyes anymore. That love was gone.

"You all right? You're usually all over me," he said.

Annie let out a breath. "I have something to tell you."

"What's up?"

"I can't marry you."

"What do you mean you can't marry me?" he asked. "What happened?"

"I met someone."

"What?" Jeff's eyes flashed with shock.

"Just listen." She put up her hands. "I took advantage of our deal. I've told you how attracted I am to other women before."

"Yeah?" He edged forward.

"Well, I slept with someone while you were gone, per our agreement, and it turned into something more."

"Oh, is that all? So you fucked someone and now we're just done? You're just breaking up with me?" Jeff's voice steadily increased in volume as his anger seemed to build. She'd never seen him that pissed before.

"I didn't want to tell you over e-mail. It happened and it spiraled." Annie swallowed then delivered the final blow. "I love her, Jeff. And I want to be with her. I'm going to be with her."

She had yet to say those words to Oksana, but she realized them as she tried to explain their situation, so Jeff would understand that she was serious, she meant it. She was in love with Oksana.

Annie watched him while his eyes scanned the floor, back and forth along the edge of the rug. Then Jeff closed his eyes in the most painful way.

"Who is she?"

"I'm not sure I want to tell you. I promised her she wouldn't get dragged into this, between us I mean."

"What do you think I'm going to do? Beat her up?"

"Her name is Oksana. We met at the gym."

"You mean your trainer. You're fucking your trainer." Annie had never mentioned more than the fact that she had a trainer to Jeff, and he never asked anything about her. She thought, at least in his mind, Annie was just going to the gym. Great. As soon as she recognized her attraction for what it was, Annie remembered wanting to keep details of Oksana to herself, especially from Jeff. She had always been someone special, and telling Jeff about her would somehow draw him into their secret world of giggling on the treadmill.

"How did you know she's my trainer?"

"Taum. She asked me if I wanted Oksana to train me too. Is this why you wanted me to go away? Is this why you were all for me taking off for a month?"

"No, Jeff. It wasn't like that. I...I told you that I've been wanting to sleep with a woman for a while. Oksana and I, we didn't mean to, but we hit it off."

"Must have been really intense," he said with biting sarcasm.

"Jeff, I swear, it started off innocent. I thought I would have my fun. I thought you'd have your fun too. Sleep with some girls in Amsterdam, maybe Paris—"

"Yeah, because nothing says commitment like bringing home herpes from your bachelor party. I didn't sleep with anyone." Jeff paused, the eerie look coming to his face. He looked at the floor and then Annie again. "I bet you hoped I would so you wouldn't feel so bad. What's going on with your brain? Cheating on me and breaking up with me isn't innocent, Annie. If you wanted to fuck around you shouldn't have agreed to marry me."

"Jeff, I swear to God it wasn't like that." But he wasn't listening to her. He whipped out his phone and a few seconds later, shoved the display in her face. Annie stared at her favorite picture of Oksana. From the Elite Fitness website.

"That's her isn't it?" Jeff said with a cruel smirk on his face. He pulled the phone back and examined the picture some more. "The one your mom hired. Irony of ironies. It's very Hollywood of you I have to say. Having an affair with your trainer." Jeff examined the picture for a while. Annie watched the various expressions pass over his face and then the focused stare he got when he was examining the composition of a photo. "She's really pretty."

"She's beautiful," Annie said softly.

Jeff tossed his phone on the table with a thud that made Annie jolt in her seat. He slid back against the couch cushions and covered his eyes with his arm. Annie watched him for a long time, afraid to move. There was nothing more she could say; all of her words were coming out wrong. There was no way she could ask him to forgive her. It was too soon, or maybe too late.

"What are you thinking about?" Annie asked after a while.

"I'm wondering what the fuck you were thinking. What the fuck was I thinking? Fuck!" Jeff let his arm flop to the side. "Should have listened to Bran."

"Why? What did Brandon say?"

"He was with me when I bought your ring. He told me not to do it. He said you liked me, but you weren't in love with me."

"What the hell?"

"Don't, okay? He was right," Jeff said. "How do you know? We've been together for almost ten years. How do you know you're not just bored? How are you sure about this chick?"

"Oksana?"

"Yeah. You told me you wanted to be with other women, but I kinda thought you were joking or just being cute."

Annie shoved aside the snide remark that immediately popped into her head and answered him honestly.

"I was, in a way. The sex was a fantasy, and I think if it had been someone else, we would have just fucked and then I would have waited for you to come home. But she's different."

"I see that."

"It's not the tattoos or the hair."

"Or that she's black?"

"What?" Annie flinched in shock.

"She's black."

"She's mixed, and what does that have to do with anything?"

"What the fuck. Look at her and then look at yourself and your friends. Look at your fucking mom. Yeah, she'd fit right in. Megan the Ice Queen would call the cops on her before she was even able to introduce herself."

"Actually, she and Megan get along just fine."

"So Megan knew about this? That's fucking great."

Annie glanced at Jeff's discarded phone, thinking of exactly what he saw in that picture of Oksana and exactly what he didn't.

"You don't…you don't know her. She's an amazing person. Sweeter than me and all of my white friends combined."

"I didn't mean it like that," Jeff said. "I meant she's probably normal. She's probably not some elitist psycho like your mom or some hypocritical snob like Megan or Feather. She probably won't go for the bullshit your family and your friends would put her through."

"So what does that say about you? Are you like that and you've just been hiding it from me?"

"No, it means I don't give a shit about your mom and your friends. I loved you and I didn't let how much they fucking suck come between us. But, hey, let's hope your trainer feels the same way. Let's hope she wants to put up with Taum's shit just to see you happy."

"She will. She already has."

Jeff laughed.

"What? What's so funny?"

"I'm just thinking about Taum. She's going to flip the fuck out; you know that, right?"

"Yeah, I do, but I can handle it."

"Can you?"

"What…what do we do?"

"*We* don't do anything. I'm going to call my parents and my friends and let them know the wedding is off. You can tell your parents. I'm not sticking around for that conversation."

"Okay. And what about your apartment? You haven't lined up a sublease, have you?"

"No." Jeff suddenly looked guilty. "I never planned to. I need my studio. Married or not, I need my space."

Annie stared at him in disbelief. "Is that what you mean by love? Needing your space?" Had Jeff always been this cold? Was Megan right the whole time? Was Jeff really a distant asshole? Annie thought he was dry and pensive, but now she was starting to see it was something else entirely.

"Whatever. Use that if you want to blame me. I guess I'll be going. Can I have my ring back?"

Annie pulled the ring box out of her pocket and placed it in Jeff's hand. He grabbed for his phone and headed for the door.

"Jeff, wait."

"For what? What do you want from me?"

"Where are you going to go?"

"Do you really care?"

"Yes. I do. I still care about you." Annie wanted to punch herself for saying something so trite, but it was the truth. She didn't hate Jeff and she hoped he wouldn't leave this angry.

"Good luck, Annie. Really. And if you care about this chick at all, maybe you should fuck everything you see before she gets serious about you. Make sure you get all that shit out of your system before she falls in love with you."

Finally, the tears hit Annie's eyes. How had she messed this up so bad? "I'm sorry," she whispered.

"Thanks. So we're done now?"

Annie nodded.

"I wish you the best, Annie. Really. I hope she ends up being exactly what you wanted. If you even know what that is."

Jeff let himself out and Annie went straight to her bedroom. She texted Oksana before she flopped onto her covers.

He's gone was all she wrote.

The tears that ran down the sides of her face made no sense. She got exactly what she wanted. She and Jeff were through. She hated herself for doing it, but as she lay on her bed, all the good times in their relationship popped into her mind. She revisited all the moments Jeff had made her smile, how happy she had been just months before. The thought of what would have really happened if Oksana hadn't come into her life made her whole body want to clench in pain. She'd been tearing herself up over the idea of being dishonest with him, but now that she was free of Jeff, she found herself wanting to make things right between them. As if she could.

Still she wondered why it had been so easy for her to leave him. There was a distinct possibility that the Jeff Annie had spent the last seven years with was a Jeff she'd created in her head. She was happy with her job, she was happy with her friends, and Jeff never gave her any problems. Maybe the lack of fights was something Annie confused with chemistry. He was right, well, Bran was. She wasn't in love with him. She was comfortable and she was lazy and Jeff was agreeable.

She sighed heavily and sniffled as the sound of Billy Squier's "The Stroke" killed the silence of her room. She didn't have to check who it was.

"Hey." Annie couldn't have sounded more devastated.

"Do you want me to come over?" Oksana asked urgently. A bad idea. Annie didn't want Oksana to see her crying. She would think the tears were for all the wrong reasons, and some of the right reasons still might upset her.

"I need some time alone," Annie said.

"Did he do something to upset you?"

"Yes and no. I'm just drained. Can we talk about it tomorrow?"

The line was silent for a few seconds too long. When she replied, Oksana's voice was quiet. "Okay."

Great.

"Babe? I'm not shutting you out, I swear," Annie said. She meant it, but now wasn't a good time for them to be together. "Sana?"

"I'm here. I'll talk to you tomorrow." Oksana hung up before Annie could say good-bye.

Chapter Fourteen

The Element of Surprise

That's great, Willow. Just one more and you're done."
Oksana counted out the last fifteen reps of her weight set, wishing she could drag out the session. She wasn't in a hurry to see Annie.

Jeff was back, and from what she understood, Annie's relationship with him was officially over, but Oksana felt uneasy. They'd barely spent a day apart in the past few weeks and not seeing Annie, right after Annie saw her fiancé made Oksana feel slightly neurotic. Annie had called her that morning to ask Oksana to lunch, right after her session with Willow. She'd apologized over the phone as well. Oksana didn't entirely buy it.

She wanted to say no to the lunch invitation, give Annie a taste of her own at arm's length medicine. Acting like an adult, though, and not avoiding your significant other was the healthier alternative. Annie most likely wanted to pretend her quick apology was enough. That's what scared Oksana, that Annie hadn't recognized her hurt, that she had been so lost in her own struggles with her ex-fiancé that she hadn't considered that being in each other's arms was exactly what they needed.

Oksana wanted to be there when Jeff left. She wanted to be the last person Annie saw before she fell asleep. She wanted to do all she could to erase Jeff from Annie's mind. It was selfish, petty want, but Oksana had become attached to Annie and she was terrified that at some point during her conversation with Jeff, Annie was starting to reconsider her future with Oksana.

Be honest; you think Annie is coming over here to break up with you in person. That's exactly what you're worried about. But you're just being paranoid. She loves you and you need to accept that.

That was the truth. Annie needed some time to process her breakup with Jeff. Oksana thought about that concept. Her girlfriend needed time to get over her fiancé. It had been backward from the beginning. There were moments when Oksana wished she hadn't caved that day in the park. She should have made Annie wait, and later, when things had been handled in a proper order, Oksana would have agreed to go out on a date with her. Jeff would be an afterthought, not a hurdle. She'd given in and now she was falling in love with someone who was probably debating her own mistakes at this very moment.

Oksana felt the foolish need to dwell on all the ifs and whats until she came face-to-face with one Annie Collins. Willow's need for guidance brought her back down to Earth.

"Should I stretch?"

"Uh, yeah. Sorry." Oksana smiled at her own stupidity. She helped Willow rack her weights and guided her over to the mats to stretch. They sat facing each other, fingers gripped together as Willow did her best to press her head to her kneecap. Oksana absently admired her flexibility.

"Good thing we're finished. I'm not sure I could have kept your attention for another hour," Willow said.

"Ignore me. You're a pro at this stuff and you're right on track."

Willow had thirty pounds to shed and she was already halfway there. Much to the studio's and Oksana's delight, they might reach her goal ahead of the schedule.

"You have something on your mind?" Willow asked. Oksana tried to ignore the lustful concern in her eyes.

No direct sexual proposition had come from Willow yet. She kept a respectful physical distance, and though they never discussed it between them, Paulo admitted that Willow had asked about Oksana's relationship status. The ass told her Oksana was sort of seeing someone. "Sort of" didn't stop Willow from flirting, constantly commenting on Oksana's smile or her eyes. A lot of clients flirted, but Oksana could tell Willow would go in for the full-on kill if she returned her affections even the slightest bit.

Things weren't perfect at the moment, but Annie was definitely on Oksana's mind and the sole occupant of her heart. Oksana had the feeling Willow wasn't going to give up until their last session. Willow was sexy and smart. She seemed genuine and reasonably grounded for a movie star. On another planet Oksana might give her a chance, but in the here and now, she was not interested.

"You could say that. Same time next week?" Oksana held out her hand to pull Willow off the mats.

"You want to talk about it? I'm an excellent listener and you see these shoulders? Great for crying on."

"I'll be fine. Thanks for the offer."

"Well, can I interest you in some lunch? A low-calorie lunch of course." Willow must have felt the countdown on the professional relationship ticking somehow faster. She'd never been this aggressive.

Oksana forced a smile and casually straightened her shoulders. "I actually have lunch plans, but make sure *you* drink plenty of water."

Willow laughed and shook her head dismissively.

"There is nothing funny about hydration."

"You're just so professional."

"It's my job." Oksana smiled back. She waited for Willow to grab her bag, then led her toward the front of the gym. Paulo's client kept up his leg presses as he stared Willow down from across the room.

"How serious is it?" she asked.

"How serious is what?"

"This relationship you're in."

Oksana hesitated to answer because there was Annie, standing outside Paulo's office. A bright smile lit up her face the second she saw Oksana coming in her direction. Oksana wanted to be crabby about the night before, give Annie at least five minutes of the cold shoulder, but Annie looked so adorable and so happy to see her and at the same time so exhausted, Oksana couldn't bring any sort of grudge to the surface.

"It's pretty serious," Oksana said.

Annie ignored Willow. "Hi. Paulo said it was cool if I waited here."

"It is. Willow, this is my girlfriend, Annie."

"Nice to meet you," Willow said. Oksana would have believed her sincerity if she wasn't sizing Annie up as if there were some sort of competition.

Willow turned to Oksana, the expression on her face business-like and friendly. Oksana returned the look with a professionally firm handshake. "I'll see you tomorrow and I'll remember, plenty of water."

When she was gone, Annie slipped her hand into Oksana's palm. Oksana had the sudden urge to cry, but Annie's smile kept that urge at bay.

"God, she's gorgeous," Annie said. "Is she still trying to get with you?"

"No, I think she's just blurring the line of friendly. Where are we going?"

"Car picnic?" Annie shrugged expectantly.

"Okay..."

Oksana followed Annie out to her Prius. They drove a few blocks away and stopped in front of a heavily shrubbed ranch house off Melrose. It was a perfect spring day. The sun was out and the street was quiet. Oksana dreaded what Annie had to say.

Once she put the hybrid in park, Annie reached behind Oksana's seat and pulled out a green and blue gift bag.

"This is for you."

Oksana peered inside. Ruffles of tissue paper hid what goodies accounted for the heavy weight. This time she did a shitty job at keeping the emotion from her face.

"Is it too much?" Annie asked.

"No, I'm just wondering if it's a bribe. Did you do something wrong?"

"Gasp. I would never! Give it back."

"No." Oksana chuckled. "I at least want to see what it is." She reached inside and pulled out a large purple dildo. One end was adequately long and thick enough for her tastes. The other end curved up into a short, bulbous nub. Underneath the toy she found a large jar of organic honey and a turkey wrap from Whole Foods.

"I'm not trying to buy you with presents, but I figured honey was a good way to apologize to a bear."

"And this?" She cocked her head to the dildo in her hand. "I thought you didn't want me to get a strap-on."

"I don't. This is for you. It's the biggest one they had. I just figured it would be easier for me to use since I've never strapped up before." Annie giggled. "The lady at the store said it was the best in double dildo technology. We could use it together?"

Okay, that's enough. She's sorry. She's begging. Give her a break.

Oksana leaned over and kissed Annie's lips. "Very thoughtful of you. Thanks." She sighed and brushed Annie's bangs away from her glasses. "I was pissed you didn't want me over last night, but I understand. You and Jeff had a tough talk and you needed a breather."

"I did, but it would have been nice to see you. I'm sorry." Annie went on to tell Oksana everything she and Jeff had talked about. In a way, she was shocked he hadn't flipped out even more. She was also overjoyed that Jeff hadn't taken Annie's mother up on her offer for the free gym membership.

"I didn't want you to think I was upset over him," Annie told her. "I was upset with how I've been living my life and how much I took for granted. But this morning I remembered if I hadn't agreed to marry Jeff I would have never met you, and I would have no one to tell me that I have no business speaking anything but a particular Southwestern dialect of English."

"So it was fate, you're saying?" Oksana smiled at the idea.

"I'm saying I want to spend my life with you, and even if it took a while, I don't care how we ended up together. I'm just glad that we did. I don't belong with Jeff, and I would have never been a part of his family and he never would have been a part of mine. He was never going to give up his loft. That's not how I envisioned married life."

"How did you see it?"

"Lots of food and tattoos. And I've always wanted a big slobbering dog."

Suddenly, the Prius wasn't big enough. They should have taken the Tahoe. Oksana wanted to drag Annie into the backseat to show her just how grateful she was for divine intervention. She kissed Annie again, this time tasting every part of her tongue, moaning as the heat spiked between her legs.

Annie panted as they came up for air. Oksana gasped just the same. She would give anything to blow off the rest of the day so they could spend it together. She welcomed Annie's hand into her lap, squirming a little until Annie's fingers were nestled between her thighs.

"When are you going to tell your parents?"

"Sunday. I'm going home so I can tell my parents in person. Do you want me to tell them about you? I'm only asking because they aren't going to be happy about my sudden switch in the batting order. I don't want you thrown into the fray if you'd rather be left out of it."

There were certain truths about a person's life that should never be kept a secret. Who you love was one of those truths. If Oksana were to ask, not only would Annie tell her parents that she was in a committed relationship with another woman, complete with hot lady-on-lady sex, but if Oksana wanted to be there for the coming out conversation, Annie wouldn't hesitate to bring her along.

"Don't tell them yet."

"You're sure?"

"Yeah. Ending the engagement is between you and Jeff and your family. Let your parents adjust to one shock before you bring up another."

"How are you so understanding?" Annie asked.

"Even though I'm still a little pissed that you wouldn't let me come comfort you, I'm not so proud that I *need* you to come out to them this week. I want this to work, and that kind of bombshell will change the whole climate of this situation."

Oksana leaned into Annie, kissing her just as the words left her lips. Annie withdrew her fingers from Oksana's lap and gently gripped her waist to deepen the caressing of their tongues. She slid her hand between Annie's legs and chuckled lightly as Annie seemed to melt under her touch and her Russian pronunciation. She rubbed with a rough thrust against the seam of Annie's jeans. Annie slid lower in the seat and let her knees fall open. Sensing Annie's impending surrender, Oksana kissed small circles around the soft skin of Annie's neck. Annie shuddered.

"Can I ask what you're doing?"

Oksana moved closer, letting the center console support her elbow. "Giving you something to think about for the rest of the day."

"You want me to go back to the office with cum-soaked panties."

"No. That would be awful."

Oksana continued with her fingers, rubbing Annie harder and harder through her pants until her hips started to pump back and forth on the seat. Annie gripped her shoulder, her low whimpers filling the car that was starting to overheat.

"Crack your window," Oksana said.

"There's an old man watching us."

Oksana's head darted up. She glanced around several times. When all she saw was an unattended mailbox and a crow hopping in the middle of the street, Annie burst out laughing.

"Just for that." Oksana reached over her and yanked the lever for the back of Annie's seat. She dropped back with a shriek, the perfect position for Oksana to pounce on her. She tore at the button on Annie's jeans and shoved her hand into her underwear. Annie's shrieks turned into deep moans as Oksana's fingers rubbed against her damp clit.

"Still think it's funny?"

"Yes! Oh my God. Keep doing that."

With a slight adjustment of her wrist, Oksana slid two fingers into Annie's wet pussy. Annie's whole body went rigid for a moment before she began to writhe and thrust against Oksana's hand. She matched the intensity below with a heated kiss, driving her tongue past Annie's lips, matching her whimpers with her own pleading moans.

Oksana's body caught up with the rhythmic wave of Annie's motions. Her own arousal consumed her every thought until Annie fell to pieces. Oksana shivered as she felt Annie's pussy contracting around her fingers, soaking them further with her sweet cum. Annie came again almost immediately, riding out the second orgasm with a low grunt that echoed in Oksana's ears.

She watched a sudden peace come to Annie's face even though her dimpled cheeks were still high with color. She eased her down, still petting and stroking her cunt and kissing her face.

"Holy shit, I can't breathe," Annie panted as she finally rolled down her window. Oksana settled back and examined the sandwich Annie had brought her while Annie adjusted her pants.

"What about you?"

Oksana held up the gift bag with a grin.

"I'll wait for later."

❖

Sergio was such a dick, and thanks to his thick skull, Annie was an hour late picking up Oksana. Her jerk boss wouldn't listen to Annie's professional opinion, the one he'd hired her for, when she told him there was no way to draw extra money for an episode of *Single Dads*. The audience favorite and father of twin girls, Ian, wanted their office to pay for an unscheduled trip to visit his brother in Florida. Annie was all for family reunions, but Ian and his brother got along great. There was no drama between them to catch on tape. The network would love to see a poor young guy struggling to manage twin toddlers through LAX, but there had to be an explosive altercation on the other end of the flight for them to foot the bill. Ian was going on a calm family vacation, nothing that would boost the show's ratings.

Sergio had dragged her into his office just as she as trying to make her escape. Baba offered to be on Kat duty for the night. Annie wanted to get Oksana back to her place, fed and naked as soon as possible. She wanted to try out Big Purple. As soon as Sergio shut the hell up and remembered it was Friday, there were no weekend shoots, and there was absolutely no reason for Annie to be sitting on the other side of his desk.

"I don't see why we can't borrow the money from Meta and her bullshit show."

Annie frowned at Sergio. He knew the procedure. He would have to call the network to approve a budget extension. Borrowing from one show to feed another was basically stealing.

"I'd like to keep my job. And even if we could 'borrow' the money, there isn't any left from *Just Dance*. I barely scraped the Paris trip together, and we still have fewer hands than I would like." Tension between Meta and Lauren was still high. Annie wanted to send Esther along to keep them from each other's throat, but between airfare, hotel, and meals, another crew member wasn't in the budget. Sergio knew this.

"You want *that* footage," Annie reminded him. "Can you imagine drunk Meta loose on Paris? You want that. You don't want to waste tape on Ian's brother playing with his nieces. If Ian wants to see his brother on tape, then book *his brother* a cheap flight on Southwest out here."

"Why didn't you say that before?"

"I did. Twice!"

"All right. All right. Get out of here. I'll have Esther arrange it. Where's Esther?"

Annie grabbed her laptop bag off the floor and heaved it over her shoulder.

"She had some birthday party to go to. I sent her home. Why are you still here?"

"Meeting the wife on this side for dinner."

"Well, I really need to go."

"Your man's back, isn't he?"

"Yeah." Annie looked down at her phone to avoid Sergio's gaze. Just a few more days and this whole crazy situation would be over with.

"Don't pull a muscle."

"You're gross. Have a good weekend." She booked it for the elevator before he decided he had some other pointless thing to discuss. She texted Oksana three times as she went. Once to say she was on her way and twice to apologize for running late.

❖

Annie almost dropped her keys and the food in her hand. Oksana's tongue tickled the edge of her earlobe and her free hand cupped her breast. Her other hand carried a certain gift bag. Annie was starving, but sex would have to come first, if she could convince Oksana that dinner could wait.

"Hurry. I'm hungry," Oksana whispered, grinding her hips against Annie's ass, pushing her closer to the back door.

"You don't mind your food cold?"

"No, I don't. I want you inside me."

Annie almost broke her keys off in the lock. They stumbled into the kitchen. Annie dumped the food on the counter and spun in Oksana's arms. She wanted to take this little interlude to the couch, get Oksana naked, upright, and exposed so Annie could devour her. She slid her hands up the front of Oksana's T-shirt. The cotton easily gave way to her wandering fingers, and in no time her bra was pushed up and out of the way.

Annie licked at Oksana's neck and gently teased her piercings.

"I want these nipples."

"They're yours," Oksana replied.

In the darkness, Annie guided her through the archway and back toward the couch, realizing a moment too late that they weren't alone. Annie froze.

"What's wrong?" Oksana asked.

"There's someone here—"

The lights flicked on. Annie screamed then bit down on her lip as she smacked heads with Oksana. They both stumbled a step apart.

Taum Collins stood in her living room. A beige Pomeranian Annie had never seen before panted happily in a pink shoulder carrier under her arm. Taum had been hitting the tanning beds hard, and it was pretty clear she'd been blasted with a fresh injection of Botox. Her lips were too tight and her eyes were strained, but her emotions were clear.

The bile in Annie's throat shot to the roof of her mouth as she looked at her mother. Out of the corner of her eye, Annie saw Oksana adjusting her shirt and her bra, but Annie didn't take her eyes off Taum or the dog.

"Mom."

"Hi, honey," Taum said, her tone oddly light.

"What are you doing here?"

"I talked to Jeff this morning; I just called him to see when he and the boys would be ready for their next fitting. You know Europe either makes you fat or skinny, but you're never the same." Her mother had never been to Europe. "He told me you were seeing someone else. Actually, he said you were sleeping with your trainer. The slut he named was pretty high on your list of priorities so I wanted to come see for myself how much of his story was true. *You* are something." She glared at Oksana.

Annie knew exactly what her mother was thinking. Throughout her childhood, she'd stood by as Taum and her friends made racist and derogatory comments about all sorts of people. At the time, Annie knew her mother's thinking was beyond flawed. She went out of her way to be a different type of person and now she was terrified of just what her mother would say to Oksana.

She looked back to Annie.

"You picked *this* over Jeff?"

Annie could feel her neck tensing. "It wasn't a matter of picking. Jeff and I aren't meant to be."

"That's not what he thinks. He's very upset, but if I can talk some sense into you, he's willing to take you back." Annie would kill him. The second her mother left, she was going downtown and she was going to murder Jeff.

"We have a reputation to uphold. Your father and I work very hard, Annie, and you can't think we can push Jeff aside and parade a tattooed, pierced, bald, black—oh, I'm sorry. Jeff pointed out the distinction for me. You're mixed. And a former porn star at that. Nice touch."

"Oh my God, Mom! Stop!" Annie cried. Her whole body was shaking. Beside her, she could feel the tension rising off Oksana. She leaned back on her heels and Annie prayed she didn't snap and try to slap Taum or run away.

"Why should I? Does she have any idea where you come from? Who your family is?"

"Who are we, Mom?" Her mother was a nobody and her father was just another faceless suit who traded numbers all day.

"We're better than this. I know that much."

"I'm going to go wait in the kitchen." Oksana said.

"No, you should hear this. I talked to your boss this afternoon," she told Oksana. "He's going to talk to you."

That was enough. Annie stepped forward and put herself between Oksana and Taum, turning her back on her mother.

"I'll talk to him, okay? He knows the truth. I'll talk to him." Annie could see it in her eyes; Oksana didn't believe her.

"Doesn't matter. He's letting her go, and she's paying for every single one of your workouts. Sweetheart, you and Jeff can make this work. He still loves you."

Annie faced her mother. "That's too bad. He might have failed to mention this to you, but I made it very clear that I love Oksana. I don't love him. I don't care how it makes you and Dad look. I'm not marrying him!"

"You are. I'm not letting you throw away all of my hard work. There is no way I can change the date at the club or get the deposit back. And there is no way I'm telling *my* friends my daughter is a lesbian involved with *that*. Say good-bye to your little friend. Actually…" Taum paused. Oksana stilled in her retreat with one foot moving toward the kitchen. "Keep her. Every good marriage has its slut on the side. Just ask your father."

"Mom!" Annie charged at her mother. She grabbed Taum's arm and yanked her out of the room. She dragged her with all her strength down the hall, into the kitchen. The little dog yapped the entire way.

"What the hell do you think you are doing? Get off me."

Annie heard the slap of Taum's hand against her face a split second before she felt it. Recoiling, she fell against the stove. Her mother had never lifted a hand to her ever.

"Six weeks. If I have to drag you down the aisle by your hair, you are marrying Jeff. And I promise, if you don't cooperate, you will regret it and so will she." Taum straightened her top and patted the dog on the head, making cooing noises until it settled down. When the little demon pooch was happy and licking the palm of her hand, she peered up at Annie. Annie held her cheek, her eyes watering from the throbbing sting, and watched as her mother pulled a green plated key out of her pocket and put it on the kitchen table. The emergency spare key she'd given Feather.

"I won't tell your father about this. I'm meeting with the caterer tomorrow morning. And I'm hiring you a new trainer. You look fat." Taum glanced toward the living room. "Call me when she knows her place. Or when it's over. Whatever. But you should apologize to your friends. You really hurt Feather's feelings."

Annie blinked, then flinched when her mother stepped closer to her side. Taum patted her hair the way she'd patted the dog's fur.

"Be a lesbian. I don't care. Just keep it under wraps. Don't...I don't know. Don't become a dyke."

After another assuming pat and an air kiss, Taum walked out the front door.

Oksana held the ice pack to Annie's cheek. Her own eyes started to sting as the tears continued to leak from Annie's eyes.

"How does it feel?" She pulled the pack away and checked the red spot before reapplying the pressure. She heard the slap Mrs. Collins laid on Annie from across the house. It took everything she had not to smack the lady down for hitting her. The last thing Oksana needed was to get arrested for assault on the weather-beaten shoe of a woman.

"It feels better. The ice is helping," Annie said. "I don't know who told her about your Ink Ladies pictures. I didn't tell anyone."

"Don't worry about it. That's the curse of the Internet. Once it's out there, it's out there."

Annie was quiet then. Oksana didn't want to speak. She couldn't help the things that were running through her head, mostly what Mrs. Collins had said and a few things in particular that came from Annie's lips.

"Sana."

"What is it, babe?" Oksana gently stroked Annie's jaw.

"I meant what I said to my mom. I love you. I didn't mean to tell you like that. I wanted it to be special, but I wanted to wait until I dealt with the wedding stuff. I wanted a clean slate so you knew what I was saying was real," Annie said. Her lip started trembling. "You can't believe anything *she* said…I…I…"

"Shh. Stop." Oksana leaned forward and kissed Annie on her lips. "Stop crying. Okay?"

Annie nodded, but the tears still flowed.

"I love you too. I was waiting for the same reasons. Jeff has always been between us and *I* wanted to wait until I had you all to myself. I love you."

"I can't believe she said that to you." Annie shook her head.

"She didn't. She said it to *you* because she was trying to hurt you. I don't know her. I know you and I love you and she was trying to hurt you so you'd let me go."

"Well, I'm not going to," Annie replied.

"I didn't think you would."

Annie took the ice pack from Oksana and sunk into a chair at the kitchen table. "I have to call Megan. And Feather. I'm going to fucking kill her. This is hers." Annie held up a loose key.

Oksana went to join her, hopefully to work out some kind of plan for the rest of the evening, but her phone vibrated in her back pocket. She took it out and stared at the display. It was Paulo.

"Fuck." She wasn't ready for this. Her senses were still humming from their run-in with Mrs. Collins. She knew this was just the eye of the shit storm. She wasn't ready to pass through to the other side.

"Who is it?" Annie asked as Oksana cursed again.

"Hold on. Hello?"

"What the fuck is going on? I'm standing in line at Pantages about to get my *Wicked* on and some crazy ass bitch calls me screaming about how she's going to sue Elite Fitness if Annie Collins isn't bride ready and in Orange County on July thirtieth. Please tell me what the fuck is going on and make it quick. I do not want to miss the opening number."

"Short version, we got busted before Annie could tell her parents on her own."

"Great. Well? Do you still want your job?"

"Uh, of course I do."

"Fine. I'll deal with her. I'm guessing this is the last time this will happen. No other clients look good to you?" Paulo was pissed, but he was making his point. This was her one fuck up, the one major headache she could give him.

"Yes. This is it."

"Okay. Tell Annie I said hi and that better be the best pussy you've ever had in your entire life. Golden ticket vagina, Oksana."

"It is." She snorted so inappropriately. "It's more than that. I'll see you tomorrow."

"Yeah. Bye," Paulo muttered.

Annie looked at Oksana with her big, sad eyes as she hung up her phone. "It's fine. He let me off with a warning."

"Are you sure?" Annie made a face and then her finger flew to her face. "Shit, that hurts." Oksana crossed the room and squatted in front of Annie.

"Here. Now, what do you want to do?" Oksana asked as she put the ice pack back on Annie's cheek.

"I have to—"

"That's not what I asked. What do you want to do? What do the butterflies want?"

"I don't deserve you." That irritated Oksana. She leaned back, taking Annie gently by the shoulders.

"Why would you say that? Don't let other people get in your head like that, okay? I love you. This isn't about deserving anything."

"What if calling Paulo isn't enough? What if she tries to hurt you more? What about Kat and Baba?"

"Kat doesn't have my restraint. She would fistfight your mom. And Baba is always packing a blade and she's got quality aim with a thirty-eight. Don't worry about us." Annie's weak smile was a welcome change. "So tell me. I still have a job. You still have me. What would you like to do?"

"I'm pretty hungry. And there's plenty of crap to watch on TV."

"Go get changed for bed and I'll get the food ready."

Annie stood and reached for Oksana's hand. The pink on her cheek was growing darker. "You want to come?"

"Give me a sec. I'll be right there."

"Okay."

Oksana braced herself against the counter and let out a long, shaky breath. Holy shit, that woman was crazy. Oksana's mother was cold. Really fucking cold and she was pretty sure heartless, but Mrs. Collins was on a new level of crazy. She was really going to try to force Annie to marry someone she had no interest in. Never mind what she had said about Oksana. She didn't want to give those cruel words any credence. Mrs. Collins was one of those women Oksana liked to pretend didn't exist. She ran into all sorts of snobby rich types through the gym, but none of them had ever had the balls to speak about Oksana that way, to her face.

Oksana knew who she was and she loved that person and she hated that Mrs. Collins's words were able to penetrate that confidence even the slightest bit. Oksana saw finally that part of her had wanted Annie's family to approve of her. She knew they wouldn't, especially from the way Annie explained her relationship with them. Still, she hoped they could see that Oksana was good for Annie. She hoped they would care that she made Annie happy, even if she didn't come in the ideal package. But Annie's happiness wasn't a factor in Mrs. Collins's plans. She was all about appearances and her own bizarre standards. The plastic strain on Mrs. Collin's face made Oksana feel a little better though, and even more thankful for her own family. All three of them would have to be there for Annie as she made her way through this swamp of bullshit.

"Sana?"

"I'm coming."

Oksana walked down the hall to Annie's bedroom. She was changed already, in loose sweats and a perfectly tight T-shirt that showed off her tits. She kissed Annie again and took a few seconds to play with her nipples through the cotton of her shirt before she took the pair of shorts Annie offered and slid out of her bra and her jeans. They lounged on the couch for a while, picking at their food and watching *Predator* until Annie drifted off. Oksana rubbed Annie's legs, trying not to think of all the ways their night had gone so wrong. They'd have to save that big purple cock thing for another time.

Sometime later, Annie's phone vibrated between them. Oksana checked the display in case it was a call from work.

It was a text from Feather. *Sorry, but you should have told me the truth.*

"Who is it?" Annie yawned and snuggled closer.

"No one, baby. Go back to sleep."

CHAPTER FIFTEEN

THE PERFECT DAY TO MOVE

At least ten times in the next week, Annie considered changing her phone number. There were calls and texts she didn't want to take and a million more calls she didn't want to make.

Every day Taum would call. Annie made the mistake of answering just once. Taum went on about things being settled with the caterers. She also gave Annie the name of two more trainers before Annie hung up on her as politely as she could. That didn't stop her mother from leaving voice mails, each more threatening and unhinged than the last.

"Your bridesmaids are cooperating. Why can't you?"

"Jeff's parents don't need to know about this. If you'll just call him we can get on with things."

"Call me back, Annie. I don't want to come back up there."

Annie had no clue how she was supposed to respond. How do you speak rationally to someone who refuses to address reality? It would be a balmy sixty degrees in hell the day she walked down the aisle to Jeff, but silence was the only way she could get her mother to see that. If Taum was crazy enough to see the ceremony through, then fine. Annie would make sure all the guests knew she wouldn't be there, and after one e-mail, she was finally able to confirm that Jeff wouldn't be there either. He was still pissed at her, but he knew they were officially done and he wasn't interested in playing Taum's insane games any more than Annie was. Taum could throw her huge wedding, and she and Feather, and maybe Shane and a few of her parents' clueless friends would be the only ones to show up. Annie hoped they would enjoy the cake.

When Taum wasn't lighting up her phone, there were texts from Feather, each more and more insulting and pathetic than the last.

I think you owe some people an apology. Including me.

You should have told me.

Why didn't you tell me?

I don't care if you're gay.

So you're just ignoring me now?

Please, Annie. Call me. I'm not mad at you anymore. Neither is Shane.

I miss you. Call me.

Annie didn't give a shit about how Feather felt. After a little investigative work on Megan's part, Annie learned that Jeff was only a small cog in the machine that had lead Taum into her living room that night. Feather had coughed up the spare key to her house. She'd also done her own research from what Jeff and Taum knew about Oksana. All it took was one glimpse at Oksana's Elite Fitness profile and Feather remembered Oksana from the Ink Ladies photos. Feather had told Taum that Annie was involved with some sort of deviant slut whose photos and videos Feather had viewed and, Annie assumed, masturbated to plenty of times. Feather was a traitor, a hypocrite, and a shitty friend.

Shane was a little annoyed that Annie and Megan had left her out of the loop, but Feather had been the fink. Even if Feather apologized to Oksana's face and offered to be her personal slave for the rest of her natural life, Feather wouldn't be hearing from Annie for a very long time.

When she wasn't avoiding her mom and her friends, Annie took what free moments she had to contact all of their guests. Most felt sorry for her, as if Jeff had dumped her. Others tried to hide their annoyance and failed. There were calls and e-mails from Jeff's family and friends too. Some were shocking, like a Facebook message she'd received from a random buddy of his calling Annie a whore. Annie spoke with Jeff's mother briefly. She wasn't amused by all the trouble Annie had caused, but she understood that Annie and Jeff had parted ways. Jeff's sister had a few choice things to say. Her voice mail was short but to the point.

"My brother dodged a bullet. Thanks." That message hit home.

Annie had hoped she would find some sort of refuge in Oksana's arms and in the warmth of Baba's home, but all of it was taking its toll on their relationship. At first Oksana sat with Annie while she made some of these calls, but after the fourth, "I'm so sorry...no, we both thought it was best," Annie could no longer handle the subtle way Oksana's body would tense beside her. She couldn't ignore the number of times Oksana excused herself for a drink or to use the bathroom. When Annie asked for a few days just to straighten things out with their guests, Oksana didn't argue. Annie couldn't wait for it all to be over.

At work, people tiptoed around her, afraid she would have some sort of abandoned bride meltdown. She told Esther the whole story and gave her permission to spread it as office gossip. Sergio bought her a bottle of tequila to express his condolences. She planned to take a few shots that night before she made the last of her calls. Hopefully, Oksana would come over after she sobered up.

Annie looked up at Jewel who was loitering in her doorway.

"You need something?" Annie asked.

"You have a package." A short man in a suit appeared behind Jewel.

"Ms. Collins?" The short man stepped into her office. He was all business.

"Yes?"

"This is for you." He handed Annie an envelope and a set of new keys.

"What is this?"

"Have a good day." He nodded and disappeared out the door. Annie could feel Jewel and Esther watching her with concern, but she ignored them. She tore into the envelope. A handwritten note from her mother was paper clipped to a letter from her parents' attorney.

Let me know when you come to your senses, the note read. Annie flipped to the first page of the letter. Her eyes skipped over certain lines as her brain refused to process what the letter was saying. Words like "forfeit" and "property" and phrases like "effective immediately" and "storage unit" stood out. Her eyes went to the top of the missive and she read the whole thing again, still holding out for the real message to come through in some hidden lines she simply couldn't see. It was a joke. Or just a push. It wasn't real.

"Tell Sergio I had an emergency," she told Esther as she gathered her things.

"Okay. What's going on?"

Annie just shook her head. "I have to go." Jewel was smart and jumped out of her way.

The drive back to Venice was a blur, the type of sightless, automatic trip that made Annie wonder how she'd avoided an accident. When she pulled up to her house, Annie knew something was off by the look of her garage. The door was down and padlocked shut. She hopped out of her car then walked toward the lock, looking at the shiny brand new metal screwed into the weathered wood. Still Annie didn't completely believe the contents of the letter. She tried her normal keys in the backdoor. They didn't work. As they shouldn't. The deadbolt was new. She found the same problem greeted her at the front door. Those locks were also new.

Annie peered through the front window because there were no curtains to stop her. Her furniture was gone. Her TV, her rugs. The house was bare. She looked some more, as if her things would magically appear. When they didn't, she dropped down on the front steps. Annie gripped her purse in her lap thinking she could read the words in the letter through the leather and the lining. Her mother had taken back possession of the house, and all of Annie's things, the items she'd paid for on her own, were now a few miles away in a storage locker. It had to be a small locker.

Annie's mind was racing. What had her mother done? Had movers staked out Annie's house before the sun came up? Had they waited for her to leave before they robbed her of her home? They must have been a pretty efficient bunch to clean her out that fast.

The sun wasn't even close to setting. She had to get her clothes at least. She had to find some place to stay.

Annie called her father.

She got him after a quick conversation with his secretary, a new woman who didn't know he had a daughter. She tried not to take that as a sign.

"Richard Collins."

"Dad?"

"Yes, Annie."

"Where am I supposed to go?"

"I don't know. I'm not sure exactly what you and your mom discussed, but your mother and I decided you are old enough to take care of yourself." Her father sounded like he was already bored with the conversation. That was when her pulse started thudding in her ears. She could barely breathe.

"I know, I…I…can." She could. She could find her things. She could find a new place to live. Everything would be fine. "This is all because I won't marry Jeff?"

"I have no feelings for Jeffery either way, but I do not approve of this new person. I will not support any life you have with her."

Annie forgot all about her things then. "Dad, I love her. Why can't you and Mom see how much that matters?"

"Perhaps the same way you can't see how reckless your behavior has been. I'm sure Megan or one of your friends will help you out. Though if this woman cares about you enough to come between you and Jeffery and enough to risk her job, then I don't see why she would have a problem taking care of you."

"Dad—"

"Annie, I have let you do exactly what you have wanted to do for years. I thought you would come around, maybe even do something respectable with your education, but I see that you don't take yourself seriously. You work in a ridiculous medium and call it a career, but you can't even afford your lifestyle. I knew I'd wasted my money on sending you to film school, and I see I've wasted more money on this wedding. Now, I want you to pay for your own selfish decisions."

"What about Mom and her dogs and that stupid store?"

"Her store is paying for itself. Unlike you, your mom understands that her actions have consequences. I wanted grandchildren, Annie, not a permanent girlfriend of yours with a pornographic history I'll have to explain to my partners. You've hurt your mother and you've embarrassed me and yourself."

"So this is it? You're disowning me?" It wasn't a matter of choosing between Oksana and her family. Her parents had already made that decision for her.

"I'm giving you a chance to grow up. This way your bad decisions are your own. I'd like you to recognize that you can't just make certain decisions because of how you *feel*. Maybe when you see that things like money and class matter, you won't be so careless."

Annie stared blankly at the ground, watching it blur behind her tears.

"You have the unit until the end of the year. Hopefully, it won't take you that long to get yourself together."

"Okay," she murmured.

"Good-bye."

Oksana was close to rubbing her head raw. She hadn't heard from Annie in almost a full twenty-four hours. That wasn't like Annie. Oksana called and left messages and she texted, but she hadn't heard a word back. Her next move was stopping by Annie's office and then her house.

She didn't think she'd done anything crazy like challenging Feather to a duel, but shit happened. Like car accidents and wildfires. And then there were the lasting effects of a Hurricane Mrs. Collins. Oksana was over all this shit with the guests and Annie feeling guilty that she'd called things off. Still, she couldn't help but picture Annie lying on her couch, crying in a fetal position over something some insensitive relative or fair-weather friend had said about her leaving Jeff. She had to know Annie was okay. As soon as she dropped Kat at home.

She took her change from the drive-thru window and handed Kat her soda. Her craving for nuggets had given Baba the night off from cooking. As Oksana pulled into traffic, her phone started buzzing in her lap.

"Hey, grab that for me." Kat hit accept and held the phone up to Oksana's ear.

"Hello?"

"Hey. It's Megan."

A deep chill ran through Oksana's skin. "Is she okay? Is she with you?"

"Yeah. She's at my place. You should come over."

"Text me your address. I'm on my way."

Minutes later, she was pulling up to Megan's apartment building. She parked in a red zone across the street with explicit instruction to Kat to watch the car.

"I got it. Just go get Annie." That was Oksana's only plan.

The doorman let her into the building, and after a quick conversation with the concierge, she was buzzed up to Megan's apartment. The door opened as soon as she knocked. Megan looked exhausted.

"Hey. She's in here." Oksana followed Megan to her living room where she found Annie crying in a fetal position on the couch. She was in some sweats that didn't belong to her. The legs and sleeves were too long. Oksana slid into the cushions beside her, pulling Annie's feet into her lap. They hadn't spent the night together in almost a week. Oksana missed Annie's heat and her softness. It took a while, a lot more crying, some hiccups, but Annie explained what had happened with her parents and her house in Venice.

Oksana turned to Megan who sat on the matching loveseat. She almost asked her to give them a second alone, but she thought better of it. Maybe Megan could help. She leaned back over Annie and brushed her hair off her face.

"Come stay with me."

"I can't."

"Why not? You think it's too soon?"

"No...that's not it."

"You can take the little house and I'll go crash up in the big house for a while."

"That's not it. I…" Annie sat up and put her feet on the floor. "I need to do this alone."

"What do you mean?"

"You were right. There's an order to things. I shouldn't have rushed you into this. I should have waited."

Oksana took a deep breath and asked. "Is this you talking or your mom?"

"No! It's me." Annie wiped her face. "I have no clue what I'm doing. I have places to sleep, but nowhere to live. I was floating with Jeff and I floated into you, and now my life is a mess. I can't bring my problems into your home."

"Do you hear yourself? I'm offering. You can come stay with us."

"I can't. I have to do this on my own."

Oksana stood and paced to the unnecessary fireplace and back to the couch. She was trying so hard to control her flaring temper, but it was too difficult. Annie had begged her for this. She'd chased Oksana, told her everything would be okay. She promised she wouldn't push her away, and here they were. Oksana was begging and Annie was shoving with all her strength.

"Is crying in Megan's living room 'doing this on your own'?" It was the wrong thing to say, but it was how Oksana felt. Annie cried even harder.

"I just need some time. I love you and I appreciate your offer. I just have to figure some stuff out." Oksana stopped near the couch and counted to ten. This wasn't a breakup. It was a break, and to Oksana it sounded pretty fucking ridiculous. They didn't need a break. Annie needed to come with Oksana. It was that simple, but Annie Collins didn't do simple. Oksana knew that from the very beginning. Everything had been a scheme or a plan, and now that the rug had been ripped out from under her, Annie needed to reassess on her own terms. Well, that was fine with Oksana. She had her own terms too. She'd reached her limit on patience.

She glanced at Megan who tossed her hand in the air with an exaggerated roll of her eyes. That one look said it all. Annie was going to be ridiculous. She was set on driving this wedge between them, and there was nothing Oksana or Megan could say in that moment to change the way Annie was thinking.

"Fine. Take all the time you need," she said as she headed for the front door.

"Oksana."

"What?" She turned as Annie stood up from the couch.

"Please. I'm sorry."

"I'm tired of hearing that, Anne. If you want to be with me then fucking be with me. If you need to go on a vision quest to find yourself, then do that. I have been so understanding with you, so patient. And you kept saying 'I know, I know. I understand. I want you to trust me. I want us to work.' Well, now you want to wallow in your own pity. So I'll let you do that. I can't offer you any more." She nodded to Megan. "I'll let myself out."

Annie called to her again, but this time Oksana didn't turn around. For once, she had to be the one to walk away.

❖

Annie woke up to the sun rising and the pungent smell of coffee. She rolled over and almost fell on the floor. Right, she thought. Still on Megan's couch. On the third try, she managed to stand up and shuffle to the kitchen. Her eyes were killing her and her head was pounding. A complete emotional breakdown led to one hell of a hangover.

She found Megan flipping through *US Weekly*, drinking a cup of coffee.

"Morning," Annie ground out. Her voice was almost gone. Another side effect of losing your mind.

"There's coffee and juice and yogurt. And I put your glasses on the mantel." Megan nodded toward her new makeshift bedroom.

"Thanks." Annie dug for a glass and poured herself some juice. She wanted a shower before she gave herself a caffeine injection.

"I take it you're all cried out?" Megan finally asked.

"Yeah, I think so. I think I ruptured something in my eye."

Megan grabbed her chin and tilted her head up. "No, you're fine. And now I have something to say."

"What?" Annie felt another lecture coming on.

"I want you out of here like ASAP. I hate sharing my space. I love the things Scooter can do to me. Love them, and he's slept here once. I love you to death, but eventually, I will kick you out and I'd like to do it soon."

"Wha—" Annie was shocked. Just the night before Megan had been welcoming, almost eager to help her out, and now she was already showing her the door. She'd stopped by her storage unit, but none of the boxes stacked to the ceiling were labeled. Annie freaked out before she called Megan, before she'd found her essentials. She didn't even have a change of clothes yet, let alone a plan for a new apartment.

Megan set down her coffee. "You're a fucking idiot. Go stay with her. Go *live* with her."

Not this again. "It's not that simple. My parents have done some shitty things, but my dad had a point. I have to slow down. I have to get out on my own for once, Megan. I have to figure out what I need and not just what I want in the moment."

"Is that all she was to you? Something for the moment, because I'm pretty sure that's exactly how you made her feel."

"No, I…" Shit.

"Think about it. From what you told me, you came on pretty strong. You pressed things when she wanted you to slow down, and then the moment shit gets rough, you freak—"

"And I shut her out."

"Exactly. You didn't ditch her at the movies, Annie. She asked you to move in with her. She's offering you a home, the ultimate invitation into her life, and you shut her down like she was asking you to chop off your thumbs to prove your love."

"Shit. Shit. Shit." The dull thudding in Annie's head escalated to a full-on pounding. "She's never going to speak to me again."

"Can you blame her? She almost got fired for you and then you're all, 'I just need a minute.' Screw your minute. She loves you. A lot. So please, get the hell off my couch and go fix things with her."

Megan was right. Annie had taken all her pain and frustration out on the worst person, the one person she didn't want to hurt. The one person she loved, and now Oksana probably thought Annie truly was a flaky, spoiled brat.

"Thanks."

"You're welcome, but really, you have to get out. I mean soon. I might not like Scooter sleeping here, but I hate fucking at his place. It's like a frat house mated with a barn." Annie laughed at that visual. "Since you have blown it for the moment, I will help you find an apartment. Some place cheap and pretty."

Annie had done a quick run-through of her available finances and kicked herself for not saving properly. Luckily, she had about enough for a small place and some pre-loved furniture. She'd have to go without things like cable and take-out for a while, but she could do it. Too bad the one person she wanted to share it with wanted nothing to do with her.

"I am so stupid." Annie sighed.

"Yes, you are. Now get dressed. We're leaving in twenty minutes." Annie looked at the clock.

"You go into the office this early?"

"Yes. Some of us have to keep this industry running."

Annie showered quickly and changed back into her clothes from the day before. Luckily, the department store near her office opened at eight. The first order of business was new jeans and underwear. The second, convince Oksana to speak to her again.

❖

A month had gone by since Oksana left Annie on Megan's couch. For two weeks, Annie apologized incessantly. Each text annoyed the hell out of Oksana, but she read them all. A bunch of *I love yous*, and *I miss yous*, and *please forgive mes*. An odd change, though, began to weaken her resolve.

Annie started sending her apologies that sort of made Oksana laugh.

Do you know how hard it is for me to reach things on high shelves without you?

My diet is suffering without Baba in my life. Please don't keep her away from me.

I'll wait till Kat's legal if that's what it takes to get close to you again.

That last one was gross, but as Oksana looked at her phone, she couldn't stop from snickering. Then came the dirty apologies, little begging notes offering to make things up to her with kisses and sex and the still packaged, big purple cock thing. Oksana wanted to be pissed. She wasn't some easy sex fiend, but as those kinds of texts continued to fill her inbox, she found herself smiling against her will and possibly finding herself a little aroused. She would think of Annie's adorable face, and her righteous tits, and then like an idiot she'd think of Annie following through with those promises, and then she'd make the even bigger mistake of thinking of the times she'd woken up in Annie's bed.

She'd think about the three and a half perfect weeks they'd spent together and gotten to know each other. Fallen in love with each other. And she almost, *almost* texted Annie back. She almost considered giving Annie a second chance. Though through all the little things that were working against her dignity, Oksana couldn't lose sight of one key factor. Annie did need to grow up and Oksana couldn't help her with that. Annie wouldn't let her.

She looked at her sister lounging across the room with her own girlfriend. They were young, but they had it right. Kat and Erica knew how to make things work. They were surprisingly respectful of each other. They kept their high school drama to a minimum, and for once, Kat had made a relationship last longer than Oksana. She also reminded Oksana of what she needed. Oksana understood the shock of being tossed out on her ass. You'd think Annie would remember that, but Oksana had been smart enough to accept help when it was offered. She was smart enough to know when it was time to go back home. She'd given Annie the same safety and Annie had rejected it. She'd rejected Oksana. So Oksana was ignoring her texts.

The universe laughed at the notion and made her phone vibrate in her lap.

"Is that Annie?" Kat asked.

"No. Shut up." Oksana hit accept on Noelle's call. "Yo, baby. Yo."

"We're headed over to Neil's. You want to come? We'll drive."

Did she ever. She had to get the fuck out of the house. "Yeah. Give me like ten minutes."

With a night's relief in sight, Oksana jogged down to the little house to change. She came back up to the big house to kiss Baba and Kat good night. As she walked out the front she was greeted by a—it wasn't exactly unpleasant—surprise.

"Hi," Annie said. She looked different. Good, but different. Slimmer in a more natural way. She'd cut her hair; a really cute bob framed her cheeks. She still wore her black-framed glasses. The strangest thing was the white bandage peeking out from the vee of her T-shirt. Oksana knew the gauze and the tape motif well, but she wasn't interested in that. Why the hell was Annie at her house?

"Hey."

"I just wanted to give you this." Annie walked up the first three steps and held out a folded piece of white paper. Oksana walked down to meet her.

"What is it?"

"My new address. I'm having a little housewarming get-together this weekend." Oksana unfolded the paper. She looked at the address and short description of the cross streets.

"Is this over by Dodgers Stadium?"

"Yeah." Annie shrugged. "It's Echo Park. I like it." Very different for someone like Annie. A whole world away from Laguna Beach and Venice.

"You don't have to come, but you're invited, and I'd love to see you again...not in your yard. Megan invited Scooter so you could come with him if you wanted."

"Okay. I'll think about it," Oksana replied. She had to get Annie out of there. Another minute and she'd do something dangerous like touch the fringe of Annie's hair. Or kiss her right on her mouth.

Annie blinked at the sudden dismissal, but she didn't push her luck. "Okay. Well, bye." Oksana watched her walk to her car. Her ass still looked delicious in the right pair of jeans.

❖

"You think I should go," Oksana said, too anxious to conjure up any Russian. She turned just as Baba lit up on the top step. She took a few drags of her cigarette before she answered.

"I think you know what it's like to lose a mother, and I think you know that sometimes you have to make a family of your own. That girl is trying to make a family and she wants you to be in it."

"What do I do if she hasn't changed? What if she really isn't ready to be with me? What if she's just lonely?"

"We all love because we are lonely, darling. We love because we need, not because we want. She loves you."

"And you think I love her." Oksana turned back to where Annie's Prius had just been.

"I know you do. I know you should go, yes."

"I was afraid you would say something like that."

❖

Oksana bobbled the potted plant Scooter shoved in her hand.

"You sure you don't want to sign the card?" he asked as she slammed the Charger door.

"No. I'm good."

"What kind of guest are you? You're supposed to bring something to a housewarming, you know, to warm the house."

"She asked me to come and I'm here. That's all the warming she gets." Oksana tried not to punch Scooter when he laughed at her. She shoved the plant back into his hands and slapped him in the back of the head instead.

Scooter howled even louder. "You're not fooling anyone."

"Shut up and walk." Oksana followed Scooter up the front steps of the narrow gray apartment building. The large front door was propped open. Inside they could hear the commotion of the party four stories up. They walked up the stairs, and as they got closer it became clear the real party was on the roof. A sign outside of apartment 308 confirmed it. When they reached the very top, a girl who introduced herself as Annie's coworker, Esther, pointed them toward a table set with wine and finger foods. Beside it stood Annie. The white Christmas lights lining the railing made her blond hair glow.

"You ready, Iron Woman?" Scooter teased.

"I said, shut up and walk," Oksana replied.

They picked their way through the guests, over the uneven rooftop. Annie looked amazing. The bandage was gone. Oksana tried not to notice.

"Hey!" Annie hugged Scooter, but when she pulled back, she looked at Oksana with a huge smile. "You came."

"I wanted to see if you followed any of my remodeling tips," Scooter said. That he had any part in Annie's move was news to Oksana, but she didn't say anything.

"You'll have to wait. I'm giving tours on the hour." Annie chuckled.

"Besides, you haven't kissed me yet." Megan appeared at Scooter's side and pulled him down for a few moments of awkward spit swapping. Oksana and Annie looked nervously to each other.

"Hey," Oksana said,

"I'm glad you came too. Can I get you some wine?"

"Sure." Oksana tried to be cordial, but as soon as she took the glass Annie handed her, she panicked and took off into the small crowd.

And that was the start of an uncomfortable night. Annie's new building was actually pretty cool though. Old, maybe built in the forties or so. The roof offered the perfect view of Dodgers Stadium and almost a whole look at the surrounding neighborhood. Oksana did the delicate dance of socializing with Megan and Scooter while Annie entertained her other guests and always found a way to disappear before Annie made her way back to them. The more people Oksana met the more she realized that *she* was some sort of guest of honor. The way their eyes would light up when she would mention her name. She wondered just how badly Annie had wanted her to show up. The attention made her less eager to want to talk to Annie, but Annie Collins wasn't one to be ignored.

Finally, she cornered Oksana by the roof door.

"It's time for the next tour," Annie said, nodding toward her imaginary watch. "You want to check out my new apartment? You're the only one who hasn't seen it."

A familiar feeling came over Oksana as she looked down at her. The same nervous excitement she'd felt that night in the Hilton Checkers Hotel. The same feeling she felt the first time Annie had smiled just for her. She tamped the emotion down so it was more of a simmer than a boil and then she nodded.

Annie's place was small, but perfect for Annie. The walls had been painted recently, a great aqua blue in the front room, which also served as the kitchen and the living room and the dining room. Somehow, they ended up in the bedroom. That was painted a lime green. It looked really nice, but the ceiling was oddly low, and dim, golden light from her decorative lamps made the space seem even smaller, more cramped. The lack of AC didn't help. Annie motioned for her to sit on the double bed that took up most of the room. Foolishly, Oksana sat. Annie joined her.

"Thanks for coming," Annie said.

"It's nice." Oksana looked around, trying to focus on the décor instead of Annie's breasts or the enormous tattoo that now covered the expanse of her cleavage.

Annie touched her knee. Oksana thought her whole leg would catch on fire. She looked Annie in the eyes instead of checking for burn marks on her pants. Why did Annie have to be so beautiful and adorable and sweet? Why did she have to be everything Oksana really wanted?

"You probably guessed I had a little speech prepared."

"Actually, no. I was used to the texts."

"I am a wee bit persistent."

"You are. So let's hear it," Oksana said. If Annie said something crazy, she could just walk out the door and catch a bus back to West Hollywood. The four bus came all the way out to the stadium, if she remembered correctly.

"Okay, here goes." Annie exhaled. "I've never messed up *big* before. And before all this, I don't think I've ever hurt anyone before either. When you asked me to come stay with you, I love you is what I should have said. And I should have told you that I was embarrassed and ashamed of my behavior. I should have told you that my last few conversations with my parents made me feel like a shitty person, too shitty to be in a relationship with anyone.

"But I should have told you that I need you and I want to be with you. Because I do. I need you. I need Baba Inna, and I need Kat. I had a family with you three and I need that back."

What the hell? Were Annie and Baba connected at the brain? Obviously not, but she hated when her grandmother was right.

"What is this?" she asked, pointing to the ink on Annie's chest. All she could make out was the head of a bird. Annie pulled down the collar of her shirt, but the fabric wouldn't give enough to show Oksana the whole piece.

"Crap." Annie reached for the bottom hem of her shirt. "Is it okay?"

"Yes. I'm able to resist you."

Annie pulled her shirt over her head and Oksana immediately ate her words. Annie's bra was light blue, the same shade as her eyes, and sheer. Oksana could see her large, hard nipples through the material. She licked her lips to contain the drool.

Above the bra was the real spectacle. A large depiction of what looked like a traditionally small bird was centered over Annie's breasts, its wing spread over the width of her collarbone. Intricate designs filled in the space around the animal, and in the center of its chest was a large heart. And in the center of that heart was the silhouette of a bear.

"It's a black-capped chickadee," Annie said.

Oksana couldn't stop her fingers from moving. Softly, she traced the bold lines of the tattoo: the wings, the beak, the bright red that shaded the middle. The body of the grizzly bear.

Her gaze flickered to Annie's eyes then back down to her chest. "What if I leave right now and I don't come back? What about this?"

"You've changed me. You've made me see myself. You'll always be here." Annie caught Oksana's hand over her heart. "No matter what happens, you'll be here."

She let Annie hold her in place for a moment, but soon she stood and put some space between them.

"This place is small," she said.

"Like me."

"Just like you." *Too small for* us.

Oksana sat back down on the bed, and before she talked herself out of it, she kissed Annie. She felt Annie's shock immediately, followed by her relief. They melded together, lips pressing harder and soon tongues searching. When she pulled away, Oksana stopped thinking about emotional bruises that had already healed and started thinking about a future that could be filled with a love they both wanted *and* needed. A place where both their giggly butterflies could roam free. She didn't know when, but she'd forgiven Annie. The cheesy metaphors for mythical creatures were proof of that.

Oksana touched Annie's hair, the way she'd been wanting to all night. "We want you. We love you. You have a family with us. We don't want you to run away."

"I know." Annie sighed and looked around her lime green bedroom. "This time has been really good for me. I *did* figure a lot of stuff out, and I saw how empty things are without you."

"It doesn't have to be that way again."

"I was hoping you'd say that. I love you." Annie kissed her this time, the same soft, sweet kiss Oksana had grown to love. A kiss that always promised so much more. "I kind of like this part of being independent, though. I earned this little rabbit hole"

"How long's the lease?" Oksana asked.

"A year."

"Let me know if you want to sublet. I'll call Ronnie. She always knows someone."

"I think I might take you up on that," Annie said softly.

"I hoped you would."

The End

About the Author

After years of meddling in her friends' love lives, Rebekah turned to writing romance as a means to surviving a stressful professional life. She has worked in various positions from library assistant, meter maid, middle school teacher, B movie production assistant, reality show crew chauffeur, D movie producer, and her most fulfilling job to date, lube and harness specialist at an erotic boutique in West Hollywood.

Her interests include Wonder Woman collectibles, cookies, James Taylor, quality hip-hop, football, American muscle cars, large breed dogs, and the ocean. When she's not writing, reading, or sleeping, she is watching Ken Burns's documentaries and cartoons or taking dance classes. If given the chance, she will cheat at UNO. She was raised in Southern New Hampshire and now lives in Southern California with an individual who is much more tech savvy than she will ever be.

You can find Rebekah at http://letusseeshallwe.blogspot.com/

Books Available from Bold Strokes Books

Burgundy Betrayal by Sheri Lewis Wohl. Park Ranger Kara Lynch has no idea she's a witch until dead bodies begin to pile up in her park, forcing her to turn to beautiful and sexy shape-shifter Camille Black Wolf for help in stopping a rogue werewolf. (978-1-60282-654-0)

LoveLife by Rachel Spangler. When Joey Lang unintentionally becomes a client of life coach Elaine Raitt, the relationship becomes complicated as they develop feelings that make them question their purpose in love and life. (978-1-60282-655-7)

The Fling by Rebekah Weatherspoon. When the ultimate fantasy of a one-night stand with her trainer, Oksana Gorinkov, suddenly turns into more, reality show producer Annie Collins opens her life to a new type of love she's never imagined. (978-1-60282-656-4)

Ill Will by J.M. Redmann. New Orleans PI Micky Knight must untangle a twisted web of health care fraud that leads to murder—and puts those closest to her most at risk. (978-1-60282-657-1)

Buccaneer Island by J.P. Beausejour. In the rough world of Caribbean piracy, a man is what he makes of himself—or what a stronger man makes of him. (978-1-60282-658-8)

Twelve O'Clock Tales by Felice Picano. The fourth collection of short fiction by legendary novelist and memoirist, Felice Picano. Eleven dark tales that will thrill and disturb, discomfort and titillate, enthrall and leave you wondering. (978-1-60282-659-5)

Night Hunt by L.L. Raand. When dormant powers ignite, the wolf Were pack is thrown into violent upheaval, and Sylvan's pregnant mate is at the center of the turmoil. A Midnight Hunters novel. (978-1-60282-647-2)

Demons are Forever by Kim Baldwin and Xenia Alexiou. Elite Operative Landis "Chase" Coolidge enlists the help of high-class call girl Heather Snyder to track down a kidnapped colleague embroiled in a global black market organ-harvesting ring. (978-1-60282-648-9)

Runaway by Anne Laughlin. When Jan Roberts is hired to find a teenager who has run away to live with a group of anti-government survivalists, she's forced to return to the life she escaped when she was a teenager herself. (978-1-60282-649-6)

Street Dreams by Tama Wise. Tyson Rua has more than his fair share of problems growing up in New Zealand—he's gay, he's falling in love, and he's run afoul of the local hip-hop crew leader just as he's trying to make it as a graffiti artist. (978-1-60282-650-2)

Women of the Dark Streets: Lesbian Paranormal edited by Radclyffe and Stacia Seaman. Erotic tales of the supernatural—a world of vampires, werewolves, witches, ghosts, and demons—by the authors of Bold Strokes Books. (978-1-60282-651-9)

Tyger, Tyger, Burning Bright by Justine Saracen. Love does not conquer all, but when all of Europe is on fire, it's better than going to hell alone. (978-1-60282-652-6)

Words to Die By by William Holden. Sixteen answers to the question: What causes a mind to curdle? (978-1-60282-653-3)

Haunting Whispers by VK Powell. Detective Rae Butler faces two challenges: a serial attacker who targets attractive women, and Audrey Everhart, a compelling woman who knows too much about the case and offers too little—professionally and personally. (978-1-60282-593-2)

Wholehearted by Ronica Black. When therapist Madison Clark and attorney Grace Hollings are forced together to help Grace's troubled nephew at Madison's healing ranch, worlds and hearts collide. (978-1-60282-594-9)

Fugitives of Love by Lisa Girolami. Artist Sinclair Grady has an unspeakable secret, but the only chance she has for love with gallery owner Brenna Wright is to reveal the secret and face the potentially devastating consequences. (978-1-60282-595-6)

Derrick Steele: Private Dick The Case of the Hollywood Hustler by Zavo. Derrick Steele, a hard-drinking, lusty private detective, is being framed for the murder of a hustler in downtown Los Angeles. When his best friend Daniel McAllister joins the investigation, their growing attraction might prove to be more explosive than the case. (978-1-60282-596-3)

Nice Butt: Gay Anal Eroticism by Shane Allison. From toys to teasing, spanking to sporting, some of the best gay erotic scribes celebrate the hottest and most creative in new erotica. (978-1-60282-635-9)

Worth the Risk by Karis Walsh. Investment analyst Jamie Callahan and Grand Prix show jumper Kaitlyn Brown are willing to risk it all in their careers—can they face a greater challenge and take a chance on love? (978-1-60282-587-1)

Bloody Claws by Winter Pennington. In the midst of aiding the police, Preternatural Private Investigator Kassandra Lyall finally finds herself at serious odds with Sheila Morris, the local werewolf pack's Alpha female, when Sheila abuses someone Kassandra has sworn to protect. (978-1-60282-588-8)

Awake Unto Me by Kathleen Knowles. In turn of the century San Francisco, two young women fight for love in a world where women are often invisible and passion is the privilege of the powerful. (978-1-60282-589-5)

Initiation by Desire by MJ Williamz. Jaded Sue and innocent Tulley find forbidden love and passion within the inhibiting confines of a sorority house filled with nosy sisters. (978-1-60282-590-1)

Toughskins by William Masswa. John and Bret are two twenty-something athletes who find that love can begin in the most unlikely of places, including a "mom and pop shop" wrestling league. (978-1-60282-591-8)

me@you.com by K.E. Payne. Is it possible to fall in love with someone you've never met? Imogen Summers thinks so because it's happened to her. (978-1-60282-592-5)

High Impact by Kim Baldwin. Thrill seeker Emery Lawson and Adventure Outfitter Pasha Dunn learn you can never truly appreciate what's important and what you're capable of until faced with a sudden and stark reminder of your own mortality. (978-1-60282-580-2)

Snowbound by Cari Hunter. "The policewoman got shot and she's bleeding everywhere. Get someone here in one hour or I'm going to put her out of her misery." It's an ultimatum that will forever change the lives of police officer Sam Lucas and Dr. Kate Myles. (978-1-60282-581-9)

Rescue Me by Julie Cannon. Tyler Logan reluctantly agrees to pose as the girlfriend of her in-the-closet gay BFF at his company's annual retreat, but she didn't count on falling for Kristin, the boss's wife. (978-1-60282-582-6)

http://www.boldstrokesbooks.com
Bold Strokes
BOOKS
victory
EDITIONS
Drama
LIBERTY
EDITION
AEROS
e
BOOKS
e-Books
Mystery
CRIME
Sci-fi
SPEC FIC
HE
erotica
Erotica
BSB
SOLILOQUY
Young
Adult
BS
BOLD
STROKES
BOOKS
MATINEE BOOKS
Romance
WEBSTORE
PRINT AND EBOOKS